THE
HORNED GOD

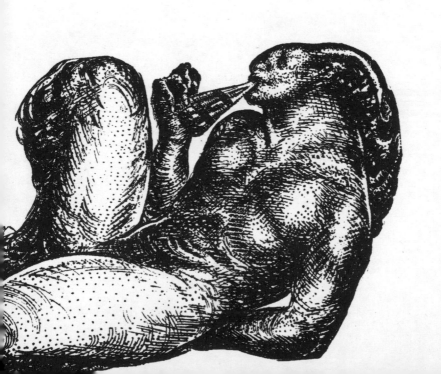

THE HORNED GOD

Weird Tales
of the
Great God Pan

Edited by
MICHAEL WHEATLEY

BRITISH LIBRARY

This collection first published in 2022 by
The British Library
96 Euston Road
London NW1 2DB

Selection, introduction and notes © 2022 Michael Wheatley
Volume copyright © 2022 The British Library Board

Cataloguing in Publication Data
A catalogue record for this publication is available from the British Library

ISBN 978 0 7123 5496 7
e-ISBN 978 0 7123 6789 9

Cover design by Mauricio Villamayor with illustration by Mag Ruhig
Text design and typesetting by Tetragon, London
Printed in England by CPI Group (UK) Ltd, Croydon, CRO 4YY

Contents

The Great God Pan

and The Inmost Light

by Arthur Machen

AUTHOR OF 'THE CHRONICLE OF
CLEMENDY,' AND TRANSLATOR
OF 'THE HEPTAMERON' AND
'LE MOYEN DE PARVENIR'

Qui perrumpit sepem, illum mordebit serpens

London : John Lane, Vigo St.

Boston : Roberts Bros., 1894

INTRODUCTION

"Suddenly from the island of Paxi was heard the voice of someone loudly calling Thamus, so that all were amazed. Thamus was an Egyptian pilot, not known by name even to many on board. Twice he was called and made no reply, but the third time he answered; and the caller, raising his voice, said, 'When you come opposite to Palodes, announce that Great Pan is dead.'"

On the Cessation of Oracles, an essay from the Greek historian Plutarch's *Moralia*, records the story of Thamus. An Egyptian sailor, Thamus heard a divine voice at sea which declared the death of Pan. This announcement, taking place during the reign of the second Roman emperor, Tiberius, was met with "a great cry of lamentation, not of one person, but of many, mingled with exclamations of amazement". Unique among the Greek pantheon of immortals, Pan alone had succumbed to mortality.

Seized upon by early Christian scholars, Pan's death was linked with the coming of Christ. The old gods were daemons, as Eusebius of Caesarea described them, cast out with the birth of the Lord. Pan, the symbol of paganistic freedoms, became their scapegoat. The conclusion was clear, even if the story was not; recent criticism questions what exactly Thamus heard. This was modern religion's victory over ancient beliefs. The plurality of Pan and his companions gave way to the monotheistic belief in God.

Yet, in death, Pan was granted new life. The goat-god has had his own resurrections, perhaps more than any other deity. Throughout our cultural history, artists, philosophers, historians and writers have habitually exhumed the corpse of Pan. And with each revival, those same minds have seemed to find new resonance.

In the Renaissance, through the writings of François Rabelais and Edmund Spenser, Pan came to be aligned with Christ instead. The death of Pan was the crucifixion of Christ upon the cross. The God of Shepherds and the Good Shepherd were one and the same. The Romantics returned to Pan as an image of pastoral power, the unseen celestial force living within the wilds. In the verse of Keats, Shelley and Byron, the landscapes of England came to echo Pan's native Arcadia.

During the *fin-de-siècle*, Pan adopted his most ominous form. Here, the horned god ran rampant, sowing panic and discord in his wake. A challenge to modernity, rationality, science and industrialism, Pan became a counter to human hubris. Yet, he also started to symbolise various personal liberties: of gender, sexuality, expression and faith. Even the occultists revisited the daemonic image of Pan, most notably in Aleister Crowley's frantic "Hymn to Pan" (1919), embracing the goat-god as a sort of satanic saviour.

If such interpretations seem contradictory, this is a necessary confusion. Pan, after all, was contradiction. Where the Greek myths frequently thematised transformation and metamorphosis, Pan remained divided; half human, half beast; half goat, half god. A liminal figure, caught between two states of being, Pan's own origin is divined through equally murky waters. In the nineteenth *Homeric Hymn*, he is the child of Hermes and a dryad. In other myths, his parents include Cronos, Zeus, Amaltheia and Penelope.

Perhaps the Christian Lord, perhaps a satanic image of countercultural liberation; perhaps a personable personification of the wilds, perhaps a vengeful spirit of the untamed wilderness. However we interpret Pan, such multiplicity has enabled his survival. Indeed, even his name has been subject to debate. Its derivation from the Greek word for "all" has largely been debunked as a persistent misconception. Instead, Pan is suggested to originate from *paean*, meaning "to pasture", or *opaōn*, meaning "companion".

Thankfully, some myth remains consistent. A lesser deity, living in the countryside rather than the splendour of Mount Olympus, Pan was the Greek god of the wild, shepherds and flocks, rustic music and impromptus. With the upper body of a human, the legs of a beast and a pair of cloven hooves, Pan is often portrayed with his panpipes or in a state of unfettered sexuality. For this reason, he is most frequently associated with Dionysus, the similarly hedonistic god of wine and ecstasy.

"The land of many springs and mother of flocks", Pan called Arcadia his home. Here, he would roam through open plains, sylvan forests, awesome mountains and crystalline streams. A keen hunter, he would foster the animals of his wilds while also blessing the success of other trackers. It is no surprise, perhaps, that artists lamenting the sheer scale of modernity frequently turned to Arcadia for escape.

This collection focuses on the representation of Pan during the late-nineteenth and early-twentieth centuries. The works selected span from 1860 to 1949. In this sense, I have included what might be considered precursors to the true pandemonium which followed. While these tales predominantly showcase what Patricia Merivale terms the "sinister Pan", expanding the scope allowed for alternative engagements with the Plutarchian (Browning), Renaissance (Lawrence) and Romantic (Grahame) interpretations.

Throughout, we see the sublime spirit of the horned god, enticing our protagonists into the wilds with sweet-sounding music. Yet, such an encounter with our sylvan saviour might just as easily destroy them in ecstasy as it would cleanse their souls. If the pagan gods were lost with the coming of Christ, defeated alongside an antiquated culture, then these tales speak of the uncanny rebirth of such banished beliefs. Collectively, artists and writers looked to the past to try to comprehend the changing present.

His most rapturous resurrection, during this period Pan captured the imaginations of such distinguished authors as Robert Louis Stevenson, D. H. Lawrence and Nathaniel Hawthorne. Arthur Machen's notorious novella, *The Great God Pan* (1894), is infamous for helping to inspire this resurgence; Pan's place among the pages of *Weird Tales* is often writ with explicit connection to Machen's masterpiece.

Due to Pan's associations with free sexuality, we also see a significant number of female and queer authors turn to the subject. Oscar Wilde, George Egerton, E. M. Forster, Saki and Elizabeth Barrett Browning are all collected here, alongside others. Seeing the human in Pan, these tales muse on themes of identity, escape and repression. Indeed, with the modern conception of homosexuality coined during this period, Pan became a symbol of resistance to the accompanying persecution.

Though all feature an element of horror, these strange stories are as diverse as Pan himself. From the Decadent stylings of Egerton to the satirical edge of Saki; the satanic panic of Toksvig alongside the devolutionary terrors of Machen. Likewise, this collection embraces an abundance of forms. While primarily a collection of short stories, illustrations, poetry and an extract from Kenneth Grahame's *The Wind in the Willows* are all included.

The selected poems feature notable works by Elizabeth Barrett Browning and Oscar Wilde, alongside more obscure pieces by Edith Hurley, Dorothy Quick and A. Lloyd Bayne. By including these lesser-known works, I hoped to reincorporate the lost tradition of verse within the pages of *Weird Tales*, and renew interest in these pulp poetics.

However, Pan still strains against the boundaries of the page. Readers interested in additional verse might turn to Elizabeth Barrett Browning's "The Dead Pan" (1840), "Pan and Luna" (1880) by Robert Browning or "A Nympholept" (1891) by Algernon Charles Swinburne. During this time, Pan also manifested in novels, such as Knut Hamsun's *Pan* (1894) and *The Blessing of Pan* (1927) by Lord Dunsany; further short stories including Henry S. Whitehead's "The People of Pan" (1929); and notable essays including Robert Louis Stevenson's "Pan's Pipes" (1878) and D. H. Lawrence's "Pan in America" (1924; 1926).

In his most recent rebirth, Pan has inspired multiple masters of horror, including Stephen King and Guillermo del Toro. Yet, despite Pan's resonance, interest appears to have waned. A figure of unstable identity, Pan challenges individualism; his hybridity suggests that we embrace the plurality of ourselves. As a guardian of the natural world, Pan would seem pertinent in the age of ecological collapse. These tales lament our severed connection from nature, and suggest a way to return to a primeval state of being, as embodied by Pan and his wilds.

If, at the moment, it seems that Pan has returned to rest, we need only remind ourselves that he is once again sleeping. Death holds no sway over the horned god, who returns when he is needed. It is only a matter of time until we look back into our history and turn to the goat-god for understanding. The sound of hooves across the hillside will soon be heard again.

MICHAEL WHEATLEY

FURTHER READING

Patricia Merivale, *Pan the Goat-God*: *His Myth in Modern Times* (Cambridge, MA: Harvard University Press, 1969).

Paul Robichaud, *Pan: The Great God's Modern Return* (London: Reaktion Books, 2021).

ILLUSTRATION SOURCES

Frontispiece: illustration by Vincent Napoli for 'Forest God' by Dorothy Quick, *Weird Tales*, November 1949.

Page 6: title page with illustration by Aubrey Beardsley of the British Library's edition of *The Great God Pan* by Arthur Machen, John Lane, 1894.

Page 116: illustration by Frederic, Lord Leighton for 'A Musical Instrument' by Elizabeth Barrett Browning in *The Cornhill Magazine*, vol. II, 1860.

Page 130: frontispiece illustration by Paul Bransom from *The Wind in the Willows* by Kenneth Grahame, Methuen and Co., 1913.

Page 132: front boards with illustration by W. Graham Robertson for *The Wind in the Willows* by Kenneth Grahame, Methuen and Co., 1912.

Page 154: illustration by Boris Dolgov from 'Great Pan is Here' by Greye La Spina in *Weird Tales*, November 1943.

Page 188: illustration by Boris Dolgov for 'Roman Remains' by Algernon Blackwood in *Weird Tales*, March 1948.

Page 216: illustration by Virgil Finlay for 'A Place in the Woods' by August Derleth, *Weird Tales*, May 1954.

Page 276: illustration for 'Bewitched' by Willard N. Marsh, *Weird Tales*, March 1945.

Page 280: illustration by A. R. Tilburne for 'The Golden Bough' by David H. Keller, *Weird Tales*, November 1942.

Page 320: illustration by Boris Dolgov for 'The Cracks of Time' by Dorothy Quick, *Weird Tales*, September 1948.

A NOTE FROM THE PUBLISHER

The original short stories reprinted in the British Library Tales of the Weird series were written and published in a period ranging across the nineteenth and twentieth centuries. There are many elements of these stories which continue to entertain modern readers; however, in some cases there are also uses of language, instances of stereotyping and some attitudes expressed by narrators or characters which may not be endorsed by the publishing standards of today. We acknowledge therefore that some elements in the stories selected for reprinting may continue to make uncomfortable reading for some of our audience. With this series British Library Publishing aims to offer a new readership a chance to read some of the rare material of the British Library's collections in an affordable paperback format, to enjoy their merits and to look back into the worlds of the past two centuries as portrayed by their writers. It is not possible to separate these stories from the history of their writing and as such the following stories are presented as they were originally published with the inclusion of minor edits made for consistency of style and sense, and with pejorative terms of an extremely offensive nature partly obscured. We welcome feedback from our readers, which can be sent to the following address:

British Library Publishing
The British Library
96 Euston Road
London, NW1 2DB
United Kingdom

PAN: A DOUBLE VILLANELLE

Oscar Wilde

Though originally born in Dublin, Oscar Wilde (1854–1900) is perhaps best remembered for the life he subsequently led in London. A pioneer of the Decadent movement, which favoured artistic excess, transgression and artificiality, Wilde was one of the preeminent literary figures writing at the end of the nineteenth century. An aesthete and a flâneur, Wilde's later life was fraught with scandal and he was branded a symbol of moral decline. In 1895, he was charged with "gross indecency" on account of his homosexuality and he spent the next two years confined to Reading Gaol, before living the remainder of his life in self-imposed exile in Europe. However, Wilde's legacy sustains through his prose, poetry and plays. This includes such notable works as *The Happy Prince and Other Tales* (1888), *The Picture of Dorian Gray* (1890), *Salomé* (1891) and *The Importance of Being Earnest* (1895).

"Pan" introduces this collection, demonstrating the breadth of interest that the horned god held over the contemporary literary imagination. Extending beyond the pages of *Weird Tales*, Pan manifested through myriad artistic forms and genres. First collected posthumously in *Poems by Oscar Wilde with the Ballad of Reading Gaol* (1907), this villanelle laments Pan's disappearance from the modern world. As with many tales in this anthology, the death of Pan coincides with a death of wonder in an increasingly industrialised Britain. Moreover, Pan's frequent positioning as a figure of sexual liberation would seem to make Wilde's choice of subject even more apt. The piece ends with a plea, as though summoning the stories to follow: "Ah, leave the hills of Arcady! This modern world hath need of thee!"

I

O goat-foot God of Arcady!
This modern world is grey and old,
And what remains to us of thee?

No more the shepherd lads in glee
Throw apples at thy wattled fold,
O goat-foot God of Arcady!

Nor through the laurels can one see
Thy soft brown limbs, thy beard of gold,
And what remains to us of thee?

And dull and dead our Thames would be,
For here the winds are chill and cold,
O goat-foot God of Arcady!

Then keep the tomb of Helice,
Thine olive-woods, thy vine-clad wold,
And what remains to us of thee?

Though many an unsung elegy
Sleeps in the reeds our rivers hold,
O goat-foot God of Arcady!
Ah, what remains to us of thee?

II

Ah, leave the hills of Arcady,
Thy satyrs and their wanton play,
This modern world hath need of thee.

No nymph or Faun indeed have we,
For Faun and nymph are old and grey,
Ah, leave the hills of Arcady!

This is the land where liberty
Lit grave-browed Milton on his way,
This modern world hath need of thee!

A land of ancient chivalry
Where gentle Sidney saw the day,
Ah, leave the hills of Arcady.

This fierce sea-lion of the sea,
This England lacks some stronger lay,
This modern world hath need of thee!

Then blow some trumpet loud and free,
And give thine oaten pipe away,
Ah, leave the hills of Arcady!
This modern world hath need of thee!

THE GREAT GOD PAN

Arthur Machen

Arthur Machen (1863–1947) was a Welsh author born in Caerleon, Monmouthshire. The son of a clergyman, Machen would develop an early interest in the occult, later blossoming into his belief in an unseen world, of the spirit and the soul, lurking just beneath the veil of ordinary experience. This, combined with fascinations for paganism, folklore and the ancient histories of his native Wales, coalesced into Machen's curious strain of weird fiction. Works such as "The White People" (1904) and *The Hill of Dreams* (1907) draw on mythology, landscape and an occult form of science to present visions of rural epiphany, where an understanding of this suppressed past can both enrich and destroy those who find it.

First published alongside a second work as *The Great God Pan and The Inmost Light* (1894), Machen's piece proved foundational for the portrayals to follow. A lost pagan history, animism, sexual liberation and the potential annihilation which meeting Pan brings are all visible in this work. Equally lauded and condemned upon its publication, *The Great God Pan* was praised by H. P. Lovecraft, who commended "the cumulative suspense and ultimate horror with which every paragraph abounds", and Oscar Wilde, who called it "un succès fou". Both Stephen King's 2008 novella, *N.*, and 2014 novel, *Revival*, also take open inspiration from the tale.

The novella focuses on Dr. Raymond who, with dubious consent, performs experimental brain surgery on a young woman named

Mary so that she might see "the Great God Pan". Dr. Raymond believes that in doing so she will attain a transcended state of mind and look beyond the veil that is reality. What follows are a series of recounted tales and patchwork narratives, with the shared theme of an unknown woman revealing a terrifying truth to those she meets. Aligning with the Decadent fictions of the time, Machen's work was initially accompanied by the following illustration by Aubrey Beardsley, who drew on similar motifs across his work.

THE EXPERIMENT

"I am glad you came, Clarke; very glad indeed. I was not sure you could spare the time."

"I was able to make arrangements for a few days; things are not very lively just now. But have you no misgivings, Raymond? Is it absolutely safe?"

The two men were slowly pacing the terrace in front of Dr. Raymond's house. The sun still hung above the western mountain-line, but it shone with a dull red glow that cast no shadows, and all the air was quiet; a sweet breath came from the great wood on the hillside above, and with it, at intervals, the soft murmuring call of the wild doves. Below, in the long lovely valley, the river wound in and out between the lonely hills, and, as the sun hovered and vanished into the west, a faint mist, pure white, began to rise from the banks. Dr. Raymond turned sharply to his friend.

"Safe? Of course it is. In itself the operation is a perfectly simple one; any surgeon could do it."

"And there is no danger at any other stage?"

"None; absolutely no physical danger whatever, I give you my word. You were always timid, Clarke, always; but you know my history. I have devoted myself to transcendental medicine for the last twenty years. I have heard myself called quack, and charlatan and impostor, but all the while I knew I was on the right path. Five years ago I reached the goal, and since then every day has been a preparation for what we shall do tonight."

"I should like to believe it is all true." Clarke knit his brows, and looked doubtfully at Dr. Raymond. "Are you perfectly sure, Raymond, that your theory is not a phantasmagoria—a splendid vision, certainly, but a mere vision after all?"

Dr. Raymond stopped in his walk and turned sharply. He was a middle-aged man, gaunt and thin, of a pale yellow complexion, but as he answered Clarke and faced him, there was a flush on his cheek.

"Look about you, Clarke. You see the mountain, and hill following after hill, as wave on wave, you see the woods and orchards, the fields of ripe corn, and the meadows reaching to the reed-beds by the river. You see me standing here beside you, and hear my voice; but I tell you that all these things—yes, from that star that has just shone out in the sky to the solid ground beneath our feet—I say that all these are but dreams and shadows: the shadows that hide the real world from our eyes. There *is* a real world, but it is beyond this glamour and this vision, beyond these 'chases in Arras, dreams in a career,' beyond them all as beyond a veil. I do not know whether any human being has ever lifted that veil; but I do know, Clarke, that you and I shall see it lifted this very night from before another's eyes. You may think all this strange nonsense; it may be strange, but it is true, and the ancients knew what lifting the veil means. They called it seeing the god Pan."

Clarke shivered; the white mist gathering over the river was chilly.

"It is wonderful indeed," he said. "We are standing on the brink of a strange world, Raymond, if what you say is true. I suppose the knife is absolutely necessary?"

"Yes; a slight lesion in the grey matter, that is all; a trifling re-arrangement of certain cells, a microscopical alteration that would escape the attention of ninety-nine brain specialists out of a hundred. I don't want to bother you with 'shop,' Clarke; I might give you a mass of technical detail which would sound very imposing, and would leave you as enlightened as you are now. But I suppose you have read, casually, in out-of-the-way corners of your paper, that immense strides have been made recently in the physiology of the brain. I saw a paragraph the other day about Digby's theory, and Browne Faber's discoveries. Theories and discoveries! Where they are standing now, I stood fifteen years ago, and I need not tell you that I have not been standing still for the last fifteen years. It will be enough if I say that five years ago I made the discovery to which I alluded when I said that then I reached the goal. After years of labour, after years of toiling and groping in the dark, after days and nights of disappointment and sometimes of despair, in which I used now and then to tremble and grow cold with the thought that perhaps there were others seeking for what I sought, at last, after so long, a pang of sudden joy thrilled my soul, and I knew the long journey was at an end. By what seemed then and still seems a chance, the suggestion of a moment's idle thought followed up upon familiar lines and paths that I had tracked a hundred times already, the great truth burst upon me, and I saw, mapped out in lines of light a whole world, a sphere unknown; continents and islands, and great oceans in which no ship has sailed (to my belief) since a Man first lifted up his eyes and beheld the sun, and the stars of heaven, and the quiet earth beneath. You will think all this high-flown language, Clarke, but it is hard to be literal. And yet; I do not know whether what I am hinting at cannot be set forth in plain and homely terms. For instance, this world of ours is pretty well girded now with the telegraph wires and cables; thought, with something less than the speed of thought, flashes from sunrise to sunset, from north to south, across the floods and the desert places. Suppose that an electrician of today were suddenly to perceive that he and his friends have merely been playing with pebbles and mistaking them for the foundations of the world; suppose that such a man saw uttermost space lie open before the current, and words of men flash forth to the sun and beyond the sun into the systems beyond, and the voices of articulate-speaking men echo in the waste void that bounds our thought. As analogies go, that is a pretty good analogy of what I have done; you can understand now a little of what I felt as I stood here one evening; it was a summer evening, and the valley looked much as it does now; I stood here, and saw before me the unutterable, the unthinkable gulf that yawns profound between two worlds, the world of matter and the world of spirit; I saw the great empty deep stretch dim before me, and in that instant a bridge of light leapt from the earth to the unknown shore, and the abyss was spanned. You may look in Browne Faber's book, if you like, and you will find that to the present day men of science are unable to account for the presence, or to specify the functions of a certain group of nerve-cells in the brain. That group is, as it were, land to let, a mere waste place for fanciful theories. I am not in the position of Browne Faber and the specialists, I am perfectly instructed as to the possible functions of those nerve-centres in the scheme of things. With a touch I can bring them into play, with a touch, I say, I can set free the current, with a touch I can complete the communication between this world of sense and—we shall be able to finish the sentence later on. Yes, the knife is necessary; but think what that knife will effect. It will level utterly the solid wall of sense, and probably, for the first time since man was made, a spirit will gaze on a spirit-world. Clarke, Mary will see the god Pan!"

"But you remember what you wrote to me? I thought it would be requisite that she—"

He whispered the rest into the doctor's ear.

"Not at all, not at all. That is nonsense, I assure you. Indeed, it is better as it is; I am quite certain of that."

"Consider the matter well, Raymond. It's a great responsibility. Something might go wrong; you would be a miserable man for the rest of your days."

"No, I think not, even if the worst happened. As you know, I rescued Mary from the gutter, and from almost certain starvation, when she was a child; I think her life is mine, to use as I see fit. Come, it is getting late; we had better go in."

Dr. Raymond led the way into the house, through the hall, and down a long dark passage. He took a key from his pocket and opened a heavy door, and motioned Clarke into his laboratory. It had once been a billiard-room, and was lighted by a glass dome in the centre of the ceiling, whence there still shone a sad grey light on the figure of the doctor as he lit a lamp with a heavy shade and placed it on a table in the middle of the room.

Clarke looked about him. Scarcely a foot of wall remained bare; there were shelves all around laden with bottles and phials of all shapes and colours, and at one end stood a little Chippendale bookcase. Raymond pointed to this.

"You see that parchment Oswald Crollius? He was one of the first to show me the way, though I don't think he ever found it himself. That is a strange saying of his: 'In every grain of wheat there lies hidden the soul of a star.'"

There was not much of furniture in the laboratory. The table in the centre, a stone slab with a drain in one corner, the two armchairs on which Raymond and Clarke were sitting; that was all, except an odd-looking chair at the furthest end of the room. Clarke looked at it, and raised his eyebrows.

"Yes, that is the chair," said Raymond. "We may as well place it in position." He got up and wheeled the chair to the light, and began raising and lowering it, letting down the seat, setting the back at various angles, and adjusting the foot-rest. It looked comfortable enough, and Clarke passed his hand over the soft green velvet, as the doctor manipulated the levers.

"Now, Clarke, make yourself quite comfortable. I have a couple of hours' work before me; I was obliged to leave certain matters to the last."

Raymond went to the stone slab, and Clarke watched him drearily as he bent over a row of phials and lit the flame under the crucible. The doctor had a small hand-lamp, shaded as the larger one, on a ledge above his apparatus, and Clarke, who sat in the shadows, looked down the great dreary room, wondering at the bizarre effects of brilliant light and undefined darkness contrasting with one another. Soon he became conscious of an odd odour, at first the merest suggestion of odour, in the room; and as it grew more decided he felt surprised that he was not reminded of the chemist's shop or the surgery. Clarke found himself idly endeavouring to analyse the sensation, and, half conscious, he began to think of a day, fifteen years ago, that he had spent in roaming through the woods and meadows near his old home. It was a burning day at the beginning of August, the heat had dimmed the outlines of all things and all distances with a faint mist, and people who observed the thermometer spoke of an abnormal register, of a temperature that was almost tropical. Strangely that wonderful hot day of 185— rose up in Clarke's imagination; the sense of dazzling all-pervading sunlight seemed to blot out the shadows and the lights of the laboratory, and he felt again the heated air beating in gusts about his face, saw the shimmer rising from the turf, and heard the myriad murmur of the summer.

"I hope the smell doesn't annoy you, Clarke; there's nothing unwholesome about it. It may make you a bit sleepy, that's all."

Clarke heard the words quite distinctly, and knew that Raymond was speaking to him, but for the life of him he could not rouse himself from his lethargy. He could only think of the lonely walk he had taken fifteen years ago; it was his last look at the fields and woods he had known since he was a child, and now it all stood out in brilliant light, as a picture, before him. Above all there came to his nostrils the scent of summer, the smell of flowers mingled, and the odour of the woods, of cool shaded places, deep in the green depths, drawn forth by the sun's heat; and the scent of the good earth, lying as it were with arms stretched forth, and smiling lips, overpowered all. His fancies made him wander, as he had wandered long ago, from the fields into the wood, tracking a little path between the shining undergrowth of beech-trees; and the trickle of water dropping from the limestone rock sounded as a clear melody in the dream. Thoughts began to go astray and to mingle with other recollections; the beech-alley was transformed to a path beneath ilex-trees, and here and there a vine climbed from bough to bough, and sent up waving tendrils and drooped with purple grapes, and the sparse grey green leaves of a wild olive-tree stood out against the dark shadows of the ilex. Clarke, in the deep folds of dream, was conscious that the path from his father's house had led him into an undiscovered country, and he was wondering at the strangeness of it all, when suddenly, in place of the hum and murmur of the summer, an infinite silence seemed to fall on all things, and the wood was hushed, and for a moment of time he stood face to face there with a presence, that was neither man nor beast, neither the living nor the dead, but all things mingled, the form of all things but devoid of all form. And in that moment, the sacrament of body and soul was dissolved, and a voice seemed to cry "let us go hence," and then the darkness of darkness beyond the stars, the darkness of everlasting.

When Clarke woke up with a start he saw Raymond pouring a few drops of some oily fluid into a green phial, which he stoppered tightly.

"You have been dozing," he said, "the journey must have tired you out. It is done now. I am going to fetch Mary; I shall be back in ten minutes."

Clarke lay back in his chair and wondered. It seemed as if he had but passed from one dream into another. He half expected to see the walls of the laboratory melt and disappear, and to awake in London, shuddering at his own sleeping fancies. But at last the door opened, and the doctor returned, and behind him came a girl of about seventeen, dressed all in white. She was so beautiful that Clarke did not wonder at what the doctor had written to him. She was blushing now over face and neck and arms, but Raymond seemed unmoved.

"Mary," he said, "the time has come. You are quite free. Are you willing to trust yourself to me entirely?"

"Yes, dear."

"You hear that, Clarke? You are my witness. Here is the chair, Mary. It is quite easy. Just sit in it and lean back. Are you ready?"

"Yes, dear, quite ready. Give me a kiss before you begin."

The doctor stooped and kissed her mouth, kindly enough. "Now shut your eyes," he said. The girl closed her eyelids, as if she were tired, and longed for sleep, and Raymond held the green phial to her nostrils. Her face grew white, whiter than her dress; she struggled faintly, and then with the feeling of submission strong within her, crossed her arms upon her breast as a little child about to say her prayers. The bright light of the lamp beat full upon her, and Clarke watched changes fleeting over that face as the changes of the hills when the summer clouds float across the sun. And then she lay all white and still, and the doctor turned up one of her eyelids. She was quite unconscious. Raymond pressed hard on one of the levers and the chair instantly sank back. Clarke saw him cutting away a circle, like a tonsure, from her hair, and the lamp was moved nearer. Raymond took a small glittering instrument from a little case, and Clarke turned away shuddering. When he looked again the doctor was binding up the wound he had made.

"She will awake in five minutes." Raymond was still perfectly cool. "There is nothing further to be done; we can only wait."

The minutes passed slowly; they could hear a slow, heavy ticking. There was an old clock in the passage. Clarke felt sick and faint; his knees shook beneath him, he could hardly stand.

Suddenly, as they watched, they heard a long-drawn sigh, and suddenly did the colour that had vanished return to the girl's cheeks, and suddenly her eyes opened. Clarke quailed before them. They shone with an awful light, looking far away, and a great wonder fell upon her face, and her hands stretched out as if to touch what was invisible; but in an instant the wonder faded, and gave place to the most awful terror. The muscles of her face were hideously convulsed, she shook from head to foot; the soul seemed struggling and shuddering within the house of flesh. It was a horrible sight, and Clarke rushed forward, as she fell shrieking to the floor.

*

Three days later Raymond took Clarke to Mary's bedside. She was lying wide-awake, rolling her head from side to side, and grinning vacantly.

"Yes," said the doctor, still quite cool, "it is a great pity; she is a hopeless idiot. However, it could not be helped; and, after all, she has seen the Great God Pan."

MR. CLARKE'S MEMOIRS

Mr. Clarke, the gentleman chosen by Dr. Raymond to witness the strange experiment of the god Pan, was a person in whose character caution and curiosity were oddly mingled; in his sober moments he thought of the unusual and the eccentric with undisguised aversion, and yet, deep in his heart, there was a wide-eyed inquisitiveness with respect to all the more recondite and esoteric elements in the nature of men. The latter tendency had prevailed when he accepted Raymond's invitation, for though his considered judgment had always repudiated the doctor's theories as the wildest nonsense, yet he secretly hugged a belief in fantasy, and would have rejoiced to see that belief confirmed. The horrors that he witnessed in the dreary laboratory were to a certain extent salutary, he was conscious of being involved in an affair not altogether reputable, and for many years afterwards he clung bravely to the commonplace, and rejected all occasions of occult investigation. Indeed, on some homœopathic principle, he for some time attended the séances of distinguished mediums, hoping that the clumsy tricks of these gentlemen would make him altogether disgusted with mysticism of every kind, but the remedy, though caustic, was not efficacious. Clarke knew that he still pined for the unseen, and little by little, the old passion began to reassert itself, as the face of Mary, shuddering and convulsed with an unknowable terror, faded slowly from his memory. Occupied all day in pursuits both serious and lucrative, the temptation to relax in the evening was too great, especially in the winter months, when the fire cast a warm glow over his snug bachelor apartment, and a bottle of some choice claret stood ready by his elbow. His dinner digested, he would make a brief pretence of reading the evening paper, but the mere catalogue of news soon palled upon him, and Clarke would find himself casting glances of warm desire in the direction of an old Japanese bureau, which stood at a pleasant distance from the hearth. Like a boy before a jam-closet, for a few minutes he would hover indecisive, but lust always prevailed, and Clarke ended by drawing up his chair, lighting a candle, and sitting down before the bureau. Its pigeon-holes and drawers teemed with documents on the most morbid subjects, and in the well reposed a large manuscript volume, in which he had painfully entered the gems of his collection. Clarke had a fine contempt for published literature; the most ghostly story ceased to interest him if it happened to be printed; his sole pleasure was in the reading, compiling, arranging, and rearranging what he called his "Memoirs to prove the Existence of the Devil," and engaged in this pursuit the evening seemed to fly and the night appeared too short.

On one particular evening, an ugly December night, black with fog, and raw with frost, Clarke hurried over his dinner, and scarcely deigned to observe his customary ritual of taking up the paper and laying it down again. He paced two or three times up and down the room, and opened the bureau, stood still a moment, and sat down. He leant back, absorbed in one of those dreams to which he was subject, and at length drew out his book, and opened it at the last entry. There were three or four pages densely covered with Clarke's round, set penmanship, and at the beginning he had written in a somewhat larger hand:

> Singular Narrative told me by my Friend, Dr. Phillips. He assures me that all the Facts related therein are strictly and wholly True, but refuses to give either the Surnames of the Persons concerned, or the Place where these Extraordinary Events occurred.

Mr. Clarke began to read over the account for the tenth time, glancing now and then at the pencil notes he had made when it was told him by his friend. It was one of his humours to pride himself on a certain literary ability; he thought well of his style, and took pains in arranging the circumstances in dramatic order. He read the following story:

The persons concerned in this statement are Helen V., who, if she is still alive, must now be a woman of twenty-three, Rachel M., since deceased, who was a year younger than the above, and Trevor W., an imbecile, aged eighteen. These persons were at the period of the story inhabitants of a village on the borders of Wales, a place of some importance in the time of the Roman occupation, but now a scattered hamlet, of not more than five hundred souls. It is situated on rising ground, about six miles from the sea, and is sheltered by a large and picturesque forest.

Some eleven years ago, Helen V. came to the village under rather peculiar circumstances. It is understood that she, being an orphan, was adopted in her infancy by a distant relative, who brought her up in his own house till she was twelve years old. Thinking, however, that it would be better for the child to have playmates of her own age, he advertised in several local papers for a good home in a comfortable farm-house for a girl of twelve, and this advertisement was answered by Mr. R., a well-to-do farmer in the above-mentioned village. His references proving satisfactory, the gentleman sent his adopted daughter to Mr. R., with a letter, in which he stipulated that the girl should have a room to herself, and stated that her guardians need be at no trouble in the matter of education, as she was already sufficiently educated for the position in life which she would occupy. In fact, Mr. R. was given to understand that the girl was to be allowed to find her own occupations, and to spend her time almost as she liked. Mr. R. duly met her at the nearest station, a town some seven miles away from his house, and seems to have remarked nothing extraordinary about the child, except that she was reticent as to her former life and her adopted father. She was, however, of a very different type from the inhabitants of the village; her skin was a pale, clear olive, and her features were strongly marked, and of a somewhat foreign character. She appears to have settled down, easily enough, into farm-house life, and became a favourite with the children, who sometimes went with her on her rambles in the forest, for this was her amusement. Mr. R. states that he has known her go out by herself directly after their early breakfast, and not return till after dusk, and that, feeling uneasy at a young girl being out alone for so many hours, he communicated with her adopted father, who replied in a brief note that Helen must do as she chose. In the winter, when the forest paths are impassable, she spent most of her time in her bedroom, where she slept alone, according to the instructions of her relative. It was on one of these expeditions to the forest, that the first of the singular incidents with which this girl is connected occurred, the date being about a year after her arrival at the village. The preceding winter had been remarkably severe, the snow drifting to a great depth, and the frost continuing for an unexampled period, and the summer following was as noteworthy for its extreme heat. On one of the very hottest days in this summer, Helen V. left the farm-house for one of her long rambles in the forest, taking with her, as usual, some bread and meat for lunch. She was seen by some men in the fields making for the old Roman Road, a green causeway which traverses the highest part of the wood, and they were astonished to observe that the girl had taken off her hat, though the heat of the sun was already almost tropical. As it happened, a labourer, Joseph W. by name, was working in the forest near the Roman Road, and at twelve o'clock, his little son, Trevor, brought the man his dinner of bread and cheese. After the meal, the boy, who was about seven years old at the time, left his father at work, and, as he says, went to look for flowers in the wood, and the man, who could hear him shouting with delight over his discoveries, felt no uneasiness. Suddenly, however, he was horrified at hearing the most dreadful screams, evidently the result of great terror, proceeding from the direction in which his son had gone, and he hastily threw down his tools and ran to see what had happened. Tracing his path by the sound, he met the little boy who was running headlong, and was evidently terribly frightened, and on questioning him the man at last elicited that after picking a posy of flowers he felt tired, and lay down on the grass and fell asleep. He was suddenly awakened, as he stated, by a peculiar noise, a sort of singing he called it, and on peeping through the branches he saw Helen V. playing on the grass with a "strange naked man," whom he seemed unable to describe further. He said he felt dreadfully frightened, and ran away crying for his father. Joseph W. proceeded in the direction indicated by his son, and found Helen V. sitting on the grass in the middle of a glade or open space left by charcoal burners. He angrily charged her with frightening his little boy, but she entirely denied the accusation and laughed at the child's story of a "strange man," to which he himself did not attach much credence. Joseph W. came to the conclusion that the boy had woke up with a sudden fright, as children sometimes do, but Trevor persisted in his story, and continued in such evident distress that at last his father took him home, hoping that his mother would be able to soothe him. For many weeks, however, the boy gave his parents much anxiety; he became nervous and strange in his manner, refusing to leave the cottage by himself, and constantly alarming the household by waking in the night with cries of "the man in the wood! father! father!" In course of time, however, the impression seemed to have worn off, and about three months later he accompanied his father to the house of a gentleman in the neighbourhood, for whom Joseph W. occasionally did work. The man was shown into the study, and the little boy was left sitting in the hall, and a few minutes later, while the gentleman was giving W. his instructions, they were both horrified by a piercing shriek and the sound of a fall, and rushing out they found the child lying senseless on the floor, his face contorted with terror. The doctor was immediately summoned, and after some examination he pronounced the child to be suffering from a kind of fit, apparently produced by a sudden shock. The boy was taken to one of the bedrooms, and after some time recovered consciousness, but only to pass into a condition described by the medical man as one of violent hysteria. The doctor exhibited a strong sedative, and in the course of two hours pronounced him fit to walk home, but in passing through the hall the paroxysms of fright returned and with additional violence. The father perceived that the child was pointing at some object, and heard the old cry, "the man in the wood," and looking in the direction indicated saw a stone head of grotesque appearance, which had been built into the wall above one of the doors. It seems that the owner of the house had recently made alterations in his premises, and on digging the foundations for some offices, the men had found a curious head, evidently of the Roman period, which had been placed in the hall in the manner described. The head is pronounced by the most experienced archæologists of the district to be that of a faun or satyr.[*]

From whatever cause arising, this second shock seemed too severe for the boy Trevor, and at the present date he suffers from a weakness of intellect, which gives but little promise of amending. The matter caused a good deal of sensation at the time, and the girl Helen was closely questioned by Mr. R., but to no purpose, she steadfastly denying that she had frightened or in any way molested Trevor.

The second event with which this girl's name is connected took place about six years ago, and is of a still more extraordinary character.

At the beginning of the summer of 188— Helen contracted a friendship of a peculiarly intimate character with Rachel M., the daughter of a prosperous farmer in the neighbourhood. This girl, who was a year younger than Helen, was considered by most people to be the prettier of the two, though Helen's features had to a great extent softened as she became older. The two girls, who were together on every available opportunity, presented a singular contrast, the one with her clear olive skin and almost Italian appearance, and the other of the proverbial red and white of our rural districts. It must be stated that the payments made to

---

[*] Dr. Phillips tells me that he has seen the head in question, and assures me that he has never received such a vivid presentment of intense evil.

Mr. R. for the maintenance of Helen were known in the village for their excessive liberality, and the impression was general that she would one day inherit a large sum of money from her relative. The parents of Rachel were therefore not averse to their daughter's friendship with the girl, and even encouraged the intimacy, though they now bitterly regret having done so. Helen still retained her extraordinary fondness for the forest, and on several occasions Rachel accompanied her, the two friends setting out early in the morning, and remaining in the wood till dusk. Once or twice after these excursions Mrs. M. thought her daughter's manner rather peculiar; she seemed languid and dreamy, and as it has been expressed, "different from herself," but these peculiarities seem to have been thought too trifling for remark. One evening, however, after Rachel had come home, her mother heard a noise which sounded like suppressed weeping in the girl's room, and on going in found her lying, half-undressed, upon the bed, evidently in the greatest distress. As soon as she saw her mother, she exclaimed, "Ah, mother, mother, why did you let me go to the forest with Helen?" Mrs. M. was astonished at so strange a question, and proceeded to make inquiries. Rachel told her a wild story. She said—

Clarke closed the book with a snap, and turned his chair towards the fire. When his friend sat one evening in that very chair, and told his story, Clarke had interrupted him at a point a little subsequent to this, had cut short his words in a paroxysm of horror, "My God!" he had exclaimed, "think, think, what you are saying. It is too incredible, too monstrous; such things can never be in this quiet world, where men and women live and die, and struggle, and conquer, or maybe fail, and fall down under sorrow, and grieve and suffer strange fortunes for many a year; but not this, Phillips, not such things as this. There must be some explanation, some way out of the terror. Why, man, if such a case were possible, our earth would be a nightmare."

But Phillips had told his story to the end, concluding:

"Her flight remains a mystery to this day; she vanished in broad sunlight, they saw her walking in a meadow, and a few moments later she was not there."

Clarke tried to conceive the thing again, as he sat by the fire, and again his mind shuddered and shrank back, appalled before the sight of such awful, unspeakable elements enthroned as it were, and triumphant in human flesh. Before him stretched the long dim vista of the green causeway in the forest, as his friend had described it: he saw the swaying leaves and the quivering shadows on the grass, he saw the sunlight and the flowers, and far away, far in the long distance, the two figures moved towards him. One was Rachel, but the other?

Clarke had tried his best to disbelieve it all, but at the end of the account, as he had written it in his book, he had placed the inscription:

ET DIABOLUS INCARNATUS EST. ET HOMO FACTUS EST.

THE CITY OF RESURRECTIONS

"Herbert! Good God! Is it possible?"

"Yes, my name's Herbert. I think I know your face too, but I don't remember your name. My memory is very queer."

"Don't you recollect Villiers of Wadham?"

"So it is, so it is. I beg your pardon, Villiers, I didn't think I was begging of an old college friend. Good-night."

"My dear fellow, this haste is unnecessary. My rooms are close by, but we won't go there just yet. Suppose we walk up Shaftesbury Avenue a little way? But how in heaven's name have you come to this pass, Herbert?"

"It's a long story, Villiers, and a strange one too, but you can hear it if you like."

"Come on, then. Take my arm, you don't seem very strong."

The ill-assorted pair moved slowly up Rupert Street; the one in dirty, evil-looking rags, and the other attired in the regulation uniform of a man about town, trim, glossy, and eminently well-to-do. Villiers had emerged from his restaurant after an excellent dinner of many courses, assisted by an ingratiating little flask of Chianti, and, in that frame of mind which was with him almost chronic, had delayed a moment by the door, peering round in the dimly-lighted street in search of those mysterious incidents and persons with which the streets of London teem in every quarter and at every hour. Villiers prided himself as a practised explorer of such obscure mazes and byways of London life, and in this unprofitable pursuit he displayed an assiduity which was worthy of more serious employment. Thus he stood beside the lamp-post surveying the passers-by with undisguised curiosity, and with that gravity only known to the systematic diner, had just enunciated in his mind the formula: "London has been called the city of encounters; it is more than that, it is the city of Resurrections," when these reflections were suddenly interrupted by a piteous whine at his elbow, and a deplorable appeal for alms. He looked round in some irritation, and with a sudden shock found himself confronted with the embodied proof of his somewhat stilted fancies. There, close beside him, his face altered and disfigured by poverty and disgrace, his body barely covered by greasy ill-fitting rags, stood his old friend Charles Herbert, who had matriculated on the same day as himself, and with whom he had been merry and wise for twelve revolving terms. Different occupations and varying interests had interrupted the friendship, and it was six years since Villiers had seen Herbert; and now he looked upon this wreck of a man with grief and dismay, mingled with a certain inquisitiveness as to what dreary chain of circumstance had dragged him down to such a doleful pass. Villiers felt together with compassion all the relish of the amateur in mysteries, and congratulated himself on his leisurely speculations outside the restaurant.

They walked on in silence for some time, and more than one passer-by stared in astonishment at the unaccustomed spectacle of a well-dressed man with an unmistakable beggar hanging on to his arm, and, observing this, Villiers led the way to an obscure street in Soho. Here he repeated his question.

"How on earth has it happened, Herbert? I always understood you would succeed to an excellent position in Dorsetshire. Did your father disinherit you? Surely not?"

"No, Villiers; I came into all the property at my poor father's death; he died a year after I left Oxford. He was a very good father to me, and I mourned his death sincerely enough. But you know what young men are; a few months later I came up to town and went a good deal into society. Of course I had excellent introductions, and I managed to enjoy myself very much in a harmless sort of way. I played a little, certainly, but never for heavy stakes, and the few bets I made on races brought me in money—only a few pounds, you know, but enough to pay for cigars and such petty pleasures. It was in my second season that the tide turned. Of course you have heard of my marriage?"

"No, I never heard anything about it."

"Yes, I married, Villiers. I met a girl, a girl of the most wonderful and most strange beauty, at the house of some people whom I knew. I cannot tell you her age; I never knew it, but, so far as I can guess, I should think she must have been about nineteen when I made her acquaintance. My friends had come to know her at Florence; she told them she was an orphan, the child of an English father and an Italian mother, and she charmed them as she charmed me. The first time I saw her was at an evening party; I was standing by the door talking to a friend, when suddenly above the hum and babble of conversation a voice, which seemed to thrill to my heart. She was singing an Italian song, I was introduced to her that evening, and in three months I married Helen. Villiers, that woman, if I can call her woman, corrupted my soul. The night of the wedding I found myself sitting in her bedroom in the hotel, listening to her talk. She was sitting up in bed, and I listened to her as she spoke in her beautiful voice, spoke of things which even now I would not dare whisper in blackest night, though I stood in the midst of a wilderness. You, Villiers, you may think you know life, and London, and what goes on, day and night, in this dreadful city; for all I can say you may have heard the talk of the vilest, but I tell you you can have no conception of what I know, no, not in your most fantastic, hideous dreams can you have imaged forth the faintest shadow of what I have heard—and seen. Yes, seen; I have seen the incredible, such horrors that even I myself sometimes stop in the middle of the street, and ask whether it is possible for a man to behold such things and live. In a year, Villiers, I was a ruined man, in body and soul,—in body and soul."

"But your property, Herbert? You had land in Dorset."

"I sold it all; the fields and woods, the dear old house—everything."

"And the money?"

"She took it all from me."

"And then left you?"

"Yes; she disappeared one night, I don't know where she went, but I am sure if I saw her again it would kill me. The rest of my story is of no interest; sordid misery, that is all. You may think, Villiers, that I have exaggerated and talked for effect; but I have not told you half. I could tell you certain things which would convince you, but you would never know a happy day again. You would pass the rest of your life, as I pass mine, a haunted man, a man who has seen hell."

Villiers took the unfortunate man to his rooms, and gave him a meal. Herbert could eat little, and scarcely touched the glass of wine set before him. He sat moody and silent by the fire, and seemed relieved when Villiers sent him away with a small present of money.

"By the way, Herbert," said Villiers, as they parted at the door, "what was your wife's name? You said Helen, I think? Helen what?"

"The name she passed under when I met her was Helen Vaughan, but what her real name was I can't say. I don't think she had a name. No, no, not in that sense. Only human beings have names, Villiers; I can't say any more. Good-bye; yes, I will not fail to call if I see any way in which you can help me. Good-night."

The man went out into the bitter night, and Villiers returned to his fireside. There was something about Herbert which shocked him inexpressibly; not his poor rags or the marks which poverty had set upon his face, but rather an indefinite terror which hung about him like a mist. He had acknowledged that he himself was not devoid of blame, the woman, he had avowed, had corrupted him body and soul, and Villiers felt that this man, once his friend, had been an actor in scenes evil beyond the power of words. His story needed no confirmation; he himself was the embodied proof of it. Villiers mused curiously over the story he had heard, and wondered whether he had heard both the first and the last of it. "No," he thought, "certainly not the last, probably only the beginning. A case like this is like a nest of Chinese boxes; you open one after another and find a quainter workmanship in every box. Most likely poor Herbert is merely one of the outside boxes; there are stranger ones to follow."

Villiers could not take his mind away from Herbert and his story, which seemed to grow wilder as the night wore on. The fire began to burn low, and the chilly air of the morning crept into the room; Villiers got up with a glance over his shoulder, and shivering slightly, went to bed.

A few days later he saw at his club a gentleman of his acquaintance, named Austin, who was famous for his intimate knowledge of London life, both in its tenebrous and luminous phases. Villiers, still full of his encounter in Soho and its consequences, thought Austin might possibly be able to shed some light on Herbert's history, and so after some casual talk he suddenly put the question:

"Do you happen to know anything of a man named Herbert—Charles Herbert?"

Austin turned round sharply and stared at Villiers with some astonishment.

"Charles Herbert? Weren't you in town three years ago? No; then you have not heard of the Paul Street case? It caused a good deal of sensation at the time."

"What was the case?"

"Well, a gentleman, a man of very good position, was found dead, stark dead, in the area of a certain house in Paul Street, off Tottenham Court Road. Of course the police did not make the discovery; if you happen to be sitting up all night and have a light in your window, the constable will ring the bell, but if you happen to be lying dead in somebody's area, you will be left alone. In this instance as in many others the alarm was raised by some kind of vagabond; I don't mean a common tramp, or a public-house loafer, but a gentleman, whose business or pleasure, or both, made him a spectator of the London Streets at five o'clock in the morning. This individual was, as he said, 'going home,' it did not appear whence or whither, and had occasion to pass through Paul Street between four and five A.M. Something or other caught his eye at Number 20; he said, absurdly enough, that the house had the most unpleasant physiognomy he had ever observed, but, at any rate, he glanced down the area, and was a good deal astonished to see a man lying on the stones, his limbs all huddled together, and his face turned up. Our gentleman thought this face looked peculiarly ghastly, and so set off at a run in search of the nearest policeman. The constable was at first inclined to treat the matter lightly, suspecting a mere drunken freak; however, he came, and after looking at the man's face changed his tone, quickly enough. The early bird, who had picked up this fine worm, was sent off for a doctor, and the policeman rang and knocked at the door till a slatternly servant girl came down looking more than half asleep. The constable pointed out the contents of the area to the maid, who screamed loudly enough to wake up the street, but she knew nothing of the man; had never seen him at the house, and so forth. Meanwhile the original discoverer had come back with a medical man, and the next thing was to get into the area. The gate was open, so the whole quartet stumped down the steps. The doctor hardly needed a moment's examination; he said the poor fellow had been dead for several hours, and he was moved away to the police-station for the time being. It was then the case began to get interesting.

The dead man had not been robbed, and in one of his pockets were papers identifying him as—well, as a man of good family and means, a favourite in society, and nobody's enemy, so far as could be known. I don't give his name, Villiers, because it has nothing to do with the story, and because it's no good raking up these affairs about the dead, when there are relations living. The next curious point was that the medical men couldn't agree as to how he met his death. There were some slight bruises on his shoulders, but they were so slight that it looked as if he had been pushed roughly out of the kitchen door, and not thrown over the railings from the street, or even dragged down the steps. But there were positively no other marks of violence about him, certainly none that would account for his death; and when they came to the autopsy there wasn't a trace of poison of any kind. Of course the police wanted to know all about the people at Number 20, and here again, so I have heard from private sources, one or two other very curious points came out. It appears that the occupants of the house were a Mr. and Mrs. Charles Herbert; he was said to be a landed proprietor, though it struck most people that Paul Street was not exactly the place to look for county gentry. As for Mrs. Herbert, nobody seemed to know who or what she was, and, between ourselves, I fancy the divers after her history found themselves in rather strange waters. Of course they both denied knowing anything about the deceased, and in default of any evidence against them they were discharged. But some very odd things came out about them. Though it was between five and six in the morning when the dead man was removed, a large crowd had collected, and several of the neighbours ran to see what was going on. They were pretty free with their comments, by all accounts, and from these it appeared that Number 20 was in very bad odour in Paul Street. The detectives tried to trace down these rumours to some solid foundation of fact, but could not get hold of anything. People shook their heads and raised their eyebrows and thought the Herberts rather 'queer,' 'would rather not be seen going into their house,' and so on, but there was nothing tangible. The authorities were morally certain that the man met his death in some way or another in the house and was thrown out by the kitchen door, but they couldn't prove it, and the absence of any indications of violence or poisoning left them helpless. An odd case, wasn't it? But curiously enough, there's something more that I haven't told you. I happened to know one of the doctors who was consulted as to the cause of death, and some time after the inquest I met him, and asked him about it. 'Do you really mean to tell me,' I said, 'that you were baffled by the case, that you actually don't know what the man died of?' 'Pardon me,' he replied, 'I know perfectly well what caused death. Blank died of fright, of sheer, awful terror; I never saw features so hideously contorted in the entire course of my practice, and I have seen the faces of a whole host of dead.' The doctor was usually a cool customer enough, and a certain vehemence in his manner struck me, but I couldn't get anything more out of him. I suppose the Treasury didn't see their way to prosecuting the Herberts for frightening a man to death; at any rate, nothing was done, and the case dropped out of men's minds. Do you happen to know anything of Herbert?"

"Well," replied Villiers, "he was an old college friend of mine."

"You don't say so? Have you ever seen his wife?"

"No, I haven't. I have lost sight of Herbert for many years."

"It's queer, isn't it, parting with a man at the college gate or at Paddington, seeing nothing of him for years, and then finding him pop up his head in such an odd place. But I should like to have seen Mrs. Herbert; people said extraordinary things about her."

"What sort of things?"

"Well, I hardly know how to tell you. Every one who saw her at the police court said she was at once the most beautiful woman and the most repulsive they had ever set eyes on. I have spoken to a man who saw her, and I assure you he positively shuddered as he tried to describe the woman, but he couldn't tell why. She seems to have been a sort of enigma; and I expect if that one dead man could have told tales, he would have told some uncommonly queer ones. And there you are again in another puzzle; what could a respectable country gentleman like Mr. Blank (we'll call him that if you don't mind) want in such a very queer house as Number 20? It's altogether a very odd case, isn't it?"

"It is indeed, Austin; an extraordinary case. I didn't think, when I asked you about my old friend, I should strike on such strange metal. Well, I must be off; good-day."

Villiers went away, thinking of his own conceit of the Chinese boxes; here was quaint workmanship indeed.

THE DISCOVERY IN PAUL STREET

A few months after Villiers's meeting with Herbert, Mr. Clarke was sitting, as usual, by his after-dinner hearth, resolutely guarding his fancies from wandering in the direction of the bureau. For more than a week he had succeeded in keeping away from the "Memoirs," and he cherished hopes of a complete self-reformation; but, in spite of his endeavours, he could not hush the wonder and the strange curiosity that that last case he had written down had excited within him. He had put the case, or rather the outline of it, conjecturally to a scientific friend, who shook his head, and thought Clarke getting queer, and on this particular evening Clarke was making an effort to rationalise the story, when a sudden knock at his door roused him from his meditations.

"Mr. Villiers to see you, sir."

"Dear me, Villiers, it is very kind of you to look me up; I have not seen you for many months; I should think nearly a year. Come in, come in. And how are you, Villiers? Want any advice about investments?"

"No, thanks, I fancy everything I have in that way is pretty safe. No, Clarke, I have really come to consult you about a rather curious matter that has been brought under my notice of late. I am afraid you will think it all rather absurd when I tell my tale, I sometimes think so myself, and that's just why I made up my mind to come to you, as I know you're a practical man."

Mr. Villiers was ignorant of the "Memoirs to prove the Existence of the Devil."

"Well, Villiers, I shall be happy to give you my advice, to the best of my ability. What is the nature of the case?"

"It's an extraordinary thing altogether. You know my ways; I always keep my eyes open in the streets, and in my time I have chanced upon some queer customers, and queer cases too, but this, I think, beats all. I was coming out of a restaurant one nasty winter night about three months ago; I had had a capital dinner and a good bottle of Chianti, and I stood for a moment on the pavement, thinking what a mystery there is about London streets and the companies that pass along them. A bottle of red wine encourages these fancies, Clarke, and I daresay I should have thought a page of small type, but I was cut short by a beggar who had come behind me, and was making the usual appeals. Of course I looked round, and this beggar turned out to be what was left of an old friend of mine, a man named Herbert. I asked him how he had come to such a wretched pass, and he told me. We walked up and down one of those long dark Soho streets, and there I listened to his story. He said he had married a beautiful girl, some years younger than himself, and, as he put it, she had corrupted him body and soul. He wouldn't go into details; he said he dare not, that what he had seen and heard haunted him by night and day, and when I looked in his face I knew he was speaking the truth. There was something about the man that made me shiver. I don't know why, but it was there. I gave him a little money and sent him away, and I assure you that when he was gone I gasped for breath. His presence seemed to chill one's blood."

"Isn't all this just a little fanciful, Villiers? I suppose the poor fellow had made an imprudent marriage, and, in plain English, gone to the bad."

"Well, listen to this." Villiers told Clarke the story he had heard from Austin.

"You see," he concluded, "there can be but little doubt that this Mr. Blank, whoever he was, died of sheer terror; he saw something so awful, so terrible, that it cut short his life. And what he saw, he most certainly saw in that house, which, somehow or other, had got a bad name in the neighbourhood. I had the curiosity to go and look at the place for myself. It's a saddening kind of street; the houses are old enough to be mean and dreary, but not old enough to be quaint. As far as I could see most of them are let in lodgings, furnished and unfurnished, and almost every door has three bells to it. Here and there the ground floors have been made into shops of the commonest kind; it's a dismal street in every way. I found Number 20 was to let, and I went to the agent's and got the key. Of course I should have heard nothing of the Herberts in that quarter, but I asked the man, fair and square, how long they have left the house, and whether there had been other tenants in the meanwhile. He looked at me queerly for a minute, and told me the Herberts had left immediately after the unpleasantness, as he called it, and since then the house had been empty."

Mr. Villiers paused for a moment.

"I have always been rather fond of going over empty houses; there's a sort of fascination about the desolate empty rooms, with the nails sticking in the walls, and the dust thick upon the window-sills. But I didn't enjoy going over Number 20 Paul Street. I had hardly put my foot inside the passage before I noticed a queer, heavy feeling about the air of the house. Of course all empty houses are stuffy, and so forth, but this was something quite different; I can't describe it to you, but it seemed to stop the breath. I went into the front room and the back room, and the kitchens downstairs; they were all dirty and dusty enough, as you would expect, but there was something strange about them all. I couldn't define it to you, I only know I felt queer. It was one of the rooms on the first floor, though, that was the worst. It was a largish room, and once on a time the paper must have been cheerful enough, but when I saw it, paint, paper, and everything were most doleful. But the room was full of horror; I felt my teeth grinding as I put my hand on the door, and when I went in, I thought I should have fallen fainting to the floor. However, I pulled myself together, and stood against the end wall, wondering what on earth there could be about the room to make my limbs tremble, and my heart beat as if I were at the hour of death. In one corner there was a pile of newspapers littered about on the floor and I began looking at them, they were papers of three or four years ago, some of them half torn, and some crumpled as if they had been used for packing. I turned the whole pile over, and amongst them I found a curious drawing; I will show it you presently. But I couldn't stay in the room; I felt it was over-powering me. I was thankful to come out, safe and sound, into the open air. People stared at me as I walked along the street, and one man said I was drunk. I was staggering about from one side of the pavement to the other, and it was as much as I could do to take the key back to the agent and get home. I was in bed for a week, suf-fering from what my doctor called nervous shock and exhaustion. One of those days I was reading the evening paper, and happened to notice a paragraph headed: 'Starved to Death.' It was the usual style of thing; a model lodging-house in Marylebone, a door locked for several days, and a dead man in his chair when they broke in. 'The deceased,' said the paragraph, 'was known as Charles Herbert, and is believed to have been once a prosperous country gentleman. His name was familiar to the public three years ago in connection with the mysterious death in Paul Street, Tottenham Court Road, the deceased being the tenant of the house Number 20, in the area of which a gentleman of good position was found dead under circumstances not devoid of suspicion.' A tragic ending, wasn't it? But after all, if what he told me were true, which I am sure it was, the man's life was all a tragedy, and a tragedy of a stranger sort than they put on the boards."

"And that is the story, is it?" said Clarke musingly.

"Yes, that is the story,"

"Well, really, Villiers, I scarcely know what to say about it. There are no doubt circumstances in the case which seem peculiar, the finding of the dead man in the area of the Herberts' house, for instance, and the extraordinary opinion of the physician as to the cause of death, but, after all, it is conceivable that the facts may be explained in a straightforward manner. As to your own sensations when you went to see the house, I would suggest that they were due to a vivid imagination; you must have been brooding, in a semi-conscious way, over what you had heard. I don't exactly see what more can be said or done in the matter; you evidently think there is a mystery of some kind, but Herbert is dead; where then do you propose to look?"

"I propose to look for the woman; the woman whom he married. *She* is the mystery."

The two men sat silent by the fireside; Clarke secretly congratulating himself on having successfully kept up the character of advocate of the commonplace, and Villiers wrapt in his gloomy fancies.

"I think I will have a cigarette," he said at last, and put his hand in his pocket to feel for the cigarette-case.

"Ah!" he said, starting slightly, "I forgot I had something to show you. You remember my saying that I had found a rather curious sketch amongst the pile of old newspapers at the house in Paul Street?—here it is."

Villiers drew out a small thin parcel from his pocket. It was covered with brown paper, and secured with string, and the knots were troublesome. In spite of himself Clarke felt inquisitive; he bent forward on his chair as Villiers painfully undid the string, and unfolded the outer covering. Inside was a second wrapping of tissue, and Villiers took it off and handed the small piece of paper to Clarke without a word.

There was dead silence in the room for five minutes or more; the two men sat so still that they could hear the ticking of the tall old-fashioned clock that stood outside in the hall, and in the mind of one of them the slow monotony of sound woke up a far, far memory. He was looking intently at the small pen-and-ink sketch of a woman's head; it had evidently been drawn with great care, and by a true artist, for the woman's soul looked out of the eyes, and the lips were parted with a strange smile. Clarke gazed still at the face; it brought to his memory one summer evening long ago; he saw again the long lovely valley, the river winding between the hills, the meadows and the cornfields, the dull red sun, and the cold white mist rising from the water. He heard a voice speaking to him across the waves of many years, and saying, "Clarke, Mary will see the God Pan!" and then he was standing in the grim room beside the doctor, listening to the heavy ticking of the clock, waiting and watching, watching the figure lying on the green chair beneath the lamplight. Mary rose up, and he looked into her eyes, and his heart grew cold within him.

"Who is this woman?" he said at last. His voice was dry and hoarse.

"That is the woman whom Herbert married."

Clarke looked again at the sketch; it was not Mary after all. There certainly was Mary's face, but there was something else, something he had not seen on Mary's features when the white-clad girl entered the laboratory with the doctor, nor at her terrible awakening, nor when she lay grinning on the bed. Whatever it was, the glance that came from those eyes, the smile on the full lips, or the expression of the whole face, Clarke shuddered before it in his inmost soul, and thought, unconsciously, of Dr. Phillips's words, "the most vivid presentment of evil I have ever seen." He turned the paper over mechanically in his hand and glanced at the back.

"Good God! Clarke, what is the matter? You are as white as death."

Villiers had started wildly from his chair, as Clarke fell back with a groan, and let the paper drop from his hands.

"I don't feel very well, Villiers, I am subject to these attacks. Pour me out a little wine; thanks, that will do. I shall be better in a few minutes."

Villiers picked up the fallen sketch and turned it over as Clarke had done.

"You saw that?" he said. "That's how I identified it as being a portrait of Herbert's wife, or I should say his widow. How do you feel now?"

"Better, thanks, it was only a passing faintness. I don't think I quite catch your meaning. What did you say enabled you to identify the picture?"

"This word—Helen—written on the back. Didn't I tell you her name was Helen? Yes; Helen Vaughan."

Clarke groaned; there could be no shadow of doubt.

"Now, don't you agree with me," said Villiers, "that in the story I have told you tonight, and in the part this woman plays in it, there are some very strange points?"

"Yes, Villiers," Clarke muttered, "it is a strange story indeed; a strange story indeed. You must give me time to think it over; I may be able to help you or I may not. Must you be going now? Well, good-night, Villiers, good-night. Come and see me in the course of a week."

THE LETTER OF ADVICE

"Do you know, Austin," said Villiers, as the two friends were pacing sedately along Piccadilly one pleasant morning in May, "do you know I am convinced that what you told me about Paul Street and the Herberts is a mere episode in an extraordinary history. I may as well confess to you that when I asked you about Herbert a few months ago I had just seen him."

"You had seen him? Where?"

"He begged of me in the street one night. He was in the most pitiable plight, but I recognised the man, and I got him to tell me his history, or at least the outline of it. In brief, it amounted to this—he had been ruined by his wife."

"In what manner?"

"He would not tell me; he would only say that she had destroyed him body and soul. The man is dead now."

"And what has become of his wife?"

"Ah, that's what I should like to know, and I mean to find her sooner or later. I know a man named Clarke, a dry fellow, in fact a man of business, but shrewd enough. You understand my meaning; not shrewd in the mere business sense of the word, but a man who really knows something about men and life. Well, I laid the case before him, and he was evidently impressed. He said it needed consideration, and asked me to come again in the course of a week. A few days later I received this extraordinary letter."

Austin took the envelope, drew out the letter, and read it curiously. It ran as follows:—

"MY DEAR VILLIERS,—I have thought over the matter on which you consulted me the other night, and my advice to you is this. Throw the portrait into the fire, blot out the story from your mind. Never give it another thought, Villiers, or you will be sorry. You will think, no doubt, that I am in possession of some secret information, and to a certain extent that is the case. But I only know a little; I am like a traveller who has peered over an abyss, and has drawn back in terror. What I know is strange enough and horrible enough, but beyond my knowledge there are depths and horrors more frightful still, more incredible than any tale told of winter nights about the fire. I have resolved, and nothing shall shake that resolve, to explore no whit further, and if you value your happiness you will make the same determination.

"Come and see me by all means; but we will talk on more cheerful topics than this."

Austin folded the letter methodically, and returned it to Villiers.

"It is certainly an extraordinary letter," he said; "what does he mean by the portrait?"

"Ah! I forgot to tell you I have been to Paul Street and have made a discovery."

Villiers told his story as he had told it to Clarke, and Austin listened in silence. He seemed puzzled.

"How very curious that you should experience such an unpleasant sensation in that room!" he said at length. "I hardly gather that it was a mere matter of the imagination; a feeling of repulsion, in short."

"No, it was more physical than mental. It was as if I were inhaling at every breath some deadly fume, which seemed to penetrate to every nerve and bone and sinew of my body. I felt racked from head to foot, my eyes began to grow dim; it was like the entrance of death."

"Yes, yes, very strange, certainly. You see, your friend confesses that there is some very black story connected with this woman. Did you notice any particular emotion in him when you were telling your tale?"

"Yes, I did. He became very faint, but he assured me that it was a mere passing attack to which he was subject."

"Did you believe him?"

"I did at the time, but I don't now. He heard what I had to say with a good deal of indifference, till I showed him the portrait. It was then he was seized with the attack of which I spoke. He looked ghastly, I assure you."

"Then he must have seen the woman before. But there might be another explanation; it might have been the name, and not the face, which was familiar to him. What do you think?"

"I couldn't say. To the best of my belief it was after turning the portrait in his hands that he nearly dropped from his chair. The name, you know, was written on the back."

"Quite so. After all, it is impossible to come to any resolution in a case like this. I hate melodrama, and nothing strikes me as more commonplace and tedious than the ordinary ghost story of commerce; but really, Villiers, it looks as if there were something very queer at the bottom of all this."

The two men had, without noticing it, turned up Ashley Street, leading northward from Piccadilly. It was a long street, and rather a gloomy one, but here and there a brighter taste had illuminated the dark houses with flowers, and gay curtains, and a cheerful paint on the doors. Villiers glanced up as Austin stopped speaking, and looked at one of these houses; geraniums, red and white, drooped from every sill, and daffodil-coloured curtains were draped back from each window.

"It looks cheerful, doesn't it?" he said.

"Yes, and the inside is still more cheery. One of the pleasantest houses of the season, so I have heard. I haven't been there myself, but I have met several men who have, and they tell me it's uncommonly jovial."

"Whose house is it?"

"A Mrs. Beaumont's."

"And who is she?"

"I couldn't tell you. I have heard she comes from South America, but, after all, who she is is of little consequence. She is a very wealthy woman, there's no doubt of that, and some of the best people have taken her up. I hear she has some wonderful claret, really marvellous wine, which must have cost a fabulous sum. Lord Argentine was telling me about it; he was there last Sunday evening. He assures me he has never tasted such a wine, and Argentine, as you know, is an expert. By the way, that reminds me, she must be an oddish sort of woman, this Mrs. Beaumont. Argentine asked her how old the wine was, and what do you think she said? 'About a thousand years, I believe.' Lord Argentine thought she was chaffing him, you know, but when he laughed she said she was speaking quite seriously, and offered to show him the jar. Of course, he couldn't say anything more after that; but it seems rather antiquated for a beverage, doesn't it? Why, here we are at my rooms. Come in, won't you?"

"Thanks, I think I will. I haven't seen the curiosity-shop for some time."

It was a room furnished richly, yet oddly, where every chair and bookcase and table, every rug and jar and ornament seemed to be a thing apart, preserving each its own individuality.

"Anything fresh lately?" said Villiers after a while.

"No; I think not; you saw those queer jugs, didn't you? I thought so. I don't think I have come across anything for the last few weeks."

Austin glanced round the room from cupboard to cupboard, from shelf to shelf, in search of some new oddity. His eyes fell at last on an old chest, pleasantly and quaintly carved, which stood in a dark corner of the room.

"Ah," he said, "I was forgetting, I have got something to show you." Austin unlocked the chest, drew out a thick quarto volume, laid it on the table, and resumed the cigar he had put down.

"Did you know Arthur Meyrick the painter, Villiers?"

"A little; I met him two or three times at the house of a friend of mine. What has become of him? I haven't heard his name mentioned for some time."

"He's dead."

"You don't say so! Quite young, wasn't he?"

"Yes; only thirty when he died."

"What did he die of?"

"I don't know. He was an intimate friend of mine, and a thoroughly good fellow. He used to come here and talk to me for hours, and he was one of the best talkers I have met. He could even talk about painting, and that's more than can be said of most painters. About eighteen months ago he was feeling rather overworked, and partly at my suggestion he went off on a sort of roving expedition, with no very definite end or aim about it. I believe New York was to be his first port, but I never heard from him. Three months ago I got this book, with a very civil letter from an English doctor practising at Buenos Ayres, stating that he had attended the late Mr. Meyrick during his illness, and that the deceased had expressed an earnest wish that the enclosed packet should be sent to me after his death. That was all."

"And haven't you written for further particulars?"

"I have been thinking of doing so. You would advise me to write to the doctor?"

"Certainly. And what about the book?"

"It was sealed up when I got it. I don't think the doctor had seen it."

"It is something very rare? Meyrick was a collector, perhaps?"

"No, I think not, hardly a collector. Now, what do you think of those Ainu jugs?"

"They are peculiar, but I like them. But aren't you going to show me poor Meyrick's legacy?"

"Yes, yes, to be sure. The fact is, it's rather a peculiar sort of thing, and I haven't shown it to any one. I wouldn't say anything about it if I were you. There it is."

Villiers took the book, and opened it at haphazard. "It isn't a printed volume then?" he said.

"No. It is a collection of drawings in black and white by my poor friend Meyrick."

Villiers turned to the first page, it was blank; the second bore a brief inscription, which he read:

Silet per diem universus, nec sine horrore secretus est; lucet nocturnis ignibus, chorus Ægipanum undique personatur: audiuntur et cantus tibiarum, et tinnitus cymbalorum per oram maritimam.

On the third page was a design which made Villiers start and look up at Austin; he was gazing abstractedly out of the window. Villiers turned page after page, absorbed, in spite of himself, in the frightful Walpurgis Night of evil, strange monstrous evil, that the dead artist had set forth in hard black and white. The figures of Fauns and Satyrs and Ægipans danced before his eyes, the darkness of the thicket, the dance on the mountain-top, the scenes by lonely shores, in green vineyards, by rocks and desert places, passed before him; a world before which the human soul seemed to shrink back and shudder. Villiers whirled over the remaining pages, he had seen enough, but the picture on the last leaf caught his eye, as he almost closed the book.

"Austin!"

"Well, what is it?"

"Do you know who that is?"

It was a woman's face, alone on the white page.

"Know who it is? No, of course not."

"I do."

"Who is it?"

"It is Mrs. Herbert."

"Are you sure?"

"I am perfectly certain of it. Poor Meyrick! He is one more chapter in her history."

"But what do you think of the designs?"

"They are frightful. Lock the book up again, Austin. If I were you I would burn it; it must be a terrible companion, even though it be in a chest."

"Yes, they are singular drawings. But I wonder what connection there could be between Meyrick and Mrs. Herbert, or what link between her and these designs?"

"Ah, who can say? It is possible that the matter may end here, and we shall never know, but in my own opinion this Helen Vaughan, or Mrs. Herbert, is only beginning. She will come back to London, Austin, depend upon it, she will come back, and we shall hear more about her then. I don't think it will be very pleasant news."

THE SUICIDES

Lord Argentine was a great favourite in London society. At twenty he had been a poor man, decked with the surname of an illustrious family, but forced to earn a livelihood as best he could, and the most speculative of money-lenders would not have intrusted him with fifty pounds on the chance of his ever changing his name for a title, and his poverty for a great fortune. His father had been near enough to the fountain of good things to secure one of the family livings, but the son, even if he had taken orders, would scarcely have obtained so much as this, and moreover felt no vocation for the ecclesiastical estate. Thus he fronted the world with no better armour than the bachelor's gown and the wits of a younger son's grandson, with which equipment he contrived in some way to make a very tolerable fight of it. At twenty-five Mr. Charles Aubernoun saw himself still a man of struggles and of warfare with the world, but out of the seven who stood between him and the high places of his family three only remained. These three, however, were "good lives," but yet not proof against the Zulu assegais and typhoid fever, and so one morning Aubernoun woke up and found himself Lord Argentine, a man of thirty who had faced the difficulties of existence, and had conquered. The situation amused him immensely, and he resolved that riches should be as pleasant to him as poverty had always been. Argentine, after some little consideration, came to the conclusion that dining, regarded as a fine art, was perhaps the most amusing pursuit open to fallen humanity, and thus his dinners became famous in London, and an invitation to his table a thing covetously desired. After ten years of lordship and dinners Argentine still declined to be jaded, still persisted in enjoying life, and by a kind of infection had become recognised as the cause of joy in others, in short as the best of company. His sudden and tragical death therefore caused a wide and deep sensation. People could scarce believe it, even though the newspaper was before their eyes, and the cry of "Mysterious Death of a Nobleman" came ringing up from the street. But there stood the brief paragraph: "Lord Argentine was found dead this morning by his valet under distressing circumstances. It is stated that there can be no doubt that his lordship committed suicide, though no motive can be assigned for the act. The deceased nobleman was widely known in society, and much liked for his genial manner and sumptuous hospitality. He is succeeded by etc. etc."

By slow degrees the details came to light, but the case still remained a mystery. The chief witness at the inquest was the dead nobleman's valet, who said that the night before his death Lord Argentine had dined with a lady of good position, whose name was suppressed in the newspaper reports. At about eleven o'clock Lord Argentine had returned, and informed his man that he should not require his services till the next morning. A little later the valet had occasion to cross the hall and was somewhat astonished to see his master quietly letting himself out at the front door. He had taken off his evening clothes, and was dressed in a Norfolk coat and knickerbockers, and wore a low brown hat. The valet had no reason to suppose that Lord Argentine had seen him, and though his master rarely kept late hours, thought little of the occurrence till the next morning, when he knocked at the bedroom door at a quarter to nine as usual. He received no answer, and, after knocking two or three times, entered the room, and saw Lord Argentine's body leaning forward at an angle from the bottom of the bed. He found that his master had tied a cord securely to one of the short bed-posts, and, after making a running noose and slipping it round his neck, the unfortunate man must have resolutely fallen forward, to die by slow strangulation. He was dressed in the light suit in which the valet had seen him go out, and the doctor who was summoned pronounced that life had been extinct for more than four hours. All papers, letters, and so forth, seemed in perfect order, and nothing was discovered which pointed in the most remote way to any scandal either great or small. Here the evidence ended; nothing more could be discovered. Several persons had been present at the dinner-party at which Lord Argentine had assisted, and to all these he seemed in his usual genial spirits. The valet, indeed, said he thought his master appeared a little excited when he came home, but he confessed that the alteration in his manner was very slight, hardly noticeable, indeed. It seemed hopeless to seek for any clew, and the suggestion that Lord Argentine had been suddenly attacked by acute suicidal mania was generally acccptcd.

It was otherwise, however, when within three weeks, three more gentlemen, one of them a nobleman, and the two others men of good position and ample means, perished miserably in almost precisely the same manner. Lord Swanleigh was found one morning in his dressing-room, hanging from a peg affixed to the wall, and Mr. Collier-Stuart and Mr. Herries had chosen to die as Lord Argentine. There was no explanation in either case; a few bald facts; a living man in the evening, and a dead body with a black swollen face in the morning. The police had been forced to confess themselves powerless to arrest or to explain the sordid murders of Whitechapel; but before the horrible suicides of Piccadilly and Mayfair, they were dumbfoundered, for not even the mere ferocity which did duty as an explanation of the crimes of the East End, could be of service in the West. Each of these men who had resolved to die a tortured shameful death was rich, prosperous, and to all appearance in love with the world, and not the acutest research could ferret out any shadow of a lurking motive in either case. There was a horror in the air, and men looked at one another's faces when they met, each wondering whether the other was to be the victim of a fifth nameless tragedy. Journalists sought in vain in their scrap-books for materials whereof to concoct reminiscent articles; and the morning paper was unfolded in many a house with a feeling of awe; no man knew when or where the blow would next light.

A short while after the last of these terrible events, Austin came to see Mr. Villiers. He was curious to know whether Villiers had succeeded in discovering any fresh traces of Mrs. Herbert, either through Clarke or by other sources, and he asked the question soon after he had sat down.

"No," said Villiers, "I wrote to Clarke, but he remains obdurate, and I have tried other channels, but without any result. I can't find out what became of Helen Vaughan after she left Paul Street, but I think she must have gone abroad. But to tell the truth, Austin, I haven't paid very much attention to the matter for the last few weeks; I knew poor Herries intimately, and his terrible death has been a great shock to me, a great shock."

"I can well believe it," answered Austin gravely, "you know Argentine was a friend of mine. If I remember rightly, we were speaking of him that day you came to my rooms."

"Yes; it was in connection with that house in Ashley Street, Mrs. Beaumont's house. You said something about Argentine's dining there."

"Quite so. Of course you know it was there Argentine dined the night before—before his death."

"No, I haven't heard that."

"Oh yes; the name was kept out of the papers to spare Mrs. Beaumont. Argentine was a great favourite of hers, and it is said she was in a terrible state for some time after."

A curious look came over Villiers's face; he seemed undecided whether to speak or not. Austin began again.

I never experienced such a feeling of horror as when I read the account of Argentine's death. I didn't understand it at the time, and I don't now. I knew him well, and it completely passes my understanding for what possible cause he—or any of the others for the matter of that—could have resolved in cold blood to die in such an awful manner. You know how men babble away each other's characters in London, you may be sure any buried scandal or hidden skeleton would have been brought to light in such a case as this; but nothing of the sort has taken place. As for the theory of mania, that is very well, of course, for the coroner's jury, but everybody knows that it's all nonsense. Suicidal mania is not smallpox."

Austin relapsed into gloomy silence. Villiers sat silent also, watching his friend. The expression of indecision still fleeted across his face, he seemed as if weighing his thoughts in the balance, and the considerations he was revolving left him still silent. Austin tried to shake off the remembrance of tragedies as hopeless and perplexed as the labyrinth of Dædalus, and began to talk in an indifferent voice of the more pleasant incidents and adventures of the season.

"That Mrs. Beaumont," he said, "of whom we were speaking, is a great success; she has taken London almost by storm. I met her the other night at Fulham's; she is really a remarkable woman."

"You have met Mrs. Beaumont?"

"Yes; she had quite a court around her. She would be called very handsome, I suppose, and yet there is something about her face which I didn't like. The features are exquisite, but the expression is strange. And all the time I was looking at her, and afterwards, when I was going home, I had a curious feeling that that very expression was in some way or other familiar to me."

"You must have seen her in the Row."

"No, I am sure I never set eyes on the woman before; it is that which makes it puzzling. And to the best of my belief I have never seen anybody like her; what I felt was a kind of dim far-off memory, vague but persistent. The only sensation I can compare it to, is that odd feeling one sometimes has in a dream, when fantastic cities and wondrous lands and phantom personages appear familiar and accustomed."

Villiers nodded and glanced aimlessly round the room, possibly in search of something on which to turn the conversation. His eyes fell on an old chest somewhat like that in which the artist's strange legacy lay hid beneath a Gothic scutcheon.

"Have you written to the doctor about poor Meyrick?" he asked.

"Yes; I wrote asking for full particulars as to his illness and death. I don't expect to have an answer for another three weeks or a month. I thought I might as well inquire whether Meyrick knew an Englishwoman named Herbert, and if so, whether the doctor could give me any information about her. But it's very possible that Meyrick fell in with her at New York, or Mexico, or San Francisco; I have no idea as to the extent or direction of his travels."

"Yes, and it's very possible that the woman may have more than one name."

"Exactly. I wish I had thought of asking you to lend me the portrait of her which you possess. I might have enclosed it in my letter to Dr. Mathews."

"So you might; that never occurred to me. We might even now do so. Hark! what are those boys calling?"

While the two men had been talking together a confused noise of shouting had been gradually growing louder. The noise rose from the eastward and swelled down Piccadilly, drawing nearer and nearer, a very torrent of sound; surging up streets usually quiet, and making every window a frame for a face, curious or excited. The cries and voices came echoing up the silent street where Villiers lived, growing more distinct as they advanced, and, as Villiers spoke, an answer rang up from the pavement:

"The West End Horrors; Another Awful Suicide; Full Details!"

Austin rushed down the stairs and bought a paper and read out the paragraph to Villiers as the uproar in the street rose and fell. The window was open and the air seemed full of noise and terror.

"Another gentleman has fallen a victim to the terrible epidemic of suicide which for the last month has prevailed in the West End. Mr. Sidney Crashaw of Stoke House, Fulham, and King's Pomeroy, Devon, was found, after a prolonged search, hanging from the branch of a tree in his garden at one o'clock today. The deceased gentleman dined last night at the Carlton Club and seemed in his usual health and spirits. He left the Club at about ten o'clock, and was seen walking leisurely up St. James's Street a little later. Subsequent to this his movements cannot be traced. On the discovery of the body medical aid was at once summoned, but life had evidently been long extinct. So far as is known Mr. Crashaw had no trouble or anxiety of any kind. This painful suicide, it will be remembered, is the fifth of the kind in the last month. The authorities at Scotland Yard are unable to suggest any explanation of these terrible occurrences."

Austin put down the paper in mute horror.

"I shall leave London tomorrow," he said, "it is a city of nightmares. How awful this is, Villiers!"

Mr. Villiers was sitting by the window quietly looking out into the street. He had listened to the newspaper report attentively, and the hint of indecision was no longer on his face.

"Wait a moment, Austin," he replied, "I have made up my mind to mention a little matter that occurred last night. It is stated, I think, that Crashaw was last seen alive in St. James's Street shortly after ten?"

"Yes, I think so. I will look again. Yes, you are quite right."

"Quite so. Well, I am in a position to contradict that statement at all events. Crashaw was seen after that; considerably later indeed."

"How do you know?"

"Because I happened to see Crashaw myself at about two o'clock this morning."

"You saw Crashaw? You, Villiers?"

"Yes, I saw him quite distinctly; indeed there were but a few feet between us."

"Where, in heaven's name, did you see him?"

"Not far from here. I saw him in Ashley Street. He was just leaving a house."

"Did you notice what house it was?"

"Yes. It was Mrs. Beaumont's."

"Villiers! Think what you are saying; there must be some mistake. How could Crashaw be in Mrs. Beaumont's house at two o'clock in the morning? Surely, surely, you must have been dreaming, Villiers, you were always rather fanciful."

"No; I was wide awake enough. Even if I had been dreaming as you say, what I saw would have roused me effectually."

"What you saw? What did you see? Was there anything strange about Crashaw? But I can't believe it; it is impossible."

"Well, if you like I will tell you what I saw, or if you please, what I think I saw, and you can judge for yourself."

"Very good, Villiers."

The noise and clamour of the street had died away, though now and then the sound of shouting still came from the distance, and the dull, leaden silence seemed like the quiet after an earthquake or a storm. Villiers turned from the window and began speaking.

"I was at a house near Regent's Park last night, and when I came away the fancy took me to walk home instead of taking a hansom. It was a clear pleasant night enough, and after a few minutes I had the streets pretty much to myself. It's a curious thing, Austin, to be alone in London at night, the gas-lamps stretching away in perspective, and the dead silence, and then perhaps the rush and clatter of a hansom on the stones, and the fire starting up under the horse's hoofs. I walked along pretty briskly, for I was feeling a little tired of being out in the night, and as the clocks were striking two I turned down Ashley Street, which, you know, is on my way. It was quieter than ever there, and the lamps were fewer, altogether it looked as dark and gloomy as a forest in winter. I had done about half the length of the street when I heard a door closed very softly, and naturally I looked up to see who was abroad like myself at such an hour. As it happens, there is a street lamp close to the house in question, and I saw a man standing on the step. He had just shut the door and his face was towards me, and I recognised Crashaw directly. I never knew him to speak to, but I had often seen him, and I am positive that I was not mistaken in my man. I looked into his face for a moment, and then—I will confess the truth—I set off at a good run, and kept it up till I was within my own door."

"Why?"

"Why? Because it made my blood run cold to see that man's face. I could never have supposed that such an infernal medley of passions could have glared out of any human eyes; I almost fainted as I looked. I knew I had looked into the eyes of a lost soul, Austin, the man's outward form remained, but all hell was within it. Furious lust, and hate that was like fire, and the loss of all hope and horror that seemed to shriek aloud to the night, though his teeth were shut; and the utter blackness of despair. I am sure he did not see me; he saw nothing that you or I can see, but he saw what I hope we never shall. I do not know when he died; I suppose in an hour, or perhaps two, but when I passed down Ashley Street and heard the closing door, that man no longer belonged to this world; it was a devil's face that I looked upon."

There was an interval of silence in the room when Villiers ceased speaking. The light was failing, and all the tumult of an hour ago was quite hushed. Austin had bent his head at the close of the story, and his hand covered his eyes.

"What can it mean?" he said at length.

"Who knows, Austin, who knows? It's a black business, but I think we had better keep it to ourselves, for the present at any rate. I will see if I cannot learn anything about that house through private channels of information, and if I do light upon anything I will let you know."

THE ENCOUNTER IN SOHO

Three weeks later Austin received a note from Villiers, asking him to call either that afternoon or the next. He chose the nearer date and found Villiers sitting as usual by the window, apparently lost in meditation on the drowsy traffic of the street. There was a bamboo table by his side, a fantastic thing, enriched with gilding and queer painted scenes, and on it lay a little pile of papers arranged and docketed as neatly as anything in Mr. Clarke's office.

"Well, Villiers, have you made any discoveries in the last three weeks?"

"I think so; I have here one or two memoranda which struck me as singular, and there is a statement to which I shall call your attention."

"And these documents relate to Mrs. Beaumont? it was really Crashaw whom you saw that night standing on the doorstep of the house in Ashley Street?"

"As to that matter my belief remains unchanged, but neither my inquiries nor their results have any special relation to Crashaw. But my investigations have had a strange issue; I have found out who Mrs. Beaumont is!"

"Who she is? In what way do you mean?"

"I mean that you and I know her better under another name."

"What name is that?"

"Herbert."

"Herbert!" Austin repeated the word, dazed with astonishment.

"Yes, Mrs. Herbert of Paul Street, Helen Vaughan of earlier adventures unknown to me. You had reason to recognise the expression of her face; when you go home look at the face in Meyrick's book of horrors, and you will know the sources of your recollection."

"And you have proof of this?"

"Yes, the best of proof; I have seen Mrs. Beaumont, or shall we say Mrs. Herbert?"

"Where did you see her?"

"Hardly in a place where you would expect to see a lady who lives in Ashley Street, Piccadilly. I saw her entering a house in one of the meanest and most disreputable streets in Soho. In fact, I had made an appointment, though not with her, and she was precise both to time and place."

"All this seems very wonderful, but I cannot call it incredible. You must remember, Villiers, that I have seen this woman, in the ordinary adventure of London society, talking and laughing, and sipping her chocolate in a commonplace drawing-room, with commonplace people. But you know what you are saying."

"I do; I have not allowed myself to be led by surmises or fancies. It was with no thought of finding Helen Vaughan that I searched for Mrs. Beaumont in the dark waters of the life of London, but such has been the issue."

"You must have been in strange places, Villiers."

"Yes, I have been in very strange places. It would have been useless, you know, to go to Ashley Street, and ask Mrs. Beaumont to kindly give me a short sketch of her previous history. No; assuming, as I had to assume, that her record was not of the cleanest, it would be pretty certain that at some previous time she must have moved in circles not quite so refined as her present ones. If you see mud on the top of a stream, you may be sure that it was once at the bottom. I went to the bottom. I have always been fond of diving into Queer Street for my amusement, and I found my knowledge of that locality and its inhabitants very useful. It is perhaps needless to say that my friends had never heard the name of Beaumont, and as I had never seen the lady, and was quite unable to describe her, I had to set to work in an indirect way. The people there know me, I have been able to do some of them a service now and again, so they made no difficulty about giving their information; they were aware I had no communication direct or indirect with Scotland Yard. I had to cast out a good many lines though, before I got what I wanted, and when I landed the fish I did not for a moment suppose it was my fish. But I listened to what I was told out of a constitutional liking for useless information, and I found myself in possession of a very curious story, though, as I imagined, not the story I was looking for. It was to this effect. Some five or six years ago a woman named Raymond suddenly made her appearance in the neighbourhood to which I am referring. She was described to me as being quite young, probably not more than seventeen or eighteen, very handsome, and looking as if she came from the country. I should be wrong in saying that she found her level in going to this particular quarter, or associating with these people, for from what I was told, I should think the worst den in London far too good for her. The person from whom I got my information, as you may suppose, no great Puritan, shuddered and grew sick in telling me of the nameless infamies which were laid to her charge. After living there for a year, or perhaps a little more, she disappeared as suddenly as she came, and they saw nothing of her till about the time of the Paul Street case. At first she came to her old haunts only occasionally, then more frequently, and finally took up her abode there as before, and remained for six or eight months. It's of no use my going into details as to the life that woman led; if you want particulars you can look at Meyrick's legacy. Those designs were not drawn from his imagination. She again disappeared, and the people of the place saw nothing of her till a few months ago. My informant told me that she had taken some rooms in a house which he pointed out, and these rooms she was in the habit of visiting two or three times a week and always at ten in the morning. I was led to expect that one of these visits would be paid on a certain day about a week ago, and I accordingly managed to be on the lookout in company with my cicerone at a quarter to ten, and the hour and the lady came with equal punctuality. My friend and I were standing under an archway, a little way back from the street, but she saw us, and gave me a glance that I shall be long in forgetting. That look was quite enough for me; I knew Miss Raymond to be Mrs. Herbert; as for Mrs. Beaumont she had quite gone out of my head. She went into the house, and I watched it till four o'clock, when she came out, and then I followed her. It was a long chase, and I had to be very careful to keep a long way in the background, and yet not to lose sight of the woman. She took me down to the Strand, and then to Westminster, and then up St. James's Street, and along Piccadilly. I felt queerish when I saw her turn up Ashley Street; the thought that Mrs. Herbert was Mrs. Beaumont came into my mind, but it seemed too improbable to be true. I waited at the corner, keeping my eye on her all the time, and I took particular care to note the house at which she stopped. It was the house with the gay curtains, the house of flowers, the house out of which Crashaw came the night he hanged himself in his garden. I was just going away with my discovery, when I saw an empty carriage come round and draw up in front of the house, and I came to the conclusion that Mrs. Herbert was going out for a drive, and I was right. I took a hansom and followed the carriage into the Park. There, as it happened, I met a man I know, and we stood talking together a little distance from the carriage-way, to which I had my back. We had not been there for ten minutes when my friend took off his hat, and I glanced round and saw the lady I had been following all day. 'Who is that?' I said, and his answer was, 'Mrs. Beaumont; lives in Ashley Street.' Of course there could be no doubt after that. I don't know whether she saw me, but I don't think she did. I went home at once, and, on consideration, I thought that I had a sufficiently good case with which to go to Clarke."

"Why to Clarke?"

"Because I am sure that Clarke is in possession of facts about this woman, facts of which I know nothing."

"Well, what then?"

Mr. Villiers leaned back in his chair and looked reflectively at Austin for a moment before he answered:

"My idea was that Clarke and I should call on Mrs. Beaumont."

"You would never go into such a house as that? No, no, Villiers, you cannot do it. Besides, consider; what result..."

"I will tell you soon. But I was going to say that my information does not end here; it has been completed in an extraordinary manner.

"Look at this neat little packet of manuscript; it is paginated, you see, and I have indulged in the civil coquetry of a ribbon of red tape. It has almost a legal air, hasn't it? Run your eye over it, Austin. It is an account of the entertainment Mrs. Beaumont provided for her choicer guests. The man who wrote this escaped with his life, but I do not think he will live many years. The doctors tell him he must have sustained some severe shock to the nerves."

Austin took the manuscript, but never read it. Opening the neat pages at haphazard his eye was caught by a word and a phrase that followed it; and, sick at heart, with white lips and a cold sweat pouring like water from his temples, he flung the paper down.

"Take it away, Villiers, never speak of this again. Are you made of stone, man? Why, the dread and horror of death itself, the thoughts of the man who stands in the keen morning air on the black platform, bound, the bell tolling in his ears, and waits for the harsh rattle of the bolt, are as nothing compared to this. I will not read it; I should never sleep again."

"Very good. I can fancy what you saw. Yes; it is horrible enough; but after all, it is an old story, an old mystery played in our day, and in dim London streets instead of amidst the vineyards and the olive gardens. We know what happened to those who chanced to meet the Great God Pan, and those who are wise know that all symbols are symbols of something, not of nothing. It was, indeed, an exquisite symbol beneath which men long ago veiled their knowledge of the most awful, most secret forces which lie at the heart of all things; forces before which the souls of men must wither and die and blacken, as their bodies blacken under the electric current. Such forces cannot be named, cannot be spoken, cannot be imagined except under a veil and a symbol, a symbol to the most of us appearing a quaint, poetic fancy, to some a foolish, silly tale. But you and I, at all events, have known something of the terror that may dwell in the secret place of life, manifested under human flesh; that which is without form taking to itself a form. Oh, Austin, how can it be? How is it that the very sunlight does not turn to blackness before this thing, the hard earth melt and boil beneath such a burden?"

Villiers was pacing up and down the room, and the beads of sweat stood out on his forehead. Austin sat silent for a while, but Villiers saw him make a sign upon his breast.

"I say again, Villiers, you will surely never enter such a house as that? You would never pass out alive."

"Yes, Austin, I shall go out alive—I, and Clarke with me."

"What do you mean? You cannot, you would not dare..."

"Wait a moment. The air was very pleasant and fresh this morning; there was a breeze blowing, even through this dull street, and I thought I would take a walk. Piccadilly stretched before me a clear, bright vista, and the sun flashed on the carriages and on the quivering leaves in the park. It was a joyous morning, and men and women looked at the sky and smiled as they went about their work or their pleasure, and the wind blew as blithely as upon the meadows and the scented gorse. But somehow or other I got out of the bustle and the gaiety, and found myself walking slowly along a quiet, dull street, where there seemed to be no sunshine and no air, and where the few foot-passengers loitered as they walked, and hung indecisively about corners and archways. I walked along,

hardly knowing where I was going or what I did there, but feeling impelled, as one sometimes is, to explore still further, with a
vague idea of reaching some unknown goal. Thus I forged up the
street, noting the small traffic of the milk-shop, and wondering at
the incongruous medley of penny pipes, black tobacco, sweets,
newspapers, and comic songs which here and there jostled one
another in the short compass of a single window. I think it was a
cold shudder that suddenly passed through me that first told me
I had found what I wanted. I looked up from the pavement and
stopped before a dusty shop, above which the lettering had faded,
where the red bricks of two hundred years ago had grimed to
black; where the windows had gathered to themselves the fog and
the dirt of winters innumerable. I saw what I required; but I think
it was five minutes before I had steadied myself and could walk in
and ask for it in a cool voice and with a calm face. I think there
must even then have been a tremor in my words, for the old man
who came out from his back parlour, and fumbled slowly amongst
his goods, looked oddly at me as he tied the parcel. I paid what he
asked, and stood leaning by the counter, with a strange reluctance
to take up my goods and go. I asked about the business, and learnt
that trade was bad and profits cut down sadly; but then the street
was not what it was before traffic had been diverted, but that was
done forty years ago, 'just before my father died,' he said. I got away
at last, and walked along sharply; it was a dismal street indeed, and
I was glad to return to the bustle and the noise. Would you like to
see my purchase?"

Austin said nothing, but nodded his head slightly; he still looked
white and sick. Villiers pulled out a drawer in the bamboo table,
and showed Austin a long coil of cord, hard and new; and at one
end was a running noose.

"It is the best hempen cord," said Villiers, "just as it used to be made for the old trade, the man told me. Not an inch of jute from end to end."

Austin set his teeth hard, and stared at Villiers, growing whiter as he looked.

"You would not do it," he murmured at last. "You would not have blood on your hands. My God!" he exclaimed, with sudden vehemence, "you cannot mean this, Villiers, that you will make yourself a hangman?"

"No. I shall offer a choice, and leave the thing alone with this cord in a locked room for fifteen minutes. If when we go in it is not done, I shall call the nearest policeman. That is all."

"I must go now. I cannot stay here any longer; I cannot bear this. Good-night."

"Good-night, Austin."

The door shut, but in a moment it was opened again, and Austin stood, white and ghastly, in the entrance.

"I was forgetting," he said, "that I too have something to tell. I have received a letter from Dr. Harding of Buenos Ayres. He says that he attended Meyrick for three weeks before his death."

"And does he say what carried him off in the prime of life? It was not fever?"

"No, it was not fever. According to the doctor, it was an utter collapse of the whole system, probably caused by some severe shock. But he states that the patient would tell him nothing, and that he was consequently at some disadvantage in treating the case."

"Is there anything more?"

"Yes. Dr. Harding ends his letter by saying: 'I think this is all the information I can give you about your poor friend. He had not been long in Buenos Ayres, and knew scarcely any one, with the exception of a person who did not bear the best of characters, and has since left—a Mrs. Vaughan.'"

THE FRAGMENTS

[Amongst the papers of the well-known physician, Dr. Robert Matheson, of Ashley Street, Piccadilly, who died suddenly, of apoplectic seizure, at the beginning of 1892, a leaf of manuscript paper was found, covered with pencil jottings. These notes were in Latin, much abbreviated, and had evidently been made in great haste. The ms. was only deciphered with great difficulty, and some words have up to the present time evaded all the efforts of the expert employed. The date, "xxv Jul. 1888," is written on the right-hand corner of the ms. The following is a translation of Dr. Matheson's manuscript.]

"Whether science would benefit by these brief notes if they could be published, I do not know, but rather doubt. But certainly I shall never take the responsibility of publishing or divulging one word of what is here written, not only on account of my oath freely given to those two persons who were present, but also because the details are too loathsome. It is probable that, upon mature consideration, and after weighing the good and evil, I shall one day destroy this paper, or at least leave it under seal to my friend D., trusting in his discretion, to use it or to burn it, as he may think fit.

"As was befitting I did all that my knowledge suggested to make sure that I was suffering under no delusion. At first astounded, I could hardly think, but in a minute's time I was sure that my pulse was steady and regular and that I was in my real and true senses. I ran over the anatomy of the foot and arm and repeated the formulæ of some of the carbon compounds, and then fixed my eyes quietly on what was before me.

"Though horror and revolting nausea rose up within me, and an odour of corruption choked my breath, I remained firm. I was then privileged or accursed, I dare not say which, to see that which was on the bed, lying there black like ink, transformed before my eyes. The skin, and the flesh, and the muscles, and the bones, and the firm structure of the human body that I had thought to be unchangeable, and permanent as adamant, began to melt and dissolve.

"I knew that the body may be separated into its elements by external agencies, but I should have refused to believe what I saw. For here there was some internal force, of which I knew nothing, that caused dissolution and change.

"Here too was all the work by which man has been made repeated before my eyes. I saw the form waver from sex to sex, dividing itself from itself, and then again reunited. Then I saw the body descend to the beasts whence it ascended, and that which was on the heights go down to the depths, even to the abyss of all being. The principle of life, which makes organism, always remained, while the outward form changed.

"The light within the room had turned to blackness, not the darkness of night, in which objects are seen dimly, for I could see clearly and without difficulty. But it was the negation of light; objects were presented to my eyes, if I may say so, without any medium, in such a manner that if there had been a prism in the room, I should have seen no colours represented in it.

"I watched, and at last I saw nothing but a substance as jelly. Then the ladder was ascended again. [*Here the MS. is illegible*]... for one instant I saw a Form, shaped in dimness before me, which I will not further describe. But the symbol of this form may be seen in ancient sculptures, and in paintings which survived beneath the lava, too foul to be spoken of... as a horrible and unspeakable shape, neither man nor beast, was changed into human form, there came finally death.

"I who saw all this, not without great horror and loathing of soul, here write my name, declaring all that I have set on this paper to be true.

"ROBERT MATHESON, MED. DR."

*

... Such, Raymond, is the story of what I know, and what I have seen. The burden of it was too heavy for me to bear alone, and yet I could tell it to none but you. Villiers, who was with me at the last knows nothing of that awful secret of the wood, of how what we both saw die, lay upon the smooth sweet turf amidst the summer flowers, half in sun and half in shadow, and holding the girl Rachel's hand, called and summoned those companions, and shaped in solid form, upon the earth we tread on, the horror which we can but hint at, which we can only name under a figure. I would not tell Villiers of this, nor of that resemblance, which struck me as with a blow upon my heart, when I saw the portrait, which filled the cup of terror at the end. What this can mean I dare not guess. I know that what I saw perish was not Mary, and yet in the last agony Mary's eyes looked into mine. Whether there be any one who can show the last link in this chain of awful mystery, I do not know, but if there be any one who can do this, you, Raymond, are the man. And if you know the secret, it rests with you to tell it or not, as you please.

I am writing this letter to you immediately on my getting back to town. I have been in the country for the last few days; perhaps you may be able to guess in what part. While the horror and wonder of London was at its height,—for "Mrs. Beaumont," as I have told you, was well known in society,—I wrote to my friend

Dr. Phillips, giving some brief outline, or rather hint, of what had happened, and asking him to tell me the name of the village where the events he had related to me occurred. He gave me the name, as he said with the less hesitation, because Rachel's father and mother were dead, and the rest of the family had gone to a relative in the State of Washington six months before. The parents, he said, had undoubtedly died of grief and horror caused by the terrible death of their daughter, and by what had gone before that death. On the evening of the day on which I received Phillips's letter I was at Caermaen, and standing beneath the mouldering Roman walls, white with the winters of seventeen hundred years, I looked over the meadow where once had stood the older temple of the "God of the Deeps," and saw a house gleaming in the sunlight. It was the house where Helen had lived. I stayed at Caermaen for several days. The people of the place, I found, knew little and had guessed less. Those whom I spoke to on the matter seemed surprised that an antiquarian (as I professed myself to be) should trouble about a village tragedy, of which they gave a very commonplace version, and, as you may imagine, I told nothing of what I knew. Most of my time was spent in the great wood that rises just above the village and climbs the hillside, and goes down to the river in the valley; such another long lovely valley, Raymond, as that on which we looked one summer night, walking to and fro before your house. For many an hour I strayed through the maze of the forest, turning now to right and now to left, pacing slowly down long alleys of undergrowth, shadowy and chill, even under the mid-day sun, and halting beneath great oaks; lying on the short turf of a clearing where the faint sweet scent of wild roses came to me on the wind and mixed with the heavy perfume of the elder whose mingled odour is like the odour of the room of the dead, a vapour of incense and corruption. I stood by rough banks at the edges of the wood, gazing at all the pomp and procession of the foxgloves towering amidst the bracken and shining red in the broad sunshine, and beyond them into deep thickets of close undergrowth where springs boil up from the rock and nourish the water-weeds, dank and evil. But in all my wanderings I avoided one part of the wood; it was not till yesterday that I climbed to the summit of the hill, and stood upon the ancient Roman road that threads the highest ridge of the wood. Here they had walked, Helen and Rachel, along this quiet causeway, upon the pavement of green turf, shut in on either side by high banks of red earth, and tall hedges of shining beech, and here I followed in their steps, looking out, now and again, through partings in the boughs, and seeing on one side the sweep of the wood stretching far to right and left, and sinking into the broad level, and beyond, the yellow sea, and the land over the sea. On the other side was the valley and the river, and hill following hill as wave on wave, and wood and meadow, and cornfield, and white houses gleaming, and a great wall of mountain, and far blue peaks in the north. And so at last, I came to the place. The track went up a gentle slope, and widened out into an open space with a wall of thick undergrowth around it, and then, narrowing again, passed on into the distance and the faint blue mist of summer heat. And into this pleasant summer glade Rachel passed a girl, and left it, who shall say what? I did not stay long there.

*

In a small town near Caermaen there is a museum, containing for the most part Roman remains which have been found in the neighbourhood at various times. On the day after my arrival at Caermaen I walked over to the town in question, and took the opportunity of inspecting this museum. After I had seen most of the sculptured stones, the coffins, rings, coins, and fragments of tessellated pavement which the place contains, I was shown a small square pillar of white stone, which had been recently discovered in the wood of which I have been speaking, and, as I found on inquiry, in that open space where the Roman road broadens out. On one side of the pillar was an inscription, of which I took a note. Some of the letters have been defaced, but I do not think there can be any doubt as to those which I supply. The inscription is as follows:

DEVOMNODENT*i*
FLA*v*IVSSENILISPOSSV*it*
PROPTERNVP*tias*
*qua*SVIDITSVBVMB*ra*

"To the great god Nodens (the god of the Great Deep or Abyss), Flavius Senilis has erected this pillar on account of the marriage which he saw beneath the shade."

The custodian of the museum informed me that local antiquaries were much puzzled, not by the inscription, or by any difficulty in translating it, but as to the circumstance or rite to which allusion is made.

*

... And now, my dear Clarke, as to what you tell me about Helen Vaughan, whom you say you saw die under circumstances of the utmost and almost incredible horror. I was interested in your account, but a good deal, nay, all of what you told me, I knew already. I can understand the strange likeness you remarked both in the portrait and in the actual face; you have seen Helen's mother.

You remember that still summer night so many years ago, when I talked to you of the world beyond the shadows, and of the god Pan. You remember Mary. She was the mother of Helen Vaughan, who was born nine months after that night.

Mary never recovered her reason. She lay, as you saw her, all the while upon her bed, and a few days after the child was born, she died. I fancy that just at the last she knew me; I was standing by the bed, and the old look came into her eyes for a second, and then she shuddered and groaned and died. It was an ill work I did that night, when you were present; I broke open the door of the house of life, without knowing or caring what might pass forth or enter in. I recollect your telling me at the time, sharply enough, and rightly enough too, in one sense, that I had ruined the reason of a human being by a foolish experiment, based on an absurd theory. You did well to blame me, but my theory was not all absurdity. What I said Mary would see, she saw, but I forgot that no human eyes could look on such a vision with impunity. And I forgot, as I have just said, that when the house of life is thus thrown open, there may enter in that for which we have no name, and human flesh may become the veil of a horror one dare not express. I played with energies which I did not understand and you have seen the ending of it. Helen Vaughan did well to bind the cord about her neck and die, though the death was horrible. The blackened face, the hideous form upon the bed, changing and melting before your eyes from woman to man, from man to beast, and from beast to worse than beast, all the strange horror that you witnessed, surprises me but little. What you say the doctor whom you sent for saw and shuddered at I noticed long ago; I knew what I had done the moment the child was born, and when it was scarcely five years old I surprised it, not once or twice but several times with a playmate, you may guess of what kind.

It was for me a constant, an incarnate horror, and after a few years I felt I could bear it no longer, and I sent Helen Vaughan away. You know now what frightened the boy in the wood. The rest of the strange story, and all else that you tell me, as discovered by your friend, I have contrived to learn from time to time, almost to the last chapter. And now Helen is with her companions...

THE END

NOTE.—*Helen Vaughan was born on August 5th, 1865, at the Red House, Breconshire, and died on July 25th, 1888, in her house in a street off Piccadilly, called Ashley Street in the story.*

PAN

George Egerton

George Egerton (1859–1945), the pen name of Mary Chavelita Dunne Bright, was a celebrated poet, novelist, playwright and translator. Born in Australia to a Welsh Protestant mother and an Irish Catholic father, her childhood was one of constant migration. Egerton spent time in New Zealand, Chile and Germany, though most of her youth was set against the backdrop of Ireland. Her travels continued into early adulthood, where she trained as a nurse in London, worked in New York, and spent two years immersing herself in the literary culture of Norway. Egerton's first collection of short stories, *Keynotes* (1893), was a critical and commercial success, and she followed this with *Discords* (1894), *Symphonies* (1897), *Fantasias* (1898) and *Flies in Amber* (1905). Egerton also wrote two novels, *The Wheel of God* (1898) and *Rosa Amorosa* (1901), as well as the plays *His Wife's Family* (1907), *Backsliders* (1910) and *Camilla States Her Case* (1925).

"Pan" is taken from Egerton's *Symphonies*. Aligned with both the Decadent and the New Woman movements, "Pan" strikes a distinct tone within this collection. Set against the landscape of the Basque Country, the story follows Tienette, at once outcast and put upon by the characters which surround her. The music of Pan has created conflict within her—"the notes of a melody that had played upon the lute strings of her soul"—with this conflict speaking to sexual longing and a desire for independence. Haunting, and with endlessly evocative descriptions, "Pan" draws comparisons with Arthur Machen's *The Great God Pan*. In Tienette, we see a female protagonist that is far from the femme fatale of Helen Vaughan, but who can be read equally as a symbol for concealed sexuality.

A honey golden noontide—blinding sun-glare beating on to a long white road in a world of quivering yellows; gold of saffron, gold of topaz, gold of jonquil and dropping laburnum bloom; a gorgeous, glowing, seething play of sunshine turning the world into an orange dream with changeful shafts of ochre and gamboge. The maize fields stood proudly like a phalanx of golden spears guarding the hill sides, and rising above them the mountains, purple-clad messengers, bent to the south—La Rune nodding to the Trois Couronnes. One could almost hear the vibrations of the heat in warm waves, between the tinkling of the neck bells and the long call of the bullock drivers; and, if one were to listen more intently, the silken swish of the waves sending a shrewd whisper to the land, heavy with scent of lime and tuberose, would fall regularly on one's ear as the breath of a sleeping child—one could see the silver cressets dance in the amber light down below, where the gorgeous pavilions and white villas with their gaily striped awnings, in the little Basque French town, clasped the bay in horseshoe form. The highway was animated, for troops of shaggy mules and pannier-laden asses filed up the winding road, great mild-eyed cream-coloured oxen—the new breed, outcome of the cross between the hardy red race of the mountains and the fighting Spanish bull, named in an impossible Basque word, the colour of the maize when ripe—dragged patiently along, peering out from under their head covers of dyed goatskins. Acquaintances met and greeted constantly, for the town was filled with bathing guests, and there had been a big market, so that commodities of every kind met with a ready sale.

The men and women swung noiselessly along like gladsome shadows, for their feet were shod in hempen solid *espartinac*, ankle-bound, with gaily coloured tapes.

The shrill laughter and guttural Basque of a group of women washing in a square stone trough built across the course of a stream-let that strove to find its way to the sea, mingled with the dull thud of their beetles as they belaboured the clothes. An old crone, with a face like a shrivelled walnut and a grizzled grey beard, peered at the passers-by, with glittering black eyes perennially young as sin. Her comments were greeted with shouts of laughter by the women, and a blush on the olive cheeks of the younger girls.

Maria Andrerea was noted all through the Basses Pyrénées as a teller of tales, tosser of cups, layer-out of cards, and vendor of philtres. She was on her way back from a secret visit to the mayor's wife of a neighbouring town, Madame having had reason to suspect M. le Maire of marital divagations. She could whisper tales of the Bassa Jauna, the goat-man who wantons in the "Akelarre," or mystic goat pastures, where the warlocks and witches hold an evil sabbat; or croon tender fancies of the "singing tree," the bird that tells the truth, and the water that makes young.

Life in all its comedy and tragedy, its pathos and irony, with the broader, more naked aspects it assumes in Southern latitudes, passed by the well with its audience of women...

The roll of wheels and the crack of a long whip broke off Maria's moralising.

"*Bon jour*, Pon Pon! How goes the widow?"

A peal of laughter followed the query, and the driver flung back a volley of Basque curses that made the girls clap their hands to their cars. A fat padre jingled by behind a richly caparisoned mule, on his way home to some Spanish border town; a troop of reformatory children in uniform of hodden grey filed silently past in charge of two seminarists in clerical dress; a little Spaniard, a well-known contrabandist, pulled up his train of mules and held a muttered conversation with the old woman, passing her a sealed package with many injunctions. Two wretched-looking prisoners manacled at the wrists and escorted by four gendarmes, halted to drink at the fountain.

"Anarchists," explained the fat sergeant, "to be banished across the border." The women, with the exception of Maria Andrerea, who made signs with one hand to the elder man, crossed themselves hurriedly at the dread name. An unkempt beggar, covered with loathsome sores, drawn in a basket chair by a miserable donkey, whined prayers, or called down curses with equal zest as the exhibition of a gangrened stump extracted alms or a shudder of disgust from those he met.

The Angelus pealed from the towers below, and tinkled at a little chapel up at the monastery; the women tied their washing into bundles and bore it away on their heads. Maria Andrerea squatted on a flat stone and sucked at a short pipe as she waited. A man's voice broke through the summer sounds, a rough bass, trolling out a Gascon drinking song. The old woman lifted her head with a grim smile of satisfaction. A peasant, tall, lithe as befitted the best pelota player in the district, clean-shaven as are all Basque men, came down the road. His blue *béret* sat insolently upon his black, crisp curls and shaggy forelock, his red brown eyes that got so easily bloodshot with excitement, looked boldly ahead; his blue trousers tapered to his ankles, and the crimson sash wound round his loins answered in colour to the flush on his tanned cheek. He had a wineskin flung over his shoulder.

"*Agour!* (Hail) Maria Andrerea."

"*Agour!* Sebastian, I've been waiting. I've got the philtre."

The man's teeth gleamed whitely as he laughed, and he laughed often.

"All right, mother. Have you seen Tienette pass yet? She gave me the slip, the hussy. What's come to the girl?—she's as shy as a hawk."

The old woman laughed, and eyed him keenly as she rose to her feet.

"There are maids and maids, *mon gars;* some must be wooed and some must be taken," with a significant wink. "*Bon jour,* Sebastian, *bon jour,* and good luck to the taking."

The man stood still a moment, and watched the retreating figure, then went on with a curious smile curving his lips.

Always the river gurgled, and rilled, and trickled, and no one passed awhile. Then a girl came up the road—a girl whose head seemed to catch and imprison the sun itself. Such hair, thick and crisp, and red-gold at the roots, and in the curls at her neck; sun-bleached like a maize leaf to a wonderful towy yellow on top; the vivid blue of the silken kerchief enclosing the braids at the back, Basque fashion, into a silken knob, offering a supreme note of contrast. Her features presented as delicately distinct an outline as the image on an Iberian coin, and, where the neck of her bodice opened, her skin showed privet white.

She swung the bundle off her head with a curve of arm that was all grace, and sat down with a sigh that was almost a dry sob. Her eyes burned under their golden lashes with a sombre fire—eyes that had something of the amethyst of the mountains, something of the green of the sea. She dabbled her hands in the water, and leant back, letting her heavy lids droop.

She had been troubled of late; her senses had quivered and tickled strangely; the notes of a melody that had played upon the lute strings of her soul all through the months, that had danced gladly by since the first voluptuous stirrings of the southern spring, awoke in her and made her heart sick; it had vibrated in between the regenerative cry of the earth in her, and around her, until she seemed to listen for it with her very blood, as if every vein were an ear, conveying it with a clutching throb to her heart, causing a sickening weakness in every limb. She pressed her hands tightly down as she thought of it, and moved her head uneasily.

When was it this had first happened to her? Early, quite early in the spring, at Easter, when Pierre and Marie Jeanne were wed. She can remember the much-talked-of player, whom the gentlemen of the town called a genius. She recalls how she laughed at his first appearance, pale and lame, with mild dove-like eyes, and silken brown curls that fell about his throat and ears like a girl's; she can see him take old Jean the fiddler's place upon the platform in the *fonda* where they held the wedding; she can hear again the wild notes of the fandango and the trip of feet upon the floor; remember how she had watched him, later on, slip out and seat himself upon a low stone wall that faced the sea. She had followed and listened as he played to the milk-warm night, and in-running sea, and starlit sky. Surely the melody must have held witchery in its cadence? It had colour in it, changeful as the rainbow gleams in the wave-mists when the spray mounts high at Socoa, and a strange call in it, like a fervid love-whisper in the dusk, and a power like the grip of a master-hand forcing one's head back to find one's mouth. It held man's need of woman, and woman's yearning for man, the primal first causes of humanity; and it had struck upon the most secret sensory fibres of her being, thrilling them and disturbing her strangely. He had come to her side for a moment, and she had felt faint, though she could have taken him up in one arm, so slight and frail was he beside her. She had stolen home early, for the click of the castanets and the shuffle of the feet hurt her like coarse blots on a beautiful fabric. Ever since the cadence of his music had sung in her; she heard it in the sea, and in the trees when she gathered firewood in the forest, in the wind as it rushed through the valleys. All these months past it had weakened her. At vespers it mingled with the organ notes and distracted her devotions, and even the white Christ on the Cross, whose feet she had kissed with a prayer for help against the imperative call of her awakened womanhood, had mild brown eyes, with the look of a maid or a dove, and helped her naught. The dry summer heat had intensified the disorder in her, and many a night she had crept out and crushed her white limbs in the cool, dew-laden moss that carpeted the wood near the cabin in which she lived with her aunt.

Every Sunday afternoon she had gone down into the town, because the melody drew her there; sometimes she had met his long, soft gaze and had cowered under it; a few times she had striven to talk with him, but he answered her in monosyllables, it almost seemed to her with reluctance. The ladies of the town spoke to him whenever they came to see the gathering, and then she had thrown herself recklessly into the fling of the dance, for no one could foot a fandango better than Estefanella or Tienette the yellow-haired.

Sebastian, with the by-name of the Toro Negro (Black Bull), courted her, and laughed when she spurned him, saying she would come to him yet. Her aunt had chided her for her refusal, for the

Toro Negro had a good farm and a share in a sardine boat, and would surely settle down when married.

She shuddered when she thought of him, for he made her afraid, and the fatal melody vibrating in her had robbed her of force to resist his power.

Suddenly she sprang to her feet and listened with quickening breath, then darted behind a flowering oleander bush. The roll of wheels, the laughter of men and women's voices, the notes of a strange wild melody came nearer, as a brake drove by, with a wedding party—the bride with myrtle and orange blossoms crowning her hair, the bridegroom with his arm round her shoulder, and sitting next the driver was the lame musician, playing as if life held no cares. She rubbed her eyes in a dazed way, swung the bundle on to her head, and sprang along the dusty road in restless haste, her sandalled feet keeping time to the fatal tune ringing in her heart.

Up where the road bent mountainwards, and the bay could be seen through a break in the trees, like a glittering sapphire held in a pearl-rimmed shell, she paused and strove for breath in the heavy lime-scented air. A man's voice, singing a stave, struck upon her ear, causing her to pale, till the heat flush died out of her cheeks, leaving the golden freckles that powdered it plainly visible.

"You are late, Tienette! I looked for you down in the market," he cried. "Did you think to escape me? You are tired. Your colour has gone," with a dance of amusement and admiration in his smile.

He took the bundle from her, bending close to her with an odd look in his eyes. The girl shrunk, but made no protest. They walked along silently. The road wound upwards, a forest of stunted oak trees, with a thick undergrowth of fern, bracken, and gorse, skirting it on either side, whilst leafy plane and chestnut trees towered above. Her limbs seemed weighted, her nerves tingled in response to the dance of the motes in the gilded sunshine, and everywhere, all round in wave and spray, and stir of heat, the witch melody that was keyed by the wan musician's hand seemed to be struck into rougher chords by the man at her side. His nearness oppressed her, as it always did, half-frightened her, until she became a mere jangle of sensory nerves and almost desired to be hurt in some way as a relief.

"Did you play pelota on Sunday last?" she asked desperately.

"Yes," with a toss of his shaggy forelock, "a match for five hundred francs. My side won. I've more than enough to start housekeeping. How long are you going to hold out?"

He placed his arm round her shoulders as he spoke, and pushed her quietly towards a wicket-gate leading into the wood.

There he faced her with his breath fanning the curls on her brow, and his bold eyes reading her disturbance. She put up her hands, palm outwards, as if to ward him off, but he only laughed a ringing laugh that seemed to find a strange echo in the wood, until the girl, true Basque as she was, fancied that the wood-spirit—the goat-man—answered him.

Then he caught her hands and pressed them to his great breast, so that she felt the mighty throb of his heart and the heave of his chest.

"How long, little one? I have been patient, and I am not patient as a rule, and I have always had my own way," with a triumphant whisper.

She had turned her head aside and was struggling to free her hands, when he bent and caught the back of her neck between his lips and crushed it roughly. She strove feebly like a half-frozen bird in a warm palm, only to give way with a stifled cry, as he snatched her up in his arms, and half carried, half led her into the wood. She made no resistance, the disturbance of the past months had come to a climax; she was worn with the warring in her strong, physical nature of forces not understood. Even the Virgin had ceased to help her, though she had prayed at her marble feet all through many a long summer night.

She was weary of it, so she let him lead her, as in a dream, further in where the bracken grew high, and one could walk ankle-deep in the maiden-hair, and the club moss bedded the ground right royally.

Once more the man and the girl stood at the wicket. He was leaning against it with his hands thrust in his trousers pockets; she was trembling violently. A dried leaf had caught in her hair, she plucked it out fiercely, and cried out a reproach.

He had been watching her with a curious look of indifference, almost of dislike, and he said:—

"Oh, what is the use of that, Stephanita?"

The girl turned as if stung, and, lifting her hand, struck him across the mouth. He laughed, but a lurid light shot in his eyes and one could see that they were too near his nose; he caught her hands and twisted them behind her, bent her face back and kissed it roughly, whispering something that made her writhe and caused the blood to leap in a flame to her cheeks, then he let her go so suddenly that she almost fell, and, waving his *béret* laughingly, called back over his shoulder as he went:—

"Remember that, my wild hawk!"

She dropped down in the moss and lay quite still, except that now and then little convulsive shivers ran through her frame; and once she turned and tore the moss with her teeth, as one has seen a magpie strip the bark off a tree in a rage at being watched.

*

November had almost run its course, mildly, even for the South. The warm smothering south wind blew over the headlands, carrying the fragrance of the sea-pinks into the valleys, distilling a wonderful memory of brine and old home gardens to many an English visitor.

Outside, the waves ran high, and the bay was full of craft unable to cross the *digue* at Bayonne; the mountains wore snowy mutches above their mantles of purple mist, and the bright blue flower stars of the chicory peered out amidst the feathery cool green of the tamarisk bushes. Away across the land the maize stalks hung in whity-brown dejection; and as the pale sun slanted over them, it struck here and there an orange speck, telling how a pumpkin had been left to ripen; the fishing, too, had commenced.

A wan reflection of Tienette the yellow-haired of the golden summer, stood at a cabin door upon the hillside, shading her eyes from the pale sun. She was watching a boy, a ragged brown urchin in tattered jersey playing a *jota* on a jew's-harp as he climbed up the path. He stopped and pulled a note out of his pocket, with a greeting.

"From the aunt, Juanito?" she queried.

"Ay, she gave it me, and the uncle gave me a whole franc to bring it. He is rich. They are saying down there," with a backward gesture of head and hand, "that he'll buy the *fonda*, La Puerta. The widow Echegarray wants to join the beguines and make her soul."

The girl read the four lines slowly, unheeding his chatter. An uncle, the elder brother of the aunt with whom she lived, had come back from Brazil after an absence of fifteen years,—report had it with much money. Now she is to go down to see him. She dreads the gossip, the prying eyes, the tongues of the women. She had felt rather than seen the half shy look of the girls, the scrutinising gaze of the matrons, in church and market-place. Her aunt's steady, watchful eyes questioned her at home,—aye, even at vespers the men's eyes have peered down from the gallery.

She placed a piece of Spanish bread, close and white as bleached sponge, upon the table, with a slab of ewes' milk cheese, and a terracotta jar of lovely shape filled with clean spring water, with an:—

"Eat Juanito, and God bless the food!"

Half an hour later she locked the door behind her, unslipped the goats from their pen, and turned the ass loose into the wood.

She had donned her black feast-day gown, wound a black kerchief about her braids, and wrapped herself in a black llama manto of the aunt's.

Her gait was heavier than in summer; the magic music has been silent in her soul; never once has she heard the witch-white melody that proved her ruin since the day when it had made her bend as wax in the grasp of the Toro Negro.

A woman stopped to greet her, and scanned her face curiously; her cheeks are hollower, and there is a pinched look about her nose; to the peasant's eye, with the wholesome love of robust health, she had lost in beauty.

"*Agour*, Étienne! I hear the uncle has come back with thousands. Congratulations; but you are not looking well, have you taken cold?" with an expressive look at the manto.

"Yes, it has hung over me all the autumn—a chill after a dance perhaps."

"Try a *tisane*, a *tisane à quatre fleurs*, borage or mallows with violets and lime blossoms, or perhaps lilies. Adieu, then!"

She parted company with Juanito at the bridge leading to the older, quainter town, the fishing colony, where every house gave some sign of the occupation of its inhabitants. Sou'westers and jerseys hung over the balconies in company with festoons of blood-red chillies, like coral necklets, slung out to dry.

Half-bred Spanish pointers yelped and fought in the gutters, a Spanish pedlar with a box slung round his neck, called vanilla pods for sale; English visitors in knickerbockers, carrying golf sticks, added an unfamiliar note to the scene.

Down in Socoa she lifted her head, setting her teeth hard, sorely conscious of eyes peering from low windows of the *fondas*, and shops; of heads popped out of the doorways of the long work-rooms where gossiping girls sat at their sewing machines and turned out *modes et robes;* of remarks made by the women and men, all acquaintances, who gave her a "good-day" as they sat outside and plaited hempen soles for *espargatas*, or covered sunshades for next year's bathing season.

The *fonda* Le Port was a straggling three-storied building, *Ici on sert à boire, à manger*, painted in great tarred letters across its pale, green-washed frontage; six stiff plane trees guarded the entrance, all bending landwards, as if shrinking from the rough caress of the ocean, and a statue of Our Lady of the Sea looked patiently out from a niche above the door. The big kitchen served as bar, parlour, eating-room, and dancing floor, when the "lads" were home. Bright copper utensils, strings of onions, and gigantic sausages, wine-skins, chillies, and castanets hung with a miscellanea of all kinds from the roof and walls. A fat Frenchwoman with long gold drops in her ears and Basque headdress greeted the girl as she entered: "Yes, the uncle is here. He has the best room, indeed the best the house affords; stands treat all round; a well-to-do man, one can see. That's what comes of going abroad." The widow sighed. "Go up the stairs one flight, the front room."

The girl knocked and went in.

A little, thin, sharp-featured woman with a meek expression sat in an armchair warming her hands over a *brassero*. She never took her eyes off the girl's face from her entrance except once, when she turned to the man dozing on the bed, and said gently: "Here is Stephana, our Anna's daughter."

The man rose, a Basque of herculean frame, with a curved nose, strong chin, and keen blue eyes. He had gold rings in his ears, and a skin tanned to the colour of an old saddle. He held out his hand and peered at the girl keenly as he shook it.

She flushed and looked back with his own look, and the old golden beauty returned for a spell. He laughed and slapped her on the shoulders.

"A handsome girl, by God! The rascal knew what he was about—but he didn't reckon with the Uncle Pierre. Sit down, girl, take off that dingy shawl, let's see you. I've brought you some silk stuff and a gold chain. The women out there are brown as coffee berries, so they like bright things. So do I. I like my wine to sparkle and my women gay as humming-birds, *por Dios* I do!"

He forced her to take some wine and eat sweetmeats, whilst he talked incessantly in guttural Basque, mixed with French and bastard Spanish.

"Well, my girl, and when is the wedding to be? The gossips say you ate the meat before you said the grace! Well, Uncle Pierre won't dwell upon that, but it will not do to wait *too* long."

The girl felt the curious steady gaze of the quiet woman in the chair lame her, as it always did. If she could only escape from it!

"I don't know. He"—with a half sob—"laughed when I spoke of it. They say he is after Laurentina, José Echaverria's daughter—she has a dowry."

The man struck his clenched fist upon the table till the glasses danced, and launched into a string of curious oaths.

"Let him look out! How much has she?"

"A thousand francs, a span of oxen, and linen."

"Young, well-favoured?"

"Turned thirty," interrupted the old woman, "with a squint, like her mother before her."

The man laughed.

"Where is he?"

"Up beyond Sare at the Palômbier, 'the pass of the pigeons.' He goes there for the sport, with Enrique. The English, too, pay to see it; they make much at it."

"We'll drive to Sare tomorrow, you'll go up to him and tell him I desire him to come down and name the day; that the Uncle Pierre stands no nonsense; that I'll give you two thousand francs to start with, and all that becomes a niece of mine in linen and housewares." A dull feeling of terror and rebellion surged up in the girl. No, no, she would sooner go away, as so many of her countrywomen had done—go to America; but a stir, so faint as to be barely felt, knocked like a tiny hand below her heart, and hushed the words on her lips.

The next morning, they set out in Pon Pon's ramshackle landau drawn by two chestnut "garrons," high-boned Rosinantes, un-groomed, half-starved looking animals that never seemed to tire and responded lazily to the crack of the long whip. Uncle Pierre lay back with a huge cigar in his mouth, and waved his *béret* gaily to any chance acquaintance. The aunt sat bolt upright with a smile of subdued triumph on her sharp face. Only twice before—at a wedding and at a funeral—had she driven in such a fashion. Tienette sat as in a dream; the cool morning air fanned the little curls about her temples; the familiar scene, the white châteaux with shutters closed for the winter, the farms with the cone-shaped stacks of bracken, each with an earthen crock inverted on a stick above them to catch the earwigs, struck her as they might a stranger. She was thought-free, almost restful. It was simply good to let oneself go, to watch the sun creep up the mountainside and scatter the mists.

They left St. Pée and Sare behind them, and then Pon Pon pointed out the opening between the mountains—"the pass of the pigeons."

"When we get to the foot of the mountain, you can see if the signal is set, they always fly a flag if there are signs of a drive. It is a good mile to the Palômbier."

Arrived there, Tienette alighted, and started up the winding unmade mountain road in which bullock waggons had cut deep ridges in the clay between the boulders. The girl's nerves were tensely strung and her breath laboured; half-way up she was forced to loosen the bands of her skirts, and seat herself upon a boulder to rest. A great stillness reigned, unbroken except by the distant call of a driver to his oxen, or the scream of an eagle—one could see them soar and drop against the blue sky. Beneath her in the valley the square church tower looked like a fortress guarding the town; above, at the cleft between the hills, the flutter of a white flag no bigger than a kerchief proclaimed the expected arrival of the birds. On the steep slope a man was busy loading bracken on to a waggon, the cream heads of his team of oxen gazing patiently out through the russet brown tangle.

She could distinguish the man, a farmer from Sare, collecting his store for the winter. (Basque peasants hold bracken rights in turbary, as an Irish peasant, turf.) She had met him once; he was a cousin of the Toro Negro on the mother's side; he recalled the object of the journey; she got up wearily and plodded on, treading the chalices of the purple and yellow autumn crocus underfoot. A farm-house, with thatched roof and a gate, barred the entrance to the pass.

"Is Sebastian here?" she asked the boy guarding the gate.

"Yes, but he's with the nets."

"How do you know when the birds are coming?"

He pointed out a tree on the northern side in which a lookout of twigs, like a giant crow's nest, was built; in this a man, known all through the district for his hawk's vision, perched each morning, with his eyes fixed on the horizon beyond which lay Bayonne, watching for the first token of the coming flock.

A shrill whistle pierced the clear air, and the boy called: "*Les palombes*, the pigeons, they come; hide behind a bush; quick, girl, quick!"

Some of the excitement in the lad's voice communicated itself to her. She ran and crouched behind a clump of furze.

The scene of the drive was in a defile cutting through a mountain that faced the south; the bottom of the cutting was a clear space, like the grass-grown bed of a dried-up river. Twelve trees grew across in a straight line, some close together, some at intervals, as if planted for the purpose by the hand of man. From those, two giant nets were suspended, invisible to the birds until retreat was too late.

A skilful arrangement of pulleys and wire enabled the men concealed behind the bushes to draw up and drop the nets. A wooden hut with a trap-door, through which the captives were thrust, stood to the right. Every bush concealed a farmer or would-be sportsman with a gun. She noticed that the tree above her head, and many of the trees on each side, held men concealed in titan nests.

She started as a whisper reached her, and Sebastian's voice made all the blood recede from her face and gather round her heart. Looking northwards, she saw what seemed to be a long streamer of grey smoke floating towards the gorge; and as it came nearer, a sound as of the rushing of a mighty wind through a tunnel; louder, ever louder, with a rhythmic beat in it—quicker, ever quicker, as it approached, quite near—a palpitating, fluttering, quivering, steady blue-grey mass of birds, that fly as if driven by some unseen power, drawn by some irresistible force to seek the south, and seek it on this wave line and no other. She has heard it said that year after year, winter after winter, never once have they been known to diverge, never once chosen another opening; always they have flown straight to their fate—one flock after the other.

She held her breath, and waited with throbbing pulses. Nearer, nearer, surely on the wings of a great wind;—beat, beat—the noise has become deafening, like the charge of hundreds of invisible aerial warriors treading the air above her. Now they have entered the pass; thousands of birds, a grey-white throbbing mass of wing-beating units, driving as one compact body straight to their doom.

They are flying rather high, but each man hidden in the nest has a wooden hawk fastened to his wrist, and as they enter he throws it high in the air above them with practised skill, and they drop with a thud—see the net too late—for those behind press the foremost on, and in one second they are trapped.

The nets fall and they are prisoned tightly. The men spring forward, seize them in handfuls, and thrust them through the trap-door. The stragglers are picked off by the gunners; those that escape soar in frightened circles to the north and east and west, only to form a new body, make a *détour* and return by the same route into the nets, as if unable to choose another passage. Tienette drew a sharp breath as the last straggler fluttered to the ground. The smell of powder and the blood-stained feathers fluttering on every side made her feel faint. The men plunged their hands into the net, clutching the struggling birds, many maimed, all half-paralysed with terror, calling out the number as they thrust them into the shed to the tally-man, who notched them on a stick dangling from a tree.

She saw the Toro Negro put his gun down with a laugh as he went by to help. How red his lips were, and how white his teeth! A feeling of hatred rose up in her against him; not a care touched him, he was filled with the zest of the sport. It flashed to her in a vague way that in that lay the gulf between man and woman.

Life to him was made of creative moments, but the woman was tied to the burden of years of mothering.

She turned back to the house, and sent the lad for him. He came, whistling gaily, his face flushed with excitement, an insolent look in his careless eyes. He beckoned to her to go down the slope out of sight of the house. There he leant against a tree and waited for her to speak. His shirt-sleeves were rolled above his elbows, his hands blood-stained, a few red fluffy feathers stuck in the hair on his sinewy arms. She shivered a little, and delivered the uncle's message in a toneless voice. He folded his arms and considered. He hated all bondage, but the farm needed a woman. Money was welcome; no other girl of his class in the district had such a dowry; and besides, the *curé* had taxed him on Sunday; the child was his. True Gascon, he calculated the advantages and decided.

"Where is the uncle?"

"At St. Pée, in the Cabaret des Palômbes."

"Very well, in an hour."

*

One evening, some weeks later, a broad band of light streamed out into the glistening roadway from the wine-cellar of José Echegarrez. Voices and laughter, the rattle of castanets and the snap of fingers, the beat of dancing feet in time to the strains of a violin playing a fandango, stole out to greet the threatening skirl of the landward-blowing wind.

The guests were footing it merrily at the wedding feast of Tienette the golden-haired. Wooden benches were placed round the walls for the older guests, the fiddler was perched upon a platform of planks stretched across two giant hogsheads of ageing grape-juice. The best man, none too steady in his gait, was going from guest to guest with a bottle of wine and a glass, out of which all drank alike. The uncle Pierre had behaved liberally; the bride had driven to church dressed in a black silk gown, her golden head crowned with orange-blossoms and myrtle, and a flowing white veil. The table had taken up the whole length of the long room of the inn Le Port, and they had sat to it for four hours, and eaten and drunk to satiety.

Only once had there been a break of an unpleasant kind. Uncle Pierre had caught sight of the lame musician, and called to him with lusty voice to join the revels; nay, more, had dragged him in by force, and compelled him to a seat opposite the bride, and called for a toast. The bride had not raised her glass in response, but had looked at him with a hunted, deep gaze that had called a flush to his thin cheeks, and made his hand shake so that the wine ran over; then she had fainted. The matrons carried her out, and Sebastian swore all women were alike, weak idiots, for he had drunk liberally, and was quarrelsome in his cups.

Later, when the twilight was falling, she stood at the door, look-ing, with hollow eyes and a strained quiver about her mouth, into

the room at the swirling round of figures. All lightness, all grace
had departed from them with the first bars of a commonplace polka;
they were keeping time with mechanical steps and a kind of forced
gravity, a tribute to the foreign nature of the music. She had donned
her sombre cashmere gown, and her white wreath sat strangely on
the yellow hair above the pale mask of her face. Sebastian looked
at her once or twice as he passed with his partner; she had been a
reproach to him all day, with her spoiled figure and gloomy eyes,
and Uncle Pierre had been bluntly offensive since he had gained
his object.

The polka came to an end with a flourish, and he swung his
partner to a seat, and went over to the woman who was as much
his property as the patient oxen who answered to his goad, or the
faithful pointer he caressed and kicked alternately. He took hold of
her arm, none too gently, between his thumb and finger.

"A malediction on your white face,—it's more fitted for a funeral
than a feast; it's a poor compliment to me. I'm sick of seeing it."

He pinched her with a quiet savagery that called the blood to
her cheeks.

"That's better; if you can't join in the dance go down and see to
the supper. Don't stand watching me; I won't have it; I've danced
to the uncle's tune all day, you'll dance to mine from this out."

He pushed her, as he spoke, into the passage, and left her with
a meaning look that held a covert threat in its sheathed glance. The
girl stood a moment; the rhythmic tramp of feet had begun again
overhead, and struck like hammer-blows on her senses. She opened
a side door leading to the street; the wind almost forced her back,
and it took all her strength to pull the door to after her.

The twilight had fallen, but there was a weird half light that
presaged a storm. She gave a great sob as she hurried along, with

the wind catching her breath and buffeting her chest; the impulse of months was crystallising into a resolve. Some of the doors on the sheltered side of the street were open, and the bright light streamed out in golden bars across the roadway, and the smell of roasting chestnuts mixed with that of ooze and brine.

She stopped a moment and looked in at one door: a woman holding a little child on her lap was laughing and talking to it in the firelight; she put its fat little fingers one by one in her mouth and pretended to bite them, and the child crowed again. The girl hurried on with a cry, past the narrow bit of road where the waves burst over in mocking spray laughter. Two men leaning over the wall gazed seaward with field-glasses. At the bridge leading to the tongue of land upon which the fort was built she paused for breath. The boats tossed uneasily in the swirling water, under it; the "Hijito del Mar" snatched a rough kiss from the "Ivonne" each time the swell came, as they rocked side by side on their chains. She looked back at the town in the distance, to the twin towers with their gleaming clock-lights, the coloured lights of the craft in the bay.

The rattle of a chain, as a safe-to-harbour steamer dropped its anchor, and the thrice three peals of the Angelus floated out across the bay to the surge-tossed ocean outside, home sounds from the shelter that the patient skill of man had devised to best the will of nature. She almost faltered in her resolve, but the thought of the dawn when she would have to go home with her half-drunken master clutched at her soul again, and she turned from the sight of the windows, blinking at her like friendly eyes, and faced the gloom.

She toiled up the cliff where the grass grew sparsely mingled with broken shells, and leant against a boulder and looked seawards. Ominous slants of bilious green showed through the rents in the cloud-masses hurtled against the sky. Battalions of wind-tossed clouds in distorted shapes drifted from north to south, gashed here and there with a livid streak like a gaping wound. And over all a background of brooding stillness hung, broken at intervals by the surge of the waters and sudden shrieks of the wind. When the wave did come it dashed with a boom like a great gun against the *digue*, and the smaller waves fell back with a rattle as of artillery. The spray mounted in a conical water-spout of foam, dissolving and scattering into spindrift. Every rush of the water expressed anger and rage and cruelty.

She crept down lower to where rough steps cut in the cliff led to the rocks below. There she crouched and stared down. At her feet the water bubbled as in a cauldron of seething foam, a giant churn in which a yellow-green liquid was tossed by invisible hands. Away through the mist beyond the curling wall of breakers, with their topping of white, and the boil and bubble and swirl of the water midst the rocks, a couple of lights and a line of smoke against a background of green told of a steamer making for shelter. She sat, and the storm lulled her. A stone or two rolled down the rough steps, as if kicked by a faltering foot, then a voice pierced through the din in a broken whisper:

"Is it you? I thought at first it was your 'fetch.' I saw you at the bridge."

She turned her head; the deep eyes stared as out of a carven mask, and met the puzzled gaze of his milder brown ones.

"Yes. Why did you follow me?"

"Why?" crouching at her side and laying his violin-case at her feet; "because the look your eyes gave me today has haunted me like the melody I hear in the wind sometimes. You are unhappy, and yet," dropping his voice, "you must have loved him."

"I have always loathed him."

"God!—then why—?"

"*You* ask me that,—*you?* Because your music got into my soul, and melted me like wax in hot weather, so that I was soft to run into any mould, and—he came at the right moment."

"God! Tienette—was it I?—I, who never dared approach you—I, a cripple, and you—you were so beautiful."

She turned and peered into his face. His words called back all the old witchery to her eyes and lips.

A blast of wind struck them both, and tore the spray-sodden wreath from her head, with a strand of her hair, and whirled it over and over till it vanished over the ledge. She laughed an odd, quiet laugh, and then she wound her arms round his neck, and kissed his eyes and mouth, and whispered:

"Play to me here in the storm the goat-man's 'call' that you played that day at the contest,—your own piece."

And she took the fiddle out of the case, and she kissed the bow before she handed it to him; and he, forgetting storm and hour and aught else but the wonder of her love and the inspiration of her caress, laid his chin to the brown wood and drew a cry from the strings that was as wonderful as the cry of a first-born to a mother; and then he played with closed eyes until the song of spring with its bursting blossoms and call of the blood rang potently through the night of winter storm.

The girl drew softly away, until she stood silhouetted against the sky on a ledge where the cliff sank steepest. The melody crept in silver notes between the skirl of the blast, now clear in the lull, now lost in the storm, rising louder and louder through a frenzy of passion and yearning to a cry of triumph; and as the last note died away the player opened his eyes as from a dream, and the wind kissed away all trace in the sand upon the ledge of the little feet of Tienette the golden-haired—but Pan still lives.

A MUSICAL INSTRUMENT

Elizabeth Barrett Browning

Elizabeth Barrett Browning (1806–1861) was an English poet and essayist born in Coxhoe Hall, Durham. Having spent her childhood in Hope End, near the Malvern Hills, Browning moved to Devon in 1832 and then to London in 1836. Her publication career started early, with her father releasing *The Battle of Marathon* (1820) privately. Browning's later collections included *The Seraphim and Other Poems* (1838), *Poems* (1844), *Sonnets from the Portuguese* (1850) and *Aurora Leigh* (1856). In 1846, she married the fellow poet, Robert Browning, who similarly explored the goat-god in his works, most notably, "Pan and Luna" (1880). Browning was also a firm campaigner for the abolition of slavery, with her family having previously profited from plantation ownership.

Alongside "The Dead Pan" (1844), which retells the death of the pagan gods against the rise of "his sole Godhead", "A Musical Instrument" (1860) is perhaps Browning's most famous Pan poem. First published in *The Cornhill Magazine*, Browning's work retells the myth of Syrinx, a chaste wood nymph who was pursued by a lustful Pan. Reaching the river's edge, Syrinx was transformed by the river nymphs into a reed so that she might hide. But, frustrated that he could not find her, Pan instead cut all the reeds asunder and fashioned them into his panpipes. Continuing Pan's associations with the wild, music and hybridity, as well as his dual nature, Browning draws on this legend to contrast creation and destruction, and to consider alternate approaches to art.

I

What was he doing, the great god Pan,
    Down in the reeds by the river?
Spreading ruin and scattering ban,
Splashing and paddling with hoofs of a goat,
And breaking the golden lilies afloat
    With the dragon-fly on the river?

II

He tore out a reed, the great god Pan,
    From the deep cool bed of the river.
The limpid water turbidly ran,
And the broken lilies a-dying lay,
And the dragon-fly had fled away,
    Ere he brought it out of the river.

III

High on the shore sate the great god Pan,
    While turbidly flowed the river,
And hacked and hewed as a great god can,
With his hard bleak steel at the patient reed,
Till there was not a sign of a leaf indeed
    To prove it fresh from the river.

IV

He cut it short, did the great god Pan,
   (How tall it stood in the river!)
Then drew the pith, like the heart of a man,
Steadily from the outside ring,
Then notched the poor dry empty thing
   In holes as he sate by the river.

V

"This is the way," laughed the great god Pan,
   (Laughed while he sate by the river!)
"The only way since gods began
To make sweet music they could succeed."
Then, dropping his mouth to a hole in the reed,
   He blew in power by the river.

VI

Sweet, sweet, sweet, O Pan,
   Piercing sweet by the river!
Blinding sweet, O great god Pan!
The sun on the hill forgot to die,
And the lilies revived, and the dragon-fly
   Came back to dream on the river.

VII

Yet half a beast is the great god Pan
  To laugh, as he sits by the river,
Making a poet out of a man.
The true gods sigh for the cost and pain,—
For the reed that grows nevermore again
  As a reed with the reeds in the river.

THE MOON-SLAVE

Barry Pain

Barry Pain (1864–1928) was an English journalist, poet, humorist and writer. Active during the late-Victorian period, Pain was a frequent contributor to a range of contemporary magazines, newspapers and periodicals, including *The Granta*, *The Cornhill Magazine*, *The Daily Chronicle*, *The Speaker* and *Punch*. Throughout his career, Pain operated in a number of genres, publishing the comic novel *Eliza* (1900), the crime collection *The Memoirs of Constantine Dix* (1905), and two selections of supernatural tales: *Stories in the Dark* (1901) and *Stories in Grey* (1911). Pain's 1897 novel, *The Octave of Claudius*, was also notably adapted into a 1922 silent horror film starring Lon Chaney—an icon of the strange, in his own right—entitled, *A Blind Bargain*.

"The Moon-Slave" was first published in the aforementioned *Stories in the Dark*. Echoing Egerton's earlier tale, we again see a protagonist weighed down by masculine pressures. Princess Viola is arranged to marry Prince Hugo, with this constraint contrasted against the paganistic freedom allowed to her by dance. "The Moon-Slave" highlights the associations of Pan with music, as well as introducing the common theme of Pan as a trickster, connecting to his parentage from the "divine trickster", Hermes. As the Princess Viola pleads with the moon to provide music for her to dance to, she finds herself caught in a new arrangement. Alongside Saki's "The Music on the Hill" and David H. Keller's "The Golden Bough", "The Moon-Slave" proves that the call of Pan is not always to be trusted.

The Princess Viola had, even in her childhood, an inevitable submission to the dance; a rhythmical madness in her blood answered hotly to the dance music, swaying her, as the wind sways trees, to movements of perfect sympathy and grace.

For the rest, she had her beauty and her long hair, that reached to her knees, and was thought lovable; but she was never very fervent and vivid unless she was dancing; at other times there almost seemed to be a touch of lethargy upon her. Now, when she was sixteen years old, she was betrothed to the Prince Hugo. With others the betrothal was merely a question of state. With her it was merely a question of obedience to the wishes of authority; it had been arranged; Hugo was *comme ci, comme ça*—no god in her eyes; it did not matter. But with Hugo it was quite different—he loved her.

The betrothal was celebrated by a banquet, and afterwards by a dance in the great hall of the palace. From this dance the Princess soon made her escape, quite discontented, and went to the furthest part of the palace gardens, where she could no longer hear the music calling her.

"They are all right," she said to herself as she thought of the men she had left, "but they cannot dance. Mechanically they are all right; they have learned it and don't make childish mistakes; but they are only one-two-three machines. They haven't the inspiration of dancing. It is so different when I dance alone."

She wandered on until she reached an old forsaken maze. It had been planned by a former king. All round it was a high crumbling wall with foxgloves growing on it. The maze itself had all its paths bordered with high opaque hedges; in the very centre was a circular open space with tall pine-trees growing round it. Many years ago the clue to the maze had been lost; it was but rarely now that anyone entered it. Its gravel paths were green with weeds, and in some places the hedges, spreading beyond their borders, had made the way almost impassable.

For a moment or two Viola stood peering in at the gate—a narrow gate with curiously twisted bars of wrought iron surmounted by a heraldic device. Then the whim seized her to enter the maze and try to find the space in the centre. She opened the gate and went in.

Outside everything was uncannily visible in the light of the full moon, but here in the dark shaded alleys the night was conscious of itself. She soon forgot her purpose, and wandered about quite aimlessly, sometimes forcing her way where the brambles had flung a laced barrier across her path, and a dragging mass of convolvulus struck wet and cool upon her cheek. As chance would have it she suddenly found herself standing under the tall pines, and looking at the open space that formed the goal of the maze. She was pleased that she had got there. Here the ground was carpeted with sand, fine and, as it seemed, beaten hard. From the summer night sky immediately above, the moonlight, unobstructed here, streamed straight down upon the scene.

Viola began to think about dancing. Over the dry, smooth sand her little satin shoes moved easily, stepping and gliding, circling and stepping, as she hummed the tune to which they moved. In the centre of the space she paused, looked at the wall of dark trees all round, at the shining stretches of silvery sand and at the moon above.

"My beautiful, moonlit, lonely, old dancing-room, why did I never find you before?" she cried; "but," she added, "you need music—there must be music here."

In her fantastic mood she stretched her soft, clasped hands upwards towards the moon.

"Sweet moon," she said in a kind of mock prayer, "make your white light come down in music into my dancing-room here, and I will dance most deliciously for you to see." She flung her head backward and let her hands fall; her eyes were half closed, and her mouth was a kissing mouth. "Ah! sweet moon," she whispered, "do this for me, and I will be your slave; I will be what you will."

Quite suddenly the air was filled with the sound of a grand invisible orchestra. Viola did not stop to wonder. To the music of a slow saraband she swayed and postured. In the music there was the regular beat of small drums and a perpetual drone. The air seemed to be filled with the perfume of some bitter spice. Viola could fancy almost that she saw a smouldering campfire and heard far off the roar of some desolate wild beast. She let her long hair fall, raising the heavy strands of it in either hand as she moved slowly to the laden music. Slowly her body swayed with drowsy grace, slowly her satin shoes slid over the silver sand.

The music ceased with a clash of cymbals. Viola rubbed her eyes. She fastened her hair up carefully again. Suddenly she looked up, almost imperiously.

"Music! more music!" she cried.

Once more the music came. This time it was a dance of caprice, pelting along over the violin-strings, leaping, laughing, wanton. Again an illusion seemed to cross her eyes. An old king was watching her, a king with the sordid history of the exhaustion of pleasure written on his flaccid face. A hook-nosed courtier by his side settled the ruffles at his wrists and mumbled, *"Ravissant! Quel Malheur que la vieillesse!"* It was a strange illusion. Faster and faster she sped to the music, stepping, spinning, pirouetting; the dance was light as thistle-down, fierce as fire, smooth as a rapid stream.

The moment that the music ceased Viola became horribly afraid. She turned and fled away from the moonlit space, through the trees, down the dark alleys of the maze, not heeding in the least which turn she took, and yet she found herself soon at the outside iron gate. From thence she ran through the palace garden, hardly ever pausing to take breath, until she reached the palace itself. In the eastern sky the first signs of dawn were showing; in the palace the festivities were drawing to an end. As she stood alone in the outer hall Prince Hugo came towards her.

"Where have you been, Viola?" he said sternly. "What have you been doing?"

She stamped her little foot.

"I will not be questioned," she replied angrily.

"I have some right to question," he said.

She laughed a little.

"For the first time in my life," she said, "I have been dancing."

He turned away in hopeless silence.

The months passed away. Slowly a great fear came over Viola, a fear that would hardly ever leave her. For every month at the full moon, whether she would or no, she found herself driven to the maze, through its mysterious walks into that strange dancing-room. And when she was there the music began once more, and once more she danced most deliciously for the moon to see. The second time that this happened she had merely thought that it was a recurrence of her own whim, and that the music was but a trick that the imagination had chosen to repeat. The third time frightened her, and she knew that the force that sways the tides had strange power over her. The fear grew as the year fell, for each month the music went on for a longer time—each month some of the pleasure had gone from the dance. On bitter nights in winter the moon called her and she came, when the breath was vapour, and the trees that circled her dancing-room were black bare skeletons, and the frost was cruel. She dared not tell anyone, and yet it was with difficulty that she kept her secret. Somehow chance seemed to favour her, and she always found a way to return from her midnight dance to her own room without being observed. Each month the summons seemed to be more imperious and urgent. Once when she was alone on her knees before the lighted altar in the private chapel of the palace she suddenly felt that the words of the familiar Latin prayer had gone from her memory. She rose to her feet, she sobbed bitterly, but the call had come and she could not resist it. She passed out of the chapel and down the palace-gardens. How madly she danced that night!

She was to be married in the spring. She began to be more gentle with Hugo now. She had a blind hope that when they were married she might be able to tell him about it, and he might be able to protect her, for she had always known him to be fearless. She could not love him, but she tried to be good to him. One day he mentioned to her that he had tried to find his way to the centre of the maze, and had failed. She smiled faintly. If only she could fail! But she never did.

On the night before the wedding day she had gone to bed and slept peacefully, thinking with her last waking moments of Hugo. Overhead the full moon came up the sky. Quite suddenly Viola was wakened with the impulse to fly to the dancing-room. It seemed to bid her hasten with breathless speed. She flung a cloak around her, slipped her naked feet into her dancing-shoes, and hurried forth. No one saw her or heard her—on the marble staircase of the palace, on down the terraces of the garden, she ran as fast as she could. A thorn-plant caught in her cloak, but she sped on, tearing it free; a sharp stone cut through the satin of one shoe, and her foot was wounded and bleeding, but she sped on. As the pebble that is flung from the cliff must fall until it reaches the sea, as the white ghost-moth must come in from cool hedges and scented darkness to a burning death in the lamp by which you sit so late—so Viola had no choice. The moon called her. The moon drew her to that circle of hard, bright sand and the pitiless music.

It was brilliant, rapid music tonight. Viola threw off her cloak and danced. As she did so, she saw that a shadow lay over a fragment of the moon's edge. It was the night of a total eclipse. She heeded it not. The intoxication of the dance was on her. She was all in white; even her face was pale in the moonlight. Every movement was full of poetry and grace.

The music would not stop. She had grown deathly weary. It seemed to her that she had been dancing for hours, and the shadow had nearly covered the moon's face, so that it was almost dark. She could hardly see the trees around her. She went on dancing, step-ping, spinning, pirouetting, held by the merciless music.

It stopped at last, just when the shadow had quite covered the moon's face, and all was dark. But it stopped only for a moment, and then began again. This time it was a slow, passionate waltz. It was useless to resist; she began to dance once more. As she did so she uttered a sudden shrill scream of horror, for in the dead dark-ness a hot hand had caught her own and whirled her round, *and she was no longer dancing alone.*

*

The search for the missing Princess lasted during the whole of the following day. In the evening Prince Hugo, his face anxious and firmly set, passed in his search the iron gate of the maze, and noticed on the stones beside it the stain of a drop of blood. Within the gate was another stain. He followed this clue, which had been left by Viola's wounded foot, until he reached that open space in the centre that had served Viola for her dancing-room. It was quite empty. He noticed that the sand round the edges was all worn down, as though someone had danced there, round and round, for a long time. But no separate footprint was distinguishable there. Just outside this track, however, he saw two footprints clearly defined close together: one was the print of a tiny satin shoe; the other was the print of a large naked foot—a cloven foot.

THE PIPER AT THE GATES OF DAWN

Kenneth Grahame

Kenneth Grahame (1859–1932) was a Scottish author born in Edinburgh. A keen student, he intended to continue his studies at Oxford University, but due to financial constraints instead pursued a career with the Bank of England. Grahame first started to publish articles in various periodicals including the *St. James Gazette* and *The Yellow Book*. He then wrote three collections of stories and essays: *Pagan Papers* (1893), *The Golden Age* (1895) and *Dream Days* (1898). Of note, "The Rural Pan", one such essay from *Pagan Papers*, reveals an early fascination with the horned god. In 1908, Grahame would publish his most famous work, *The Wind in the Willows*. Endlessly adapted, versions include A. A. Milne's *Toad of Toad Hall* (1929), Walt Disney Productions' *The Adventures of Ichabod and Mr. Toad* (1949) and Alan Bennett's *The Wind in the Willows* (1991).

"The Piper at the Gates of Dawn", while also the title of Pink Floyd's debut album, is the seventh chapter from *The Wind in the Willows*. This strange interlude finds Rat and Mole venturing upstream in search of Otter's missing child, Portly. Aligning with the pastoral image of Pan, who speaks to the awesome divinity of Nature, Rat and Mole experience sublime fear as they venture into Pan's domain. Indeed, the strangeness of this extract is all the more marked for the context in which it was published: a children's tale of anthropomorphic animals. Yet, perhaps this form was the ideal conduit for the horned god. Through their human-animal hybridity, the characters of *The Wind in the Willows* come to echo Pan's own divided form. Included below is the front board of the 1908 Methuen edition, which depicts Rat and Mole among the reeds of Pan, their heads bowed in sleep or worship.

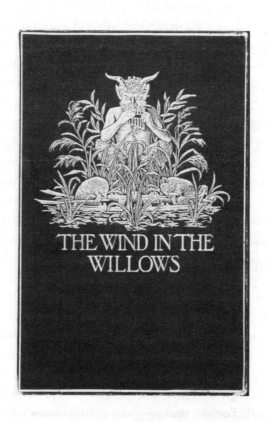

The Willow-Wren was twittering his thin little song, hidden himself in the dark selvedge of the river bank. Though it was past ten o'clock at night, the sky still clung to and retained some lingering skirts of light from the departed day; and the sullen heats of the torrid afternoon broke up and rolled away at the dispersing touch of the cool fingers of the short midsummer night. Mole lay stretched on the bank, still panting from the stress of the fierce day that had been cloudless from dawn to late sunset, and waited for his friend to return. He had been on the river with some companions, leaving the Water Rat free to keep an engagement of long standing with Otter; and he had come back to find the house dark and deserted, and no sign of Rat, who was doubtless keeping it up late with his old comrade. It was still too hot to think of staying indoors, so he lay on some cool dock-leaves, and thought over the past day and its doings, and how very good they all had been.

The Rat's light footfall was presently heard approaching over the parched grass. "O, the blessed coolness!" he said, and sat down, gazing thoughtfully into the river, silent and preoccupied.

"You stayed to supper, of course?" said the Mole presently.

"Simply had to," said the Rat. "They wouldn't hear of my going before. You know how kind they always are. And they made things as jolly for me as ever they could, right up to the moment I left. But I felt a brute all the time, as it was clear to me they were very unhappy, though they tried to hide it. Mole, I'm afraid they're in trouble. Little Portly is missing again; and you know what a lot his father thinks of him, though he never says much about it."

"What, that child?" said the Mole lightly. "Well, suppose he is; why worry about it? He's always straying off and getting lost, and turning up again; he's so adventurous. But no harm ever happens to him. Everybody hereabouts knows him and likes him, just as they do old Otter, and you may be sure some animal or other will come across him and bring him back again all right. Why, we've found him ourselves, miles from home, and quite self-possessed and cheerful!"

"Yes; but this time it's more serious," said the Rat gravely. "He's been missing for some days now, and the Otters have hunted everywhere, high and low, without finding the slightest trace. And they've asked every animal, too, for miles around, and no one knows anything about him. Otter's evidently more anxious than he'll admit. I got out of him that young Portly hasn't learnt to swim very well yet, and I can see he's thinking of the weir. There's a lot of water coming down still, considering the time of the year, and the place always had a fascination for the child. And then there are—well, traps and things—*you* know. Otter's not the fellow to be nervous about any son of his before it's time. And now he *is* nervous. When I left, he came out with me—said he wanted some air, and talked about stretching his legs. But I could see it wasn't that, so I drew him out and pumped him, and got it all from him at last. He was going to spend the night watching by the ford. You know the place where the old ford used to be, in by-gone days before they built the bridge?"

"I know it well," said the Mole. "But why should Otter choose to watch there?"

"Well, it seems that it was there he gave Portly his first swimming-lesson," continued the Rat. "From that shallow, gravelly spit near the bank. And it was there he used to teach him fishing, and there young Portly caught his first fish, of which he was so very proud.

The child loved the spot, and Otter thinks that if he came wandering back from wherever he is—if he *is* anywhere by this time, poor little chap—he might make for the ford he was so fond of; or if he came across it he'd remember it well, and stop there and play, perhaps. So Otter goes there every night and watches—on the chance, you know, just on the chance!"

They were silent for a time, both thinking of the same thing—the lonely, heart-sore animal, crouched by the ford, watching and waiting, the long night through—on the chance.

"Well, well," said the Rat presently, "I suppose we ought to be thinking about turning in." But he never offered to move.

"Rat," said the Mole, "I simply can't go and turn in, and go to sleep, and *do* nothing, even though there doesn't seem to be anything to be done. We'll get the boat out, and paddle upstream. The moon will be up in an hour or so, and then we will search as well as we can—anyhow, it will be better than going to bed and doing *nothing*."

"Just what I was thinking myself," said the Rat. "It's not the sort of night for bed anyhow; and daybreak is not so very far off, and then we may pick up some news of him from early risers as we go along."

They got the boat out, and the Rat took the sculls, paddling with caution. Out in midstream, there was a clear, narrow track that faintly reflected the sky; but wherever shadows fell on the water from bank, bush, or tree, they were as solid to all appearance as the banks themselves, and the Mole had to steer with judgment accordingly. Dark and deserted as it was, the night was full of small noises, song and chatter and rustling, telling of the busy little population who were up and about, plying their trades and vocations through the night till sunshine should fall on them at last and send them off to their well-earned repose. The water's own noises, too, were more apparent than by day, its gurglings and "cloops" more unexpected and near at hand; and constantly they started at what seemed a sudden clear call from an actual articulate voice.

The line of the horizon was clear and hard against the sky, and in one particular quarter it showed black against a silvery climbing phosphorescence that grew and grew. At last, over the rim of the waiting earth the moon lifted with slow majesty till it swung clear of the horizon and rode off, free of moorings; and once more they began to see surfaces—meadows wide-spread, and quiet gardens, and the river itself from bank to bank, all softly disclosed, all washed clean of mystery and terror, all radiant again as by day, but with a difference that was tremendous. Their old haunts greeted them again in other raiment, as if they had slipped away and put on this pure new apparel and come quietly back, smiling as they shyly waited to see if they would be recognised again under it.

Fastening their boat to a willow, the friends landed in this silent, silver kingdom, and patiently explored the hedges, the hollow trees, the runnels and their little culverts, the ditches and dry water-ways. Embarking again and crossing over, they worked their way up the stream in this manner, while the moon, serene and detached in a cloudless sky, did what she could, though so far off, to help them in their quest; till her hour came and she sank earthwards reluctantly, and left them, and mystery once more held field and river.

Then a change began slowly to declare itself. The horizon became clearer, field and tree came more into sight, and somehow with a different look; the mystery began to drop away from them. A bird piped suddenly, and was still; and a light breeze sprang up and set the reeds and bulrushes rustling. Rat, who was in the stern of the boat, while Mole sculled, sat up suddenly and listened with a passionate intentness. Mole, who with gentle strokes was just keeping the boat moving while he scanned the banks with care, looked at him with curiosity.

"It's gone!" sighed the Rat, sinking back in his seat again. "So beautiful and strange and new! Since it was to end so soon, I almost wish I had never heard it. For it has roused a longing in me that is pain, and nothing seems worth while but just to hear that sound once more and go on listening to it for ever. No! There it is again!" he cried, alert once more. Entranced, he was silent for a long space, spellbound.

"Now it passes on and I begin to lose it," he said presently. "O Mole! the beauty of it! The merry bubble and joy, the thin, clear, happy call of the distant piping! Such music I never dreamed of, and the call in it is stronger even than the music is sweet! Row on, Mole, row! For the music and the call must be for us."

The Mole, greatly wondering, obeyed. "I hear nothing myself," he said, "but the wind playing in the reeds and rushes and osiers."

The Rat never answered, if indeed he heard. Rapt, transported, trembling, he was possessed in all his senses by this new divine thing that caught up his helpless soul and swung and dandled it, a powerless but happy infant in a strong sustaining grasp.

In silence Mole rowed steadily, and soon they came to a point where the river divided, a long backwater branching off to one side. With a slight movement of his head Rat, who had long dropped the rudder-lines, directed the rower to take the backwater. The creeping tide of light gained and gained, and now they could see the colour of the flowers that gemmed the water's edge.

"Clearer and nearer still," cried the Rat joyously. "Now you must surely hear it! Ah—at last—I see you do!"

Breathless and transfixed, the Mole stopped rowing as the liquid run of that glad piping broke on him like a wave, caught him up, and possessed him utterly. He saw the tears on his comrade's cheeks, and bowed his head and understood. For a space they hung there, brushed by the purple loosestrife that fringed the bank; then the clear imperious summons that marched hand-in-hand with the intoxicating melody imposed its will on Mole, and mechanically he bent to his oars again. And the light grew steadily stronger, but no birds sang as they were wont to do at the approach of dawn; and but for the heavenly music all was marvellously still.

On either side of them, as they glided onwards, the rich meadow-grass seemed that morning of a freshness and a greenness unsurpassable. Never had they noticed the roses so vivid, the willow-herb so riotous, the meadow-sweet so odorous and pervading. Then the murmur of the approaching weir began to hold the air, and they felt a consciousness that they were nearing the end, whatever it might be, that surely awaited their expedition.

A wide half-circle of foam and glinting lights and shining shoulders of green water, the great weir closed the backwater from bank to bank, troubled all the quiet surface with twirling eddies and floating foam-streaks, and deadened all other sounds with its solemn and soothing rumble. In midmost of the stream, embraced in the weir's shimmering arm-spread, a small island lay anchored, fringed close with willow and silver birch and alder. Reserved, shy, but full of significance, it hid whatever it might hold behind a veil, keeping it till the hour should come, and, with the hour, those who were called and chosen.

Slowly, but with no doubt or hesitation whatever, and in something of a solemn expectancy, the two animals passed through the broken, tumultuous water and moored their boat at the flowery margin of the island. In silence they landed, and pushed through the blossom and scented herbage and undergrowth that led up to the level ground, till they stood on a little lawn of a marvellous green, set round with Nature's own orchard-trees—crab-apple, wild cherry, and sloe.

"This is the place of my song-dream, the place the music played to me," whispered the Rat, as if in a trance. "Here, in this holy place, here if anywhere, surely we shall find Him!"

Then suddenly the Mole felt a great Awe fall upon him, an awe that turned his muscles to water, bowed his head, and rooted his feet to the ground. It was no panic terror—indeed he felt wonderfully at peace and happy—but it was an awe that smote and held him and, without seeing, he knew it could only mean that some august Presence was very, very near. With difficulty he turned to look for his friend, and saw him at his side, cowed, stricken, and trembling violently. And still there was utter silence in the populous bird-haunted branches around them; and still the light grew and grew.

Perhaps he would never have dared to raise his eyes, but that, though the piping was now hushed, the call and the summons seemed still dominant and imperious. He might not refuse, were Death himself waiting to strike him instantly, once he had looked with mortal eye on things rightly kept hidden. Trembling he obeyed, and raised his humble head; and then, in that utter clearness of the imminent dawn, while Nature, flushed with fulness of incredible colour, seemed to hold her breath for the event, he looked in the very eyes of the Friend and Helper; saw the backward sweep of the curved horns, gleaming in the growing daylight; saw the stern, hooked nose between the kindly eyes that were looking down on them humorously, while the bearded mouth broke into a half-smile at the corners; saw the rippling muscles on the arm that lay across the broad chest, the long supple hand still holding the panpipes only just fallen away from the parted lips; saw the splendid curves of the shaggy limbs disposed in majestic ease on the sward; saw, last of all, nestling between his very hooves, sleeping soundly in entire peace and contentment, the little, round, podgy, childish form of the baby otter. All this he saw, for one moment breathless and intense, vivid on the morning sky; and still, as he looked, he lived; and still, as he lived, he wondered.

"Rat!" he found breath to whisper, shaking. "Are you afraid?"

"Afraid?" murmured the Rat, his eyes shining with unutterable love. "Afraid! Of *Him*? O, never, never! And yet—and yet—O, Mole, I am afraid!"

Then the two animals, crouching to the earth, bowed their heads and did worship.

Sudden and magnificent, the sun's broad golden disc showed itself over the horizon facing them; and the first rays, shooting across the level water-meadows, took the animals full in the eyes and dazzled them. When they were able to look once more, the Vision had vanished, and the air was full of the carol of birds that hailed the dawn.

As they stared blankly, in dumb misery deepening as they slowly realised all they had seen and all they had lost, a capricious little breeze, dancing up from the surface of the water, tossed the aspens, shook the dewy roses, and blew lightly and caressingly in their faces; and with its soft touch came instant oblivion. For this is the last best gift that the kindly demi-god is careful to bestow on those to whom he has revealed himself in their helping: the gift of forgetfulness. Lest the awful remembrance should remain and grow, and overshadow mirth and pleasure, and the great haunting memory should spoil all the after-lives of little animals helped out of difficulties, in order that they should be happy and light-hearted as before.

Mole rubbed his eyes and stared at Rat, who was looking about him in a puzzled sort of way. "I beg your pardon; what did you say, Rat?" he asked.

"I think I was only remarking," said Rat slowly, "that this was the right sort of place, and that here, if anywhere, we should find him. And look! Why, there he is, the little fellow!" And with a cry of delight he ran towards the slumbering Portly.

But Mole stood still a moment, held in thought. As one wakened suddenly from a beautiful dream, who struggles to recall it, and can recapture nothing but a dim sense of the beauty of it, the beauty! Till that, too, fades away in its turn, and the dreamer bitterly accepts the hard, cold waking and all its penalties; so Mole, after struggling with his memory for a brief space, shook his head sadly and followed the Rat.

Portly woke up with a joyous squeak, and wriggled with pleasure at the sight of his father's friends, who had played with him so often in past days. In a moment, however, his face grew blank, and he fell to hunting round in a circle with pleading whine. As a child that has fallen happily asleep in its nurse's arms, and wakes to find itself alone and laid in a strange place, and searches corners and cupboards, and runs from room to room, despair growing silently in its heart, even so Portly searched the island and searched, dogged and unwearying, till at last the black moment came for giving it up, and sitting down and crying bitterly.

The Mole ran quickly to comfort the little animal; but Rat, lingering, looked long and doubtfully at certain hoof-marks deep in the sward.

"Some—great—animal—has been here," he murmured slowly and thoughtfully; and stood musing, musing; his mind strangely stirred.

"Come along, Rat!" called the Mole. "Think of poor Otter, waiting up there by the ford!"

Portly had soon been comforted by the promise of a treat—a jaunt on the river in Mr. Rat's real boat; and the two animals conducted him to the water's side, placed him securely between them in the bottom of the boat, and paddled off down the backwater. The sun was fully up by now, and hot on them, birds sang lustily and without restraint, and flowers smiled and nodded from either bank, but somehow—so thought the animals—with less of richness and blaze of colour than they seemed to remember seeing quite recently somewhere—they wondered where.

The main river reached again, they turned the boat's head upstream, towards the point where they knew their friend was keeping his lonely vigil. As they drew near the familiar ford, the Mole took the boat in to the bank, and they lifted Portly out and set him on his legs on the tow-path, gave him his marching orders and a friendly farewell pat on the back, and shoved out into midstream. They watched the little animal as he waddled along the path contentedly and with importance; watched him till they saw his muzzle suddenly lift and his waddle break into a clumsy amble as he quickened his pace with shrill whines and wriggles of recognition. Looking up the river, they could see Otter start up, tense and rigid, from out of the shallows where he crouched in dumb patience, and could hear his amazed and joyous bark as he bounded up through the osiers on to the path. Then the Mole, with a strong pull on one oar, swung the boat round and let the full stream bear them down again whither it would, their quest now happily ended.

"I feel strangely tired, Rat," said the Mole, leaning wearily over his oars, as the boat drifted. "It's being up all night, you'll say, perhaps; but that's nothing. We do as much half the nights of the week, at this time of the year. No; I feel as if I had been through something very exciting and rather terrible, and it was just over; and yet nothing particular has happened."

"Or something very surprising and splendid and beautiful," murmured the Rat, leaning back and closing his eyes. "I feel just as you do, Mole; simply dead tired, though not body-tired. It's lucky we've got the stream with us, to take us home. Isn't it jolly to feel the sun again, soaking into one's bones! And hark to the wind playing in the reeds!"

"It's like music—far-away music," said the Mole, nodding drowsily.

"So I was thinking," murmured the Rat, dreamful and languid. "Dance-music—the lilting sort that runs on without a stop—but with words in it, too—it passes into words and out of them again—I catch them at intervals—then it is dance-music once more, and then nothing but the reeds' soft thin whispering."

"You hear better than I," said the Mole sadly. "I cannot catch the words."

"Let me try and give you them," said the Rat softly, his eyes still closed. "Now it is turning into words again—faint but clear—*Lest the awe should dwell—And turn your frolic to fret—You shall look on my power at the helping hour—But then you shall forget!* Now the reeds take it up—*forget, forget*, they sigh, and it dies away in a rustle and a whisper. Then the voice returns—

"*Lest limbs be reddened and rent—I spring the trap that is set—As I loose the snare you may glimpse me there—For surely you shall forget!* Row nearer, Mole, nearer to the reeds! It is hard to catch, and grows each minute fainter.

"*Helper and healer, I cheer—Small waifs in the woodland wet— Strays I find in it, wounds I bind in it—Bidding them all forget!*

Nearer, Mole, nearer! No, it is no good; the song has died away into reed-talk."

"But what do the words mean?" asked the wondering Mole.

"That I do not know," said the Rat simply. "I passed them on to you as they reached me. Ah! now they return again, and this time full and clear! This time, at last, it is the real, the unmistakable thing, simple—passionate—perfect—"

"Well, let's have it, then," said the Mole, after he had waited patiently for a few minutes, half-dozing in the hot sun.

But no answer came. He looked, and understood the silence. With a smile of much happiness on his face, and something of a listening look still lingering there, the weary Rat was fast asleep.

THE MUSIC ON THE HILL

Saki

Saki (1870–1916), otherwise known as Hector Hugh Munro, was a British writer and journalist famed for his short fiction. Born in Burma, Munro was sent home to England at the age of two, where he lived with his siblings under the care of his grandmother and aunts. In 1896, Munro moved to London where he began his journalistic career, writing for *The Westminster Gazette*, *The Morning Post* and *The Daily Express*. He then adopted the pen name Saki for his satirical debut, *The Westminster Alice* (1902), a series of pastiche vignettes illustrated by the cartoonist Francis Carruthers Gould. Saki's subsequent writings would continue to lampoon Edwardian culture, contrasting stuffy conservative values with the unforgiving wildness of nature. Mischievous and macabre, his works include *Reginald* (1904), *Reginald in Russia* (1910), and his final collection, *Beasts and Super-Beasts* (1914), published before his death in World War I.

"The Music on the Hill" is one such playful work, first published in *The Chronicles of Clovis* (1911). The story centres on Sylvia Seltoun, a prototypical socialite, who is familiar with a wholly beatified image of nature. Having persuaded her husband, Mortimer, to relocate to their country manor, Sylvia starts to encounter strange events in the surrounding landscape. But, confident in her rationality, she ignores her husband's warnings of Pan. "The Music on the Hill" furthers Pan's presentation as a trickster, with a darkly comic ending, while also hinting at the queer undertones present in Saki's other works. An altogether more sinister interpretation of the god of the wild, the tale also cautions that the natural world is not to be easily tamed.

Sylvia Seltoun ate her breakfast in the morning room at Yessney with a pleasant sense of ultimate victory, such as a fervent Ironside might have permitted himself on the morrow of Worcester fight. She was scarcely pugnacious by temperament, but belonged to that more successful class of fighters who are pugnacious by circumstance. Fate had willed that her life should be occupied with a series of small struggles, usually with the odds slightly against her, and usually she had just managed to come through winning. And now she felt that she had brought her hardest and certainly her most important struggle to a successful issue. To have married Mortimer Seltoun, "Dead Mortimer" as his more intimate enemies called him, in the teeth of the cold hostility of his family, and in spite of his unaffected indifference to women, was indeed an achievement that had needed some determination and adroitness to carry through; yesterday she had brought her victory to its concluding stage by wrenching her husband away from Town and its group of satellite watering places and "settling him down," in the vocabulary of her kind, in this remote wood-girt manor-farm which was his country house. "You will never get Mortimer to go," his mother had said carpingly, "but if he once goes he'll stay; Yessney throws almost as much a spell over him as Town does. One can understand what holds him to Town, but Yessney—" and the dowager had shrugged her shoulders.

There was a sombre almost savage wildness about Yessney that was certainly not likely to appeal to town-bred tastes, and Sylvia, notwithstanding her name, was accustomed to nothing much more sylvan than "leafy Kensington." She looked on the country as something excellent and wholesome in its way, which was apt to become troublesome if you encouraged it overmuch. Distrust of town-life had been a new thing with her, born of her marriage with Mortimer, and she had watched with satisfaction the gradual fading of what she called "the Jermyn-street-look" in his eyes as the woods and heather of Yessney had closed in on them yesternight. Her will power and strategy had prevailed; Mortimer would stay.

Outside the morning room windows was a triangular slope of turf, which the indulgent might call a lawn, and beyond its low hedge of neglected fuchsia bushes a steeper slope of heather and bracken dropped down into cavernous combes overgrown with oak and yew. In its wild open savagery there seemed a stealthy linking of the joy of life with the terror of unseen things. Sylvia smiled complacently as she gazed with a School-of-Art appreciation at the landscape, and then of a sudden she almost shuddered.

"It is very wild," she said to Mortimer who had joined her; "one could almost think that in such a place the worship of Pan had never quite died out."

"The worship of Pan never has died out," said Mortimer. "Other newer gods have drawn aside his votaries from time to time, but he is the Nature-God to whom all must come back at last. He has been called the Father of all the Gods, but most of his children have been still-born."

Sylvia was religious in an honest vaguely devotional kind of way, and did not like to hear her beliefs spoken of as mere aftergrowths, but it was at least something new and hopeful to hear Dead Mortimer speak with such energy and conviction on any subject.

"You don't really believe in Pan?" she asked incredulously.

"I've been a fool in most things," said Mortimer quietly, "but I'm not such a fool as not to believe in Pan when I'm down here. And if you're wise you won't disbelieve in him too boastfully while you're in his country."

It was not till a week later, when Sylvia had exhausted the attractions of the woodland walks round Yessney, that she ventured on a tour of inspection of the farm buildings. A farmyard suggested in her mind a scene of cheerful bustle, with churns and flails and smiling dairymaids, and teams of horses drinking knee-deep in duck-crowded ponds. As she wandered among the gaunt grey buildings of Yessney manor-farm her first impression was one of crushing stillness and desolation, as though she had happened on some lone deserted homestead long given over to owls and cobwebs; then came a sense of furtive watchful hostility, the same shadow of unseen things that seemed to lurk in the wooded combes and coppices. From behind heavy doors and shuttered windows came the restless stamp of hoof or rasp of chain halter, and at times a muffled bellow from some stalled beast. From a distant corner a shaggy dog watched her with intent unfriendly eyes; as she drew near it slipped quietly into its kennel, and slipped out again as noiselessly when she had passed by. A few hens, questing for food under a rick, stole away under a gate at her approach. Sylvia felt that if she had come across any human beings in this wilderness of barn and byre they would have fled wraith-like from her gaze. At last, turning a corner quickly, she came upon a living thing that did not fly from her. Astretch in a pool of mud was an enormous sow, gigantic beyond the town-woman's wildest computation of swine-flesh, and speedily alert to resent and if necessary repel the unwonted intrusion. It was Sylvia's turn to make an unobtrusive retreat. As she threaded her way past rickyards and cowsheds and long blank walls, she started suddenly at a strange sound—the echo of a boy's laughter, golden and equivocal. Jan, the only boy employed on the farm, a tow-headed, wizen-faced yokel, was visibly at work on a potato clearing half-way up the nearest hillside, and Mortimer, when questioned, knew of no other probable or possible begetter of the hidden mockery that had ambushed Sylvia's retreat. The memory of that untraceable echo was added to her other impressions of a furtive sinister "something" that hung around Yessney.

Of Mortimer she saw very little; farm and woods and trout-streams seemed to swallow him up from dawn till dusk. Once, following the direction she had seen him take in the morning, she came to an open space in a nut copse, further shut in by huge yew trees, in the centre of which stood a stone pedestal surmounted by a small bronze figure of a youthful Pan. It was a beautiful piece of workmanship, but her attention was chiefly held by the fact that a newly cut bunch of grapes had been placed as an offering at its feet. Grapes were none too plentiful at the manor house, and Sylvia snatched the bunch angrily from the pedestal. Contemptuous annoyance dominated her thoughts as she strolled slowly home-ward, and then gave way to a sharp feeling of something that was very near fright; across a thick tangle of undergrowth a boy's face was scowling at her, brown and beautiful, with unutterably evil eyes. It was a lonely pathway, all pathways round Yessney were lonely for the matter of that, and she sped forward without waiting to give a closer scrutiny to this sudden apparition. It was not till she had reached the house that she discovered that she had dropped the bunch of grapes in her flight.

"I saw a youth in the wood today," she told Mortimer that even-ing, "brown-faced and rather handsome, but a scoundrel to look at. A gipsy lad, I suppose."

"A reasonable theory," said Mortimer, "only there aren't any gipsies in these parts at present."

"Then who was he?" asked Sylvia, and as Mortimer appeared to have no theory of his own she passed on to recount her finding of the votive offering.

"I suppose it was your doing" she observed; "it's a harmless piece of lunacy, but people would think you dreadfully silly if they knew of it."

"Did you meddle with it in any way?" asked Mortimer.

"I—I threw the grapes away. It seemed so silly," said Sylvia, watching Mortimer's impassive face for a sign of annoyance.

"I don't think you were wise to do that," he said reflectively. "I've heard it said that the Wood Gods are rather horrible to those who molest them."

"Horrible perhaps to those that believe in them, but you see I don't," retorted Sylvia.

"All the same," said Mortimer in his even, dispassionate tone, "I should avoid the woods and orchards if I were you, and give a wide berth to the horned beasts on the farm."

It was all nonsense, of course, but in that lonely wood-girt spot nonsense seemed able to rear a bastard brood of uneasiness.

"Mortimer," said Sylvia suddenly, "I think we will go back to Town some time soon."

Her victory had not been so complete as she had supposed; it had carried her on to ground that she was already anxious to quit.

"I don't think you will ever go back to Town," said Mortimer. He seemed to be paraphrasing his mother's prediction as to himself.

Sylvia noted with dissatisfaction and some self-contempt that the course of her next afternoon's ramble took her instinctively clear of the network of woods. As to the horned cattle, Mortimer's warning was scarcely needed, for she had always regarded them as of doubtful neutrality at the best; her imagination unsexed the most matronly dairy cows and turned them into bulls liable to "see red" at any moment. The ram who fed in the narrow paddock below the orchards she had adjudged, after ample and cautious probation, to be of docile temper; today, however, she decided to leave his docility untested, for the usually tranquil beast was roaming with every sign of restlessness from corner to corner of his meadow. A low, fitful piping, as of some reedy flute, was coming from the depth of a neighbouring copse, and there seemed to be some subtle connection between the animal's restless pacing and the wild music from the wood. Sylvia turned her steps in an upward direction and climbed the heather-clad slopes that stretched in rolling shoulders high above Yessney. She had left the piping notes behind her, but across the wooded combes at her feet the wind brought her another kind of music, the straining bay of hounds in full chase. Yessney was just on the outskirts of the Devon-and-Somerset country, and the hunted deer sometimes came that way. Sylvia could presently see a dark body, breasting hill after hill, and sinking again and again out of sight as he crossed the combes, while behind him steadily swelled that relentless chorus, and she grew tense with the excited sympathy that one feels for any hunted thing in whose capture one is not directly interested. And at last he broke through the outermost line of oak scrub and fern and stood panting in the open, a fat September stag carrying a well-furnished head. His obvious course was to drop down to the brown pools of Undercombe and thence make his way towards the red deer's favoured sanctuary, the sea. To Sylvia's surprise, however, he turned his head to the upland slope and came lumbering resolutely onward over the heather. "It will be dreadful," she thought, "the hounds will pull him down under my very eyes." But the music of the pack seemed to have died away for a moment, and in its place she heard again that wild piping, which rose now on this side, now on that, as though urging the failing stag to a final effort. Sylvia stood well aside from his path, half hidden in a thick growth of whortle bushes, and watched him swing stiffly upward, his flanks dark with sweat, the coarse hair on his neck showing light by contrast. The pipe music shrilled suddenly around her, seeming to come from the bushes at her very feet, and at the same moment the great beast slewed round and bore directly down upon her. In an instant her pity for the hunted animal was changed to wild terror at her own danger; the thick heather roots mocked her scrambling efforts at flight, and she looked frantically downward for a glimpse of oncoming hounds. The huge antler spikes were within a few yards of her, and in a flash of numbing fear she remembered Mortimer's warning, to beware of horned beasts on the farm. And then with a quick throb of joy she saw that she was not alone; a human figure stood a few paces aside, knee-deep in the whortle bushes.

"Drive it off!" she shrieked. But the figure made no answering movement.

The antlers drove straight at her breast, the acrid smell of the hunted animal was in her nostrils, but her eyes were filled with the horror of something she saw other than her oncoming death. And in her ears rang the echo of a boy's laughter, golden and equivocal.

THE HAUNTED FOREST

Edith Hurley

Edith Hurley (1903–1997) was an American poet and playwright born in Roanoke, Virginia. An early supporter of *Weird Tales*—in the letters column of the October 1934 issue, she noted how she had "been a reader... since its inception"—Hurley contributed five poems to the magazine, with equally uplifting titles: "The Haunted Forest" (1929), "Sonnet of Death" (1930), "The City of Death" (1939), "The Dream" (1939) and "The Great God Death" (1940). These poems were later republished in her 1977 collection, *Faint Echo*. Hurley published further verse in *Contemporary American Women Poets*, *The Rotarian* and the *New York Times*. Her dramatic works include *A More Perfect Union* (1964) and *We The People* (1965).

"The Haunted Forest" was the first of Hurley's contributions to *Weird Tales*, published in July 1929. Similar to Oscar Wilde, Hurley's poem grieves Pan's disappearance from the modern world. However, she suggests that the horned god's presence can still be felt "on mystic nights in May" – that we might reconnect with our banished pagan past. Evoking the language of nature, ritual and myth, "The Haunted Forest" suggests that even in death, Pan still lives on.

There is a forest deep and dark.
    Where never sunbeam strays;
Untravelled are its winding paths,
    And all untrod its ways.

And there are dusky violets
    In little, silent dells.
And a dim cave within a rock
    Where Pan, the goat-god, dwells.

And in one still and hidden spot
    There is a crystal pool;
Serene its surface as a glass.
    And weirdly beautiful.

No wind disturbs those ancient trees,
    And nothing living stirs;
For broken are the shrines of Pan,
    And gone his worshippers.

Yet on some mystic nights in May,
    Safe from the eyes of man.
Above a strange wind's crying.
    Long call the pipes of Pan.

And from the hills and hollows
   The fairy people come.
With flute and lute and viol
   And beat of tiny drum.

Near by the pool's green edges
   They dance the long hours through,
And golden is the moonlight.
   And silver is the dew.

Their songs are all sung softly.
   And gently do they tread;
For lo, the place is haunted
   By ghosts of men long dead.

THE STORY OF A PANIC

E. M. Forster

E. M. Forster (1879–1970) was an English writer born in Marylebone, London. Following his father's death from tuberculosis, Forster relocated with his mother to Hertfordshire. During his early adulthood, he travelled extensively, exploring Greece, Italy, Germany and India. At the age of twenty-six, Forster published his first novel, *Where Angels Fear to Tread* (1905). This was followed by works of equal renown, including *A Room with a View* (1908), *Howards End* (1910) and *A Passage to India* (1924). Forster also published short fiction, such as those collected in *The Eternal Moment and Other Stories* (1928). His works often explored class differences and sexuality. Impacted by the trial of Oscar Wilde, Forster's own homosexuality was kept secret except to his closest friends, and his early works focused instead on heterosexual partners. Only in his later writings, often published posthumously, does homosexual love prove a key theme. These pieces include *Maurice* (1971) and *The Life to Come and Other Stories* (1972).

"The Story of a Panic" was first published in *The Celestial Omnibus and Other Stories* (1911). It follows a group of tourists holidaying in Italy who, venturing into the mountains, are startled by the shaded appearance of Pan. Eustace, a young boy outcast from the group already because of his apparent idleness and failures of masculinity, seems altered by this encounter. Alongside E. F. Benson's "The Man Who Went Too Far" (1912), "The Story of a

Panic" thus invites itself to be read as a story of queer realisation. Indeed, with Eustace finding liberation at the end of the tale, Forster challenges the death and persecution to which he would have been accustomed.

I

E ustace's career—if career it can be called—certainly dates from that afternoon in the chestnut woods above Ravello. I confess at once that I am a plain, simple man, with no pretensions to literary style. Still, I do flatter myself that I can tell a story without exaggerating, and I have therefore decided to give an unbiased account of the extraordinary events of eight years ago.

Ravello is a delightful place with a delightful little hotel in which we met some charming people. There were the two Miss Robinsons, who had been there for six weeks with Eustace, their nephew, then a boy of about fourteen. Mr. Sandbach had also been there some time. He had held a curacy in the north of England, which he had been compelled to resign on account of ill-health, and while he was recruiting at Ravello he had taken in hand Eustace's education— which was then sadly deficient—and was endeavouring to fit him for one of our great public schools. Then there was Mr. Leyland, a would-be artist, and, finally, there was the nice landlady, Signora Scafetti, and the nice English-speaking waiter, Emmanuele—though at the time of which I am speaking Emmanuele was away, visiting a sick father.

To this little circle, I, my wife, and my two daughters made, I venture to think, a not unwelcome addition. But though I liked most of the company well enough, there were two of them to whom I did not take at all. They were the artist, Leyland, and the Miss Robinsons' nephew, Eustace.

Leyland was simply conceited and odious, and, as those qualities will be amply illustrated in my narrative, I need not enlarge upon them here. But Eustace was something besides: he was indescribably repellent.

I am fond of boys as a rule, and was quite disposed to be friendly. I and my daughters offered to take him out—"No, walking was such a fag." Then I asked him to come and bathe—"No, he could not swim."

"Every English boy should be able to swim," I said, "I will teach you myself."

"There, Eustace dear," said Miss Robinson; "here is a chance for you."

But he said he was afraid of the water!—a boy afraid!—and of course I said no more.

I would not have minded so much if he had been a really studious boy, but he neither played hard nor worked hard. His favourite occupations were lounging on the terrace in an easy chair and loafing along the high road, with his feet shuffling up the dust and his shoulders stooping forward. Naturally enough, his features were pale, his chest contracted, and his muscles undeveloped. His aunts thought him delicate; what he really needed was discipline.

That memorable day we all arranged to go for a picnic up in the chestnut woods—all, that is, except Janet, who stopped behind to finish her water-colour of the Cathedral—not a very successful attempt, I am afraid.

I wander off into these irrelevant details, because in my mind I cannot separate them from an account of the day; and it is the same with the conversation during the picnic: all is imprinted on my brain together. After a couple of hours' ascent, we left the donkeys that had carried the Miss Robinsons and my wife, and all proceeded on foot to the head of the valley—Vallone Fontana Caroso is its proper name, I find.

I have visited a good deal of fine scenery before and since, but have found little that has pleased me more. The valley ended in a vast hollow, shaped like a cup, into which radiated ravines from the precipitous hills around. Both the valley and the ravines and the ribs of hill that divided the ravines were covered with leafy chestnut, so that the general appearance was that of a many-fingered green hand, palm upwards, which was clutching convulsively to keep us in its grasp. Far down the valley we could see Ravello and the sea, but that was the only sign of another world.

"Oh, what a perfectly lovely place," said my daughter Rose. "What a picture it would make!"

"Yes," said Mr. Sandbach. "Many a famous European gallery would be proud to have a landscape a tithe as beautiful as this upon its walls."

"On the contrary," said Leyland, "it would make a very poor picture. Indeed, it is not paintable at all."

"And why is that?" said Rose, with far more deference than he deserved.

"Look, in the first place," he replied, "how intolerably straight against the sky is the line of the hill. It would need breaking up and diversifying. And where we are standing the whole thing is out of perspective. Besides, all the colouring is monotonous and crude."

"I do not know anything about pictures," I put in, "and I do not pretend to know: but I know what is beautiful when I see it, and I am thoroughly content with this."

"Indeed, who could help being contented!" said the elder Miss Robinson; and Mr. Sandbach said the same.

"Ah!" said Leyland, "you all confuse the artistic view of Nature with the photographic."

Poor Rose had brought her camera with her, so I thought this positively rude. I did not wish any unpleasantness; so I merely turned away and assisted my wife and Miss Mary Robinson to put out the lunch—not a very nice lunch.

"Eustace, dear," said his aunt, "come and help us here."

He was in a particularly bad temper that morning. He had, as usual, not wanted to come, and his aunts had nearly allowed him to stop at the hotel to vex Janet. But I, with their permission, spoke to him rather sharply on the subject of exercise; and the result was that he had come, but was even more taciturn and moody than usual.

Obedience was not his strong point. He invariably questioned every command, and only executed it grumbling. I should always insist on prompt and cheerful obedience, if I had a son.

"I'm—coming—Aunt—Mary," he at last replied, and dawdled to cut a piece of wood to make a whistle, taking care not to arrive till we had finished.

"Well, well, sir!" said I, "you stroll in at the end and profit by our labours." He sighed, for he could not endure being chaffed. Miss Mary, very unwisely, insisted on giving him the wing of the chicken, in spite of all my attempts to prevent her. I remember that I had a moment's vexation when I thought that, instead of enjoying the sun, and the air, and the woods, we were all engaged in wrangling over the diet of a spoilt boy.

But, after lunch, he was a little less in evidence. He withdrew to a tree trunk, and began to loosen the bark from his whistle. I was thankful to see him employed, for once in a way. We reclined, and took a *dolce far niente*.

Those sweet chestnuts of the South are puny striplings compared with our robust Northerners. But they clothed the contours of the hills and valleys in a most pleasing way, their veil being only broken by two clearings, in one of which we were sitting.

And because these few trees were cut down, Leyland burst into a petty indictment of the proprietor.

"All the poetry is going from Nature," he cried, "her lakes and marshes are drained, her seas banked up, her forests cut down. Everywhere we see the vulgarity of desolation spreading."

I have had some experience of estates, and answered that cutting was very necessary for the health of the larger trees. Besides, it was unreasonable to expect the proprietor to derive no income from his lands.

"If you take the commercial side of landscape, you may feel pleasure in the owner's activity. But to me the mere thought that a tree is convertible into cash is disgusting."

"I see no reason," I observed politely, "to despise the gifts of Nature because they are of value."

It did not stop him. "It is no matter," he went on, "we are all hopelessly steeped in vulgarity. I do not except myself. It is through us, and to our shame, that the Nereids have left the waters and the Oreads the mountains, that the woods no longer give shelter to Pan."

"Pan!" cried Mr. Sandbach, his mellow voice filling the valley as if it had been a great green church, "Pan is dead. That is why the woods do not shelter him." And he began to tell the striking story of the mariners who were sailing near the coast at the time of the birth of Christ, and three times heard a loud voice saying: "The great God Pan is dead."

"Yes. The great God Pan is dead," said Leyland. And he abandoned himself to that mock misery in which artistic people are so fond of indulging. His cigar went out, and he had to ask me for a match.

"How very interesting," said Rose. "I do wish I knew some ancient history."

"It is not worth your notice," said Mr. Sandbach. "Eh, Eustace?"

Eustace was finishing his whistle. He looked up, with the irritable frown in which his aunts allowed him to indulge, and made no reply.

The conversation turned to various topics and then died out. It was a cloudless afternoon in May, and the pale green of the young chestnut leaves made a pretty contrast with the dark blue of the sky. We were all sitting at the edge of the small clearing for the sake of the view, and the shade of the chestnut saplings behind us was manifestly insufficient. All sounds died away—at least that is my account: Miss Robinson says that the clamour of the birds was the first sign of uneasiness that she discerned. All sounds died away, except that, far in the distance, I could hear two boughs of a great chestnut grinding together as the tree swayed. The grinds grew shorter and shorter, and finally that sound stopped also. As I looked over the green fingers of the valley, everything was absolutely motionless and still; and that feeling of suspense which one so often experiences when Nature is in repose, began to steal over me.

Suddenly, we were all electrified by the excruciating noise of Eustace's whistle. I never heard any instrument give forth so ear-splitting and discordant a sound.

"Eustace, dear," said Miss Mary Robinson, "you might have thought of your poor Aunt Julia's head."

Leyland who had apparently been asleep, sat up.

"It is astonishing how blind a boy is to anything that is elevating or beautiful," he observed. "I should not have thought he could have found the wherewithal out here to spoil our pleasure like this."

Then the terrible silence fell upon us again. I was now standing up and watching a catspaw of wind that was running down one of the ridges opposite, turning the light green to dark as it travelled. A fanciful feeling of foreboding came over me; so I turned away, to find to my amazement, that all the others were also on their feet, watching it too.

It is not possible to describe coherently what happened next: but I, for one, am not ashamed to confess that, though the fair blue sky was above me, and the green spring woods beneath me, and the kindest of friends around me, yet I became terribly frightened, more frightened than I ever wish to become again, frightened in a way I never have known either before or after. And in the eyes of the others, too, I saw blank, expressionless fear, while their mouths strove in vain to speak and their hands to gesticulate. Yet, all around us were prosperity, beauty, and peace, and all was motionless, save the catspaw of wind, now travelling up the ridge on which we stood.

Who moved first has never been settled. It is enough to say that in one second we were tearing away along the hillside. Leyland was in front, then Mr. Sandbach, then my wife. But I only saw for a brief moment; for I ran across the little clearing and through the woods and over the undergrowth and the rocks and down the dry torrent beds into the valley below. The sky might have been black as I ran, and the trees short grass, and the hillside a level road; for I saw nothing and heard nothing and felt nothing, since all the channels of sense and reason were blocked. It was not the spiritual fear that one has known at other times, but brutal overmastering physical fear, stopping up the ears, and dropping clouds before the eyes, and filling the mouth with foul tastes. And it was no ordinary humiliation that survived; for I had been afraid, not as a man, but as a beast.

II

I cannot describe our finish any better than our start; for our fear passed away as it had come, without cause. Suddenly I was able to see, and hear, and cough, and clear my mouth. Looking back, I saw that the others were stopping too; and, in a short time, we were all together, though it was long before we could speak, and longer before we dared to.

No one was seriously injured. My poor wife had sprained her ankle, Leyland had torn one of his nails on a tree trunk, and I myself had scraped and damaged my ear. I never noticed it till I had stopped.

We were all silent, searching one another's faces. Suddenly Miss Mary Robinson gave a terrible shriek. "Oh, merciful heavens! where is Eustace?" And then she would have fallen, if Mr. Sandbach had not caught her.

"We must go back, we must go back at once," said my Rose, who was quite the most collected of the party. "But I hope—I feel he is safe."

Such was the cowardice of Leyland, that he objected. But, finding himself in a minority, and being afraid of being left alone, he gave in. Rose and I supported my poor wife, Mr. Sandbach and Miss Robinson helped Miss Mary, and we returned slowly and silently, taking forty minutes to ascend the path that we had descended in ten.

Our conversation was naturally disjointed, as no one wished to offer an opinion on what had happened. Rose was the most talkative: she startled us all by saying that she had very nearly stopped where she was.

"Do you mean to say that you weren't—that you didn't feel compelled to go?" said Mr. Sandbach.

"Oh, of course, I did feel frightened"—she was the first to use the word—"but I somehow felt that if I could stop on it would be quite different, that I shouldn't be frightened at all, so to speak." Rose never did express herself clearly: still, it is greatly to her credit that she, the youngest of us, should have held on so long at that terrible time.

"I should have stopped, I do believe," she continued, "if I had not seen mamma go."

Rose's experience comforted us a little about Eustace. But a feeling of terrible foreboding was on us all, as we painfully climbed the chestnut-covered slopes and neared the little clearing. When we reached it our tongues broke loose. There, at the further side, were the remains of our lunch, and close to them, lying motionless on his back, was Eustace.

With some presence of mind I at once cried out: "Hey, you young monkey! jump up!" But he made no reply, nor did he answer when his poor aunts spoke to him. And, to my unspeakable horror, I saw one of those green lizards dart out from under his shirt-cuff as we approached.

We stood watching him as he lay there so silently, and my ears began to tingle in expectation of the outbursts of lamentations and tears.

Miss Mary fell on her knees beside him and touched his hand, which was convulsively entwined in the long grass.

As she did so, he opened his eyes and smiled.

I have often seen that peculiar smile since, both on the possessor's face and on the photographs of him that are beginning to get into the illustrated papers. But, till then, Eustace had always worn a peevish, discontented frown; and we were all unused to this disquieting smile, which always seemed to be without adequate reason.

His aunts showered kisses on him, which he did not reciprocate, and then there was an awkward pause. Eustace seemed so natural and undisturbed; yet, if he had not had astonishing experiences himself, he ought to have been all the more astonished at our extraordinary behaviour. My wife, with ready tact, endeavoured to behave as if nothing had happened.

"Well, Mr. Eustace," she said, sitting down as she spoke, to ease her foot, "how have you been amusing yourself since we have been away?"

"Thank you, Mrs. Tytler, I have been very happy."

"And where have you been?"

"Here."

"And lying down all the time, you idle boy?"

"No, not all the time."

"What were you doing before?"

"Oh; standing or sitting."

"Stood and sat doing nothing! Don't you know the poem 'Satan finds some mischief still for—'"

"Oh, my dear madam, hush! hush!" Mr. Sandbach's voice broke in; and my wife, naturally mortified by the interruption, said no more and moved away. I was surprised to see Rose immediately take her place, and, with more freedom than she generally displayed, run her fingers through the boy's tousled hair.

"Eustace! Eustace!" she said, hurriedly, "tell me everything— every single thing."

Slowly he sat up—till then he had lain on his back.

"Oh, Rose—," he whispered, and, my curiosity being aroused, I moved nearer to hear what he was going to say. As I did so, I caught sight of some goats' footmarks in the moist earth beneath the trees.

"Apparently you have had a visit from some goats," I observed. "I had no idea they fed up here."

Eustace laboriously got on to his feet and came to see; and when he saw the footmarks he lay down and rolled on them, as a dog rolls in dirt.

After that there was a grave silence, broken at length by the solemn speech of Mr. Sandbach.

"My dear friends," he said, "it is best to confess the truth bravely. I know that what I am going to say now is what you are all now feeling. The Evil One has been very near us in bodily form. Time may yet discover some injury that he has wrought among us. But, at present, for myself at all events, I wish to offer up thanks for a merciful deliverance."

With that he knelt down, and, as the others knelt, I knelt too, though I do not believe in the Devil being allowed to assail us in visible form, as I told Mr. Sandbach afterwards. Eustace came too, and knelt quietly enough between his aunts after they had beckoned to him. But when it was over he at once got up, and began hunting for something.

"Why! Someone has cut my whistle in two," he said. (I had seen Leyland with an open knife in his hand—a superstitious act which I could hardly approve.)

"Well, it doesn't matter," he continued.

"And why doesn't it matter?" said Mr. Sandbach, who has ever since tried to entrap Eustace into an account of that mysterious hour.

"Because I don't want it any more."

"Why?"

At that he smiled; and, as no one seemed to have anything more to say, I set off as fast as I could through the wood, and hauled up a donkey to carry my poor wife home. Nothing occurred in my absence, except that Rose had again asked Eustace to tell her what had happened; and he, this time, had turned away his head, and had not answered her a single word.

As soon as I returned, we all set off. Eustace walked with difficulty, almost with pain, so that, when we reached the other donkeys, his aunts wished him to mount one of them and ride all the way home. I make it a rule never to interfere between relatives, but I put my foot down at this. As it turned out, I was perfectly right, for the healthy exercise, I suppose, began to thaw Eustace's sluggish blood and loosen his stiffened muscles. He stepped out manfully, for the first time in his life, holding his head up and taking deep draughts of air into his chest. I observed with satisfaction to Miss Mary Robinson, that Eustace was at last taking some pride in his personal appearance.

Mr. Sandbach sighed, and said that Eustace must be carefully watched, for we none of us understood him yet. Miss Mary Robinson being very much—over much, I think—guided by him, sighed too.

"Come, come, Miss Robinson," I said, "there's nothing wrong with Eustace. Our experiences are mysterious, not his. He was astonished at our sudden departure, that's why he was so strange when we returned. He's right enough—improved, if anything."

"And is the worship of athletics, the cult of insensate activity, to be counted as an improvement?" put in Leyland, fixing a large, sorrowful eye on Eustace, who had stopped to scramble on to a rock to pick some cyclamen. "The passionate desire to rend from Nature the few beauties that have been still left her—that is to be counted as an improvement too?"

It is mere waste of time to reply to such remarks, especially when they come from an unsuccessful artist, suffering from a damaged finger. I changed the conversation by asking what we should say at the hotel. After some discussion, it was agreed that we should say nothing, either there or in our letters home. Importunate truth-telling, which brings only bewilderment and discomfort to the hearers, is, in my opinion, a mistake; and, after a long discussion, I managed to make Mr. Sandbach acquiesce in my view.

Eustace did not share in our conversation. He was racing about, like a real boy, in the wood to the right. A strange feeling of shame prevented us from openly mentioning our fright to him. Indeed, it seemed almost reasonable to conclude that it had made but little impression on him. So it disconcerted us when he bounded back with an armful of flowering acanthus, calling out:

"Do you suppose Gennaro'll be there when we get back?"

Gennaro was the stop-gap waiter, a clumsy, impertinent fisher-lad, who had been had up from Minori in the absence of the nice English-speaking Emmanuele. It was to him that we owed our scrappy lunch; and I could not conceive why Eustace desired to see him, unless it was to make mock with him of our behaviour.

"Yes, of course he will be there," said Miss Robinson. "Why do you ask, dear?"

"Oh, I thought I'd like to see him."

"And why?" snapped Mr. Sandbach.

"Because, because I do, I do; because, because I do." He danced away into the darkening wood to the rhythm of his words.

"This is very extraordinary," said Mr. Sandbach. "Did he like Gennaro before?"

"Gennaro has only been here two days," said Rose, "and I know that they haven't spoken to each other a dozen times."

Each time Eustace returned from the wood his spirits were higher. Once he came whooping down on us as a wild Indian, and

another time he made believe to be a dog. The last time he came
back with a poor dazed hare, too frightened to move, sitting on
his arm. He was getting too uproarious, I thought; and we were all
glad to leave the wood, and start upon the steep staircase path that
leads down into Ravello. It was late and turning dark; and we made
all the speed we could, Eustace scurrying in front of us like a goat.

Just where the staircase path debouches on the white high
road, the next extraordinary incident of this extraordinary day
occurred. Three old women were standing by the wayside. They,
like ourselves, had come down from the woods, and they were
resting their heavy bundles of fuel on the low parapet of the road.
Eustace stopped in front of them, and, after a moment's delibera-
tion, stepped forward and—kissed the left-hand one on the cheek!

"My good fellow!" exclaimed Mr. Sandbach, "are you quite
crazy?"

Eustace said nothing, but offered the old woman some of his
flowers, and then hurried on. I looked back; and the old woman's
companions seemed as much astonished at the proceeding as we
were. But she herself had put the flowers in her bosom, and was
murmuring blessings.

This salutation of the old lady was the first example of Eustace's
strange behaviour, and we were both surprised and alarmed. It
was useless talking to him, for he either made silly replies, or else
bounded away without replying at all.

He made no reference on the way home to Gennaro, and I
hoped that that was forgotten. But, when we came to the Piazza,
in front of the Cathedral, he screamed out: "Gennaro! Gennaro!"
at the top of his voice, and began running up the little alley that
led to the hotel. Sure enough, there was Gennaro at the end of it,
with his arms and legs sticking out of the nice little English-speaking

waiter's dress suit, and a dirty fisherman's cap on his head—for, as the poor landlady truly said, however much she superintended his toilette, he always managed to introduce something incongruous into it before he had done.

Eustace sprang to meet him, and leapt right up into his arms, and put his own arms round his neck. And this in the presence, not only of us, but also of the landlady, the chambermaid, the facchino, and of two American ladies who were coming for a few days' visit to the little hotel.

I always make a point of behaving pleasantly to Italians, however little they may deserve it; but this habit of promiscuous intimacy was perfectly intolerable, and could only lead to familiarity and mortification for all. Taking Miss Robinson aside, I asked her permission to speak seriously to Eustace on the subject of intercourse with social inferiors. She granted it; but I determined to wait till the absurd boy had calmed down a little from the excitement of the day. Meanwhile, Gennaro, instead of attending to the wants of the two new ladies, carried Eustace into the house, as if it was the most natural thing in the world.

"*Ho capito*," I heard him say as he passed me. "*Ho capito*" is the Italian for "I have understood"; but, as Eustace had not spoken to him, I could not see the force of the remark. It served to increase our bewilderment, and, by the time we sat down at the dinner-table, our imaginations and our tongues were alike exhausted.

I omit from this account the various comments that were made, as few of them seem worthy of being recorded. But, for three or four hours, seven of us were pouring forth our bewilderment in a stream of appropriate and inappropriate exclamations. Some traced a connection between our behaviour in the afternoon and the behaviour of Eustace now. Others saw no connection at all. Mr. Sandbach still held to the possibility of infernal influences, and also said that he ought to have a doctor. Leyland only saw the development of "that unspeakable Philistine, the boy." Rose maintained, to my surprise, that everything was excusable; while I began to see that the young gentleman wanted a sound thrashing. The poor Miss Robinsons swayed helplessly about between these diverse opinions; inclining now to careful supervision, now to acquiescence, now to corporal chastisement, now to Eno's Fruit Salt.

Dinner passed off fairly well, though Eustace was terribly fidgety, Gennaro as usual dropping the knives and spoons, and hawking and clearing his throat. He only knew a few words of English, and we were all reduced to Italian for making known our wants. Eustace, who had picked up a little somehow, asked for some oranges. To my annoyance, Gennaro, in his answer made use of the second person singular—a form only used when addressing those who are both intimates and equals. Eustace had brought it on himself; but an impertinence of this kind was an affront to us all, and I was determined to speak, and to speak at once.

When I heard him clearing the table I went in, and, summoning up my Italian, or rather Neapolitan—the Southern dialects are execrable—I said, "Gennaro! I heard you address Signor Eustace with 'Tu.'"

"It is true."

"You are not right. You must use 'Lei' or 'Voi'—more polite forms. And remember that, though Signor Eustace is sometimes silly and foolish—this afternoon for example—yet you must always behave respectfully to him; for he is a young English gentleman, and you are a poor Italian fisher-boy."

I know that speech sounds terribly snobbish, but in Italian one can say things that one would never dream of saying in English.

Besides, it is no good speaking delicately to persons of that class. Unless you put things plainly, they take a vicious pleasure in misunderstanding you.

An honest English fisherman would have landed me one in the eye in a minute for such a remark, but the wretched down-trodden Italians have no pride. Gennaro only sighed, and said: "It is true."

"Quite so," I said, and turned to go. To my indignation I heard him add: "But sometimes it is not important."

"What do you mean?" I shouted.

He came close up to me with horrid gesticulating fingers.

"Signor Tytler, I wish to say this. If Eustazio asks me to call him 'Voi,' I will call him 'Voi.' Otherwise, no."

With that he seized up a tray of dinner things, and fled from the room with them; and I heard two more wine-glasses go on the courtyard floor.

I was now fairly angry, and strode out to interview Eustace. But he had gone to bed, and the landlady, to whom I also wished to speak, was engaged. After more vague wonderings, obscurely expressed owing to the presence of Janet and the two American ladies, we all went to bed, too, after a harassing and most extraordinary day.

III

But the day was nothing to the night.

I suppose I had slept for about four hours, when I woke suddenly thinking I heard a noise in the garden. And, immediately, before my eyes were open, cold terrible fear seized me—not fear of something that was happening, like the fear in the wood, but fear of something that might happen.

Our room was on the first floor, looking out on to the garden—
or terrace, it was rather: a wedge-shaped block of ground covered
with roses and vines, and intersected with little asphalt paths. It
was bounded on the small side by the house; round the two long
sides ran a wall, only three feet above the terrace level, but with a
good twenty feet drop over it into the olive yards, for the ground
fell very precipitously away.

Trembling all over I stole to the window. There, pattering up
and down the asphalt paths, was something white. I was too much
alarmed to see clearly; and in the uncertain light of the stars the
thing took all manner of curious shapes. Now it was a great dog,
now an enormous white bat, now a mass of quickly travelling cloud.
It would bounce like a ball, or take short flights like a bird, or glide
slowly like a wraith. It gave no sound—save the pattering sound of
what, after all, must be human feet. And at last the obvious explanation forced itself upon my disordered mind; and I realised that
Eustace had got out of bed, and that we were in for something more.

I hastily dressed myself, and went down into the dining-room
which opened upon the terrace. The door was already unfastened.
My terror had almost entirely passed away, but for quite five minutes
I struggled with a curious cowardly feeling, which bade me not
interfere with the poor strange boy, but leave him to his ghostly
patterings, and merely watch him from the window, to see he took
no harm.

But better impulses prevailed and, opening the door, I called out:
"Eustace! what on earth are you doing? Come in at once."

He stopped his antics, and said: "I hate my bedroom. I could
not stop in it, it is too small."

"Come! come! I'm tired of affectation. You've never complained
of it before."

"Besides I can't see anything—no flowers, no leaves, no sky: only a stone wall." The outlook of Eustace's room certainly was limited; but, as I told him, he had never complained of it before.

"Eustace, you talk like a child. Come in! Prompt obedience, if you please."

He did not move.

"Very well: I shall carry you in by force," I added, and made a few steps towards him. But I was soon convinced of the futility of pursuing a boy through a tangle of asphalt paths, and went in instead, to call Mr. Sandbach and Leyland to my aid.

When I returned with them he was worse than ever. He would not even answer us when we spoke, but began singing and chattering to himself in a most alarming way.

"It's a case for the doctor now," said Mr. Sandbach, gravely tapping his forehead.

He had stopped his running and was singing, first low, then loud—singing five-finger exercises, scales, hymn tunes, scraps of Wagner—anything that came into his head. His voice—a very untuneful voice—grew stronger and stronger, and he ended with a tremendous shout which boomed like a gun among the mountains, and awoke everyone who was still sleeping in the hotel. My poor wife and the two girls appeared at their respective windows, and the American ladies were heard violently ringing their bell.

"Eustace," we all cried, "stop! stop, dear boy, and come into the house."

He shook his head, and started off again—talking this time. Never have I listened to such an extraordinary speech. At any other time it would have been ludicrous, for here was a boy, with no sense of beauty and a puerile command of words, attempting to tackle themes which the greatest poets have found almost beyond their power. Eustace Robinson, aged fourteen, was standing in his nightshirt saluting, praising, and blessing, the great forces and manifestations of Nature.

He spoke first of night and the stars and planets above his head, of the swarms of fire-flies below him, of the invisible sea below the fire-flies, of the great rocks covered with anemones and shells that were slumbering in the invisible sea. He spoke of the rivers and waterfalls, of the ripening bunches of grapes, of the smoking cone of Vesuvius and the hidden fire-channels that made the smoke, of the myriads of lizards who were lying curled up in the crannies of the sultry earth, of the showers of white rose-leaves that were tangled in his hair. And then he spoke of the rain and the wind by which all things are changed, of the air through which all things live, and of the woods in which all things can be hidden.

Of course, it was all absurdly high faluting: yet I could have kicked Leyland for audibly observing that it was "a diabolical caricature of all that was most holy and beautiful in life."

"And then,"—Eustace was going on in the pitiable conversational doggerel which was his only mode of expression—"and then there are men, but I can't make them out so well." He knelt down by the parapet, and rested his head on his arms.

"Now's the time," whispered Leyland. I hate stealth, but we darted forward and endeavoured to catch hold of him from behind. He was away in a twinkling, but turned round at once to look at us. As far as I could see in the starlight, he was crying. Leyland rushed at him again, and we tried to corner him among the asphalt paths, but without the slightest approach to success.

We returned, breathless and discomfited, leaving him to his madness in the further corner of the terrace. But my Rose had an inspiration.

"Papa," she called from the window, "if you get Gennaro, he might be able to catch him for you."

I had no wish to ask a favour of Gennaro, but, as the landlady had by now appeared on the scene, I begged her to summon him from the charcoal-bin in which he slept, and make him try what he could do.

She soon returned, and was shortly followed by Gennaro, attired in a dress coat, without either waistcoat, shirt, or vest, and a ragged pair of what had been trousers, cut short above the knees for purposes of wading. The landlady, who had quite picked up English ways, rebuked him for the incongruous and even indecent appearance which he presented.

"I have a coat and I have trousers. What more do you desire?"

"Never mind, Signora Scafetti," I put in. "As there are no ladies here, it is not of the slightest consequence." Then, turning to Gennaro, I said: "The aunts of Signor Eustace wish you to fetch him into the house."

He did not answer.

"Do you hear me? He is not well. I order you to fetch him into the house."

"Fetch! fetch!" said Signora Scafetti, and shook him roughly by the arm.

"Eustazio is well where he is."

"Fetch! fetch!" Signora Scafetti screamed, and let loose a flood of Italian, most of which, I am glad to say, I could not follow. I glanced up nervously at the girls' window, but they hardly know as much as I do, and I am thankful to say that none of us caught one word of Gennaro's answer.

The two yelled and shouted at each other for quite ten minutes, at the end of which Gennaro rushed back to his charcoal-bin and

Signora Scafetti burst into tears, as well she might, for she greatly valued her English guests.

"He says," she sobbed, "that Signor Eustace is well where he is, and that he will not fetch him. I can do no more."

But I could, for, in my stupid British way, I have got some insight into the Italian character. I followed Mr. Gennaro to his place of repose, and found him wriggling down on to a dirty sack.

"I wish you to fetch Signor Eustace to me," I began.

He hurled at me an unintelligible reply.

"If you fetch him, I will give you this." And out of my pocket I took a new ten lira note.

This time he did not answer.

"This note is equal to ten lire in silver," I continued, for I knew that the poor-class Italian is unable to conceive of a single large sum.

"I know it."

"That is, two hundred soldi."

"I do not desire them. Eustazio is my friend."

I put the note into my pocket.

"Besides, you would not give it me."

"I am an Englishman. The English always do what they promise."

"That is true." It is astonishing how the most dishonest of nations trust us. Indeed they often trust us more than we trust one another. Gennaro knelt up on his sack. It was too dark to see his face, but I could feel his warm garlicky breath coming out in gasps, and I knew that the eternal avarice of the South had laid hold upon him.

"I could not fetch Eustazio to the house. He might die there."

"You need not do that," I replied patiently. "You need only bring him to me; and I will stand outside in the garden." And to this, as if it were something quite different, the pitiable youth consented.

"But give me first the ten lire."

"No"—for I knew the kind of person with whom I had to deal. Once faithless, always faithless.

We returned to the terrace, and Gennaro, without a single word, pattered off towards the pattering that could be heard at the remoter end. Mr. Sandbach, Leyland, and myself moved away a little from the house, and stood in the shadow of the white climbing roses, practically invisible.

We heard "Eustazio" called, followed by absurd cries of pleasure from the poor boy. The pattering ceased, and we heard them talking. Their voices got nearer, and presently I could discern them through the creepers, the grotesque figure of the young man, and the slim little white-robed boy. Gennaro had his arm round Eustace's neck, and Eustace was talking away in his fluent, slip-shod Italian.

"I understand almost everything," I heard him say. "The trees, hills, stars, water, I can see all. But isn't it odd! I can't make out men a bit. Do you know what I mean?"

"*Ho capito*," said Gennaro gravely, and took his arm off Eustace's shoulder. But I made the new note crackle in my pocket; and he heard it. He stuck his hand out with a jerk; and the unsuspecting Eustace gripped it in his own.

"It is odd!" Eustace went on—they were quite close now—"It almost seems as if—as if—"

I darted out and caught hold of his arm, and Leyland got hold of the other arm, and Mr. Sandbach hung on to his feet. He gave shrill heart-piercing screams; and the white roses, which were falling early that year, descended in showers on him as we dragged him into the house.

As soon as we entered the house he stopped shrieking; but floods of tears silently burst forth, and spread over his upturned face.

"Not to my room," he pleaded. "It is so small."

His infinitely dolorous look filled me with strange pity, but what could I do? Besides, his window was the only one that had bars to it.

"Never mind, dear boy," said kind Mr. Sandbach. "I will bear you company till the morning."

At this his convulsive struggles began again. "Oh, please, not that. Anything but that. I will promise to lie still and not to cry more than I can help, if I am left alone."

So we laid him on the bed, and drew the sheets over him, and left him sobbing bitterly, and saying: "I nearly saw everything, and now I can see nothing at all."

We informed the Miss Robinsons of all that had happened, and returned to the dining-room, where we found Signora Scafetti and Gennaro whispering together. Mr. Sandbach got pen and paper, and began writing to the English doctor at Naples. I at once drew out the note, and flung it down on the table to Gennaro.

"Here is your pay," I said sternly, for I was thinking of the Thirty Pieces of Silver.

"Thank you very much, sir," said Gennaro, and grabbed it.

He was going off, when Leyland, whose interest and indifference were always equally misplaced, asked him what Eustace had meant by saying "he could not make out men a bit."

"I cannot say. Signor Eustazio" (I was glad to observe a little deference at last) "has a subtle brain. He understands many things."

"But I heard you say you understood," Leyland persisted.

"I understand, but I cannot explain. I am a poor Italian fisher-lad. Yet, listen: I will try." I saw to my alarm that his manner was changing, and tried to stop him. But he sat down on the edge of the table and started off, with some absolutely incoherent remarks.

"It is sad," he observed at last. "What has happened is very sad. But what can I do? I am poor. It is not I."

I turned away in contempt. Leyland went on asking questions. He wanted to know who it was that Eustace had in his mind when he spoke.

"That is easy to say," Gennaro gravely answered. "It is you, it is I. It is all in this house, and many outside it. If he wishes for mirth, we discomfort him. If he asks to be alone, we disturb him. He longed for a friend, and found none for fifteen years. Then he found me, and the first night I—I who have been in the woods and understood things too—betray him to you, and send him in to die. But what could I do?"

"Gently, gently," said I.

"Oh, assuredly he will die. He will lie in the small room all night, and in the morning he will be dead. That I know for certain."

"There, that will do," said Mr. Sandbach. "I shall be sitting with him."

"Filomena Giusti sat all night with Caterina, but Caterina was dead in the morning. They would not let her out, though I begged, and prayed, and cursed, and beat the door, and climbed the wall. They were ignorant fools, and thought I wished to carry her away. And in the morning she was dead."

"What is all this?" I asked Signora Scafetti.

"All kinds of stories will get about," she replied, "and he, least of anyone, has reason to repeat them."

"And I am alive now," he went on, "because I had neither parents nor relatives nor friends, so that, when the first night came, I could run through the woods, and climb the rocks, and plunge into the water, until I had accomplished my desire!"

We heard a cry from Eustace's room—a faint but steady sound, like the sound of wind in a distant wood, heard by one standing in tranquillity.

"That," said Gennaro, "was the last noise of Caterina. I was hanging on to her window then, and it blew out past me."

And, lifting up his hand, in which my ten lira note was safely packed, he solemnly cursed Mr. Sandbach, and Leyland, and myself, and Fate, because Eustace was dying in the upstairs room. Such is the working of the Southern mind; and I verily believe that he would not have moved even then, had not Leyland, that unspeakable idiot, upset the lamp with his elbow. It was a patent self-extinguishing lamp, bought by Signora Scafetti, at my special request, to replace the dangerous thing that she was using. The result was, that it went out; and the mere physical change from light to darkness had more power over the ignorant animal nature of Gennaro than the most obvious dictates of logic and reason.

I felt, rather than saw, that he had left the room, and shouted out to Mr. Sandbach: "Have you got the key of Eustace's room in your pocket?" But Mr. Sandbach and Leyland were both on the floor, having mistaken each other for Gennaro, and some more precious time was wasted in finding a match. Mr. Sandbach had only just time to say that he had left the key in the door, in case the Miss Robinsons wished to pay Eustace a visit, when we heard a noise on the stairs, and there was Gennaro, carrying Eustace down.

We rushed out and blocked up the passage, and they lost heart and retreated to the upper landing.

"Now they are caught," cried Signora Scafetti. "There is no other way out."

We were cautiously ascending the staircase, when there was a terrific scream from my wife's room, followed by a heavy thud on the asphalt path. They had leapt out of her window.

I reached the terrace just in time to see Eustace jumping over the parapet of the garden wall. This time I knew for certain he would be killed. But he alighted in an olive tree, looking like a great white moth, and from the tree he slid on to the earth. And as soon as his bare feet touched the clods of earth he uttered a strange loud cry, such as I should not have thought the human voice could have produced, and disappeared among the trees below.

"He has understood and he is saved," cried Gennaro, who was still sitting on the asphalt path. "Now, instead of dying he will live!"

"And you, instead of keeping the ten lire, will give them up," I retorted, for at this theatrical remark I could contain myself no longer.

"The ten lire are mine," he hissed back, in a scarcely audible voice. He clasped his hand over his breast to protect his ill-gotten gains, and, as he did so, he swayed forward and fell upon his face on the path. He had not broken any limbs, and a leap like that would never have killed an Englishman, for the drop was not great. But those miserable Italians have no stamina. Something had gone wrong inside him, and he was dead.

The morning was still far off, but the morning breeze had begun, and more rose leaves fell on us as we carried him in. Signora Scafetti burst into screams at the sight of the dead body, and, far down the valley towards the sea, there still resounded the shouts and the laughter of the escaping boy.

THE TOUCH OF PAN

Algernon Blackwood

Algernon Blackwood (1869–1951) was an English writer and broadcaster born in Shooter's Hill, Kent. His early life was marked by a flurry of different jobs, working as a model, a violin teacher and a journalist for the *New York Times*. Deeply spiritual, Blackwood's beliefs drew on Buddhist philosophy and often centred around pantheism: the alignment of nature with the divine, and the interconnectedness of all life. These spiritual beliefs led Blackwood to join The Ghost Club, a contemporary order of paranormal research and investigation, and the Hermetic Order of the Golden Dawn. A renowned author of the weird, Blackwood's works include the "The Willows" (1907), the *John Silence* series (1908–1914), "The Wendigo" (1910) and *Pan's Garden: A Volume of Nature Stories* (1912). His 1908 short story, "Ancient Sorceries", was also adapted into the formative horror film, *Cat People* (1942).

"The Touch of Pan" was first published in Blackwood's *Day and Night Stories* (1917). The story concerns Heber and Elspeth, equally disenchanted by the house party they are attending. As with Saki's "The Music on the Hill" and E. M. Forster's "The Story of a Panic", Blackwood uses the figure of Pan to tease traditional values; in this instance, heteronormative relationships. With its moonlit orgy, Blackwood's tale is perhaps the most explicit of all the works in this collection, and speaks to an embracing of alternate sexualities and paganistic freedom. Blackwood would later revisit the subject of Pan in his 1948 tale, "Roman Remains".

An idiot, Heber understood, was a person in whom intelligence had been arrested—instinct acted, but not reason. A lunatic, on the other hand, was some one whose reason had gone awry—the mechanism of the brain was injured. The lunatic was out of relation with his environment; the idiot had merely been delayed *en route*.

Be that as it might, he knew at any rate that a lunatic was not to be listened to, whereas an idiot—well, the one he fell in love with certainly had the secret of some instinctual knowledge that was not only joy, but a kind of sheer natural joy. Probably it was that sheer natural joy of living that reason argues to be untaught, degraded. In any case—at thirty—he married her instead of the daughter of a duchess he was engaged to. They lead today that happy, natural, vagabond life called idiotic, unmindful of that world the majority of reasonable people live only to remember.

Though born into an artificial social clique that made it difficult, Heber had always loved the simple things. Nature, especially, meant much to him. He would rather see a woodland misty with bluebells than all the châteaux on the Loire; the thought of a mountain valley in the dawn made his feet lonely in the grandest houses. Yet in these very houses was his home established. Not that he under-estimated worldly things—their value was too obvious—but that it was another thing he wanted. Only he did not know precisely *what* he wanted until this particular idiot made it plain.

Her case was a mild one, possibly; the title bestowed by implication rather than by specific mention. Her family did not say that she was imbecile or half-witted, but that she "was not all there" they probably did say. Perhaps she saw men as trees walking, perhaps she saw through a glass darkly. Heber, who had met her once or twice, though never yet to speak to, did not analyse her degree of sight, for in him, personally, she woke a secret joy and wonder that almost involved a touch of awe. The part of her that was not "all there" dwelt in an "elsewhere" that he longed to know about. He wanted to share it with her. She seemed aware of certain happy and desirable things that reason and too much thinking hide.

He just felt this instinctively without analysis. The values they set upon the prizes of life were similar. Money to her was just stamped metal, fame a loud noise of sorts, position nothing. Of people she was aware as a dog or bird might be aware—they were kind or unkind. Her parents, having collected much metal and achieved position, proceeded to make a loud noise of sorts with some success; and since she did not contribute, either by her appearance or her tastes, to their ambitions, they neglected her and made excuses. They were ashamed of her existence. Her father in particular justified Nietzsche's shrewd remark that no one with a loud voice can listen to subtle thoughts.

She was, perhaps, sixteen—for, though she looked it, eighteen or nineteen was probably more in accord with her birth certificate. Her mother was content, however, that she should dress the lesser age, preferring to tell strangers that she was childish, rather than admit that she was backward.

"You'll never marry at all, child, much less marry as you might," she said, "if you go about with that rabbit expression on your face. That's not the way to catch a nice young man of the sort we get down to stay with us now. Many a chorus-girl with less than you've got has caught them easily enough. Your sister's done well. Why not do the same? There's nothing to be shy or frightened about."

"But I'm not shy or frightened, mother. I'm bored. I mean *they* bore me."

It made no difference to the girl; she was herself. The bored expression in the eyes—the rabbit, not-all-there expression—gave place sometimes to another look. Yet not often, nor with anybody. It was this other look that stirred the strange joy in the man who fell in love with her. It is not to be easily described. It was very wonderful. Whether sixteen or nineteen, she then looked—a thousand.

The house-party was of that up-to-date kind prevalent in Heber's world. Husbands and wives were not asked together. There was a cynical disregard of the decent (not the stupid) conventions that savoured of abandon, perhaps of decadence. He only went himself in the hope of seeing the backward daughter once again. Her millionaire parents afflicted him, the smart folk tired him. Their peculiar affectation of a special language, their strange belief that they were of importance, their treatment of the servants, their calculated self-indulgence, all jarred upon him more than usual. At bottom he heartily despised the whole vapid set. He felt uncomfortable and out of place. Though not a prig, he abhorred the way these folk believed themselves the climax of fine living. Their open immorality disgusted him, their indiscriminate love-making was merely rather nasty; he watched the very girl he was at last to settle down with behaving as the tone of the clique expected over her final fling— and, bored by the strain of so much "modernity," he tried to get away. Tea was long over, the sunset interval invited, he felt hungry for trees and fields that were not self-conscious—and he escaped.

The flaming June day was turning chill. Dusk hovered over the ancient house, veiling the pretentious new wing that had been added. And he came across the idiot girl at the bend of the drive, where the birch trees shivered in the evening wind. His heart gave a leap.

She was leaning against one of the dreadful statues—it was a satyr—that sprinkled the lawn. Her back was to him; she gazed at a group of broken pine trees in the park beyond. He paused an instant, then went on quickly, while his mind scurried to recall her name. They were within easy speaking range.

"Miss Elizabeth!" he cried, yet not too loudly lest she might vanish as suddenly as she had appeared. She turned at once. Her eyes and lips were smiling welcome at him without pretence. She showed no surprise.

"You're the first one of the lot who's said it properly," she exclaimed, as he came up. "Everybody calls me Elizabeth instead of Elspeth. It's idiotic. They don't even take the trouble to get a name right."

"It is," he agreed. "Quite idiotic." He did not correct her. Possibly he had said Elspeth after all—the names were similar. Her perfectly natural voice was grateful to his ear, and soothing. He looked at her all over with an open admiration that she noticed and, without concealment, liked. She was very untidy, the grey stockings on her vigorous legs were torn, her short skirt was spattered with mud. Her nut-brown hair, glossy and plentiful, flew loose about neck and shoulders. In place of the usual belt she had tied a coloured handkerchief round her waist. She wore no hat. What she had been doing to get in such a state, while her parents entertained a "distinguished" party, he did not know, but it was not difficult to guess. Climbing trees or riding bareback and astride was probably the truth. Yet her dishevelled state became her well, and the welcome in her face delighted him. She remembered him, she was glad. He, too, was glad, and a sense both happy and reckless stirred in his heart. "Like a wild animal," he said, "you come out in the dusk—"

"To play with my kind," she answered in a flash, throwing him a glance of invitation that made his blood go dancing.

He leaned against the statue a moment, asking himself why this young Cinderella of a parvenu family delighted him when all the London beauties left him cold. There was a lift through his whole being as he watched her, slim and supple, grace shining through the untidy modern garb—almost as though she wore no clothes. He thought of a panther standing upright. Her poise was so alert—one arm upon the marble ledge, one leg bent across the other, the hip-line showing like a bird's curved wing. Wild animal or bird, flashed across his mind: something untamed and natural. Another second, and she might leap away—or spring into his arms.

It was a deep, stirring sensation in him that produced the mental picture. "Pure and natural," a voice whispered with it in his heart, "as surely as *they* are just the other thing!" And the thrill struck with unerring aim at the very root of that unrest he had always known in the state of life to which he was called. She made it natural, clean, and pure. This girl and himself were somehow kin. The primitive thing broke loose in him.

In two seconds, while he stood with her beside the vulgar statue, these thoughts passed through his mind. But he did not at first give utterance to any of them. He spoke more formally, although laughter, due to his happiness, lay behind:

"They haven't asked you to the party, then? Or you don't care about it? Which is it?"

"Both," she said, looking fearlessly into his face. "But I've been here ten minutes already. Why were you so long?"

This outspoken honesty was hardly what he expected, yet in another sense he was not surprised. Her eyes were very penetrating, very innocent, very frank. He felt her as clean and sweet as some young fawn that asks plainly to be stroked and fondled. He told the truth: "I couldn't get away before. I had to play about and—" when she interrupted with impatience:

"*They* don't really want you," she exclaimed scornfully. "I do."

And, before he could choose one out of the several answers that rushed into his mind, she nudged him with her foot, holding it out a little so that he saw the shoelace was unfastened. She nodded her head towards it, and pulled her skirt up half an inch as he at once stooped down.

"And, anyhow," she went on as he fumbled with the lace, touching her ankle with his hand, "you're going to marry one of them. I read it in the paper. It's idiotic. You'll be miserable."

The blood rushed to his head, but whether owing to his stooping or to something else, he could not say.

"I only came—I only accepted," he said quickly, "because I wanted to see *you* again."

"Of course. I made mother ask you."

He did an impulsive thing. Kneeling as he was, he bent his head a little lower and suddenly kissed the soft grey stocking—then stood up and looked her in the face. She was laughing happily, no sign of embarrassment in her anywhere, no trace of outraged modesty. She just looked very pleased.

"I've tied a knot that won't come undone in a hurry—" he began, then stopped dead. For as he said it, gazing into her smiling face, another expression looked forth at him from the two big eyes of hazel. Something rushed from his heart to meet it. It may have been that playful kiss, it may have been the way she took it; but, at any rate, there was a strength in the new emotion that made him unsure of who he was and of whom he looked at. He forgot the place, the time, his own identity and hers. The lawn swept from beneath his feet, the English sunset with it. He forgot his host and hostess, his fellow guests, even his father's name and his own into the bargain. He was carried away upon a great tide, the girl always beside him. He left the shore-line in the distance, already half forgotten, the shore-line of his education, learning, manners, social point of view—everything to which his father had most carefully brought him up as the scion of an old-established English family. This girl had torn up the anchor. Only the anchor had previously been loosened a little by his own unconscious and restless efforts...

Where was she taking him to? Upon what island would they land?

"I'm younger than you—a good deal," she broke in upon his rushing mood. "But that doesn't matter a bit, does it? We're about the same age really."

With the happy sound of her voice the extraordinary sensation passed—or, rather, it became normal. But that it had lasted an appreciable time was proved by the fact that they had left the statue on the lawn, the house was no longer visible behind them, and they were walking side by side between the massive rhododendron clumps. They brought up against a five-barred gate into the park. They leaned upon the topmost bar, and he felt her shoulder touching his—edging into it—as they looked across to the grove of pines.

"I feel absurdly young," he said without a sign of affectation, "and yet I've been looking for you a thousand years and more."

The afterglow lit up her face; it fell on her loose hair and tumbled blouse, turning them amber red. She looked not only soft and

comely, but extraordinarily beautiful. The strange expression haunted
the deep eyes again, the lips were a little parted, the young breast
heaving slightly, joy and excitement in her whole presentment.
And as he watched her he knew that all he had just felt was due to
her close presence, to her atmosphere, her perfume, her physical
warmth and vigour. It had emanated directly from her being.

"Of course," she said, and laughed so that he felt her breath
upon his face. He bent lower to bring his own on a level, gazing
straight into her eyes that were fixed upon the field beyond. They
were clear and luminous as pools of water, and in their centre, sharp
as a photograph, he saw the reflection of the pine grove, perhaps a
hundred yards away. With detailed accuracy he saw it, empty and
motionless in the glimmering June dusk.

Then something caught his eye. He examined the picture more
closely. He drew slightly nearer. He almost touched her face with
his own, forgetting for a moment whose were the eyes that served
him for a mirror. For, looking intently thus, it seemed to him that
there was a movement, a passing to and fro, a stirring as of figures
among the trees... Then suddenly the entire picture was obliterated.
She had dropped her lids. He heard her speaking—the warm breath
was again upon his face:

"In the heart of that wood dwell I."

His heart gave another leap—more violent than the first—for
the wonder and beauty of the sentence caught him like a spell.
There was a lilt and rhythm in the words that made it poetry. She
laid emphasis upon the pronoun and the nouns. It seemed the last
line of some delicious runic verse:

"In the *heart* of the *wood*—dwell *I*..."

And it flashed across him: That living, moving, inhabited pine
wood was her thought. It was thus she saw it. Her nature flung

back to a life she understood, a life that needed, claimed her. The ostentatious and artificial values that surrounded her, she denied, even as the distinguished house-party of her ambitious, masquerading family neglected her. Of course she was unnoticed by them, just as a swallow or a wild-rose were unnoticed.

He knew her secret then, for she had told it to him. It was his own secret too. They were akin, as the birds and animals were akin. They belonged together in some free and open life, natural, wild, untamed. That unhampered life was flowing about them now, rising, beating with delicious tumult in her veins and his, yet innocent as the sunlight and the wind—because it was as freely recognised.

"Elspeth!" he cried, "come, take me with you! We'll go at once. Come—hurry—before we forget to be happy, or remember to be wise again—!"

His words stopped half-way towards completion, for a perfume floated past him, born of the summer dusk, perhaps, yet sweet with a penetrating magic that made his senses reel with some remembered joy. No flower, no scented garden bush delivered it. It was the perfume of young, spendthrift life, sweet with the purity that reason had not yet stained. The girl moved closer. Gathering her loose hair between her fingers, she brushed his cheeks and eyes with it, her slim, warm body pressing against him as she leaned over laughingly.

"In the darkness," she whispered in his ear; "when the moon puts the house upon the statue!"

And he understood. Her world lay behind the vulgar, staring day. He turned. He heard the flutter of skirts—just caught the grey stockings, swift and light, as they flew behind the rhododendron masses. And she was gone.

He stood a long time, leaning upon that five-barred gate... It was the dressing-gong that recalled him at length to what seemed the present. By the conservatory door, as he went slowly in, he met his distinguished cousin—who was helping the girl he himself was to marry to enjoy her "final fling." He looked at his cousin. He realised suddenly that he was merely vicious. There was no sun and wind, no flowers—there was depravity only, lust instead of laughter, excitement in place of happiness. It was calculated, not spontaneous. His mind was in it. Without joy it was. He was not natural.

"Not a girl in the whole lot fit to look at," he exclaimed with peevish boredom, excusing himself stupidly for his illicit conduct. "I'm off in the morning." He shrugged his blue-blooded shoulders. "These millionaires! Their shooting's all right, but their mixum-gatherum week-ends—bah!" His gesture completed all he had to say about this one in particular. He glanced sharply, nastily, at his companion. "*You* look as if you'd found something!" he added, with a suggestive grin. "Or have you seen the ghost that was paid for with the house?" And he guffawed and let his eyeglass drop. "Lady Hermione will be asking for an explanation—eh?"

"Idiot!" replied Heber, and ran upstairs to dress for dinner.

But the word was wrong, he remembered, as he closed his door. It was lunatic he had meant to say, yet something more as well. He saw the smart, modern philanderer somehow as a beast.

II

It was nearly midnight when he went up to bed, after an evening of intolerable amusement. The abandoned moral attitude, the common rudeness, the contempt of all others but themselves, the ugly jests, the horseplay of tasteless minds that passed for gaiety, above all the shamelessness of the women that behind the cover of fine breeding aped emancipation, afflicted him to a boredom that touched desperation.

He understood now with a clarity unknown before. As with his cousin, so with these. They took life, he saw, with a brazen effrontery they thought was freedom, while yet it was life that they denied. He felt vampired and degraded; spontaneity went out of him. The fact that the geography of bedrooms was studied openly seemed an affirmation of vice that sickened him. Their ways were nauseous merely. He escaped—unnoticed.

He locked his door, went to the open window, and looked out into the night—then started. For silver dressed the lawn and park, the shadow of the building lay dark across the elaborate garden, and the moon, he noticed, was just high enough to put the house upon the statue. The chimney-stacks edged the pedestal precisely.

"Odd!" he exclaimed. "Odd that I should come at the very moment!" then smiled as he realised how his proposed adventure would be misinterpreted, its natural innocence and spirit ruined—if he were seen. "And some one would be sure to see me on a night like this. There are couples still hanging about in the garden." And he glanced at the shrubberies and secret paths that seemed to float upon the warm June air like islands.

He stood for a moment framed in the glare of the electric light, then turned back into the room; and at that instant a low sound like a bird-call rose from the lawn below. It was soft and flutey, as though some one played two notes upon a reed, a piping sound. He had been seen, and she was waiting for him. Before he knew it, he had made an answering call, of oddly similar kind, then switched the light out. Three minutes later, dressed in simpler clothes, with a cap pulled over his eyes, he reached the back lawn by means of the conservatory and the billiard-room. He paused a moment to look about him. There was no one, although the lights were still ablaze. "I am an idiot," he chuckled to himself. "I'm acting on instinct!" He ran.

The sweet night air bathed him from head to foot; there was strength and cleansing in it. The lawn shone wet with dew. He could almost smell the perfume of the stars. The fumes of wine, cigars and artificial scent were left behind, the atmosphere exhaled by civilisation, by heavy thoughts, by bodies overdressed, unwisely stimulated—all, all forgotten. He passed into a world of magical enchantment. The hush of the open sky came down. In black and white the garden lay, brimmed full with beauty, shot by the ancient silver of the moon, spangled with the stars' old-gold. And the night wind rustled in the rhododendron masses as he flew between them.

In a moment he was beside the statue, engulfed now by the shadow of the building, and the girl detached herself silently from the blur of darkness. Two arms were flung about his neck, a shower of soft hair fell on his cheek with a heady scent of earth and leaves and grass, and the same instant they were away together at full speed—towards the pine wood. Their feet were soundless on the soaking grass. They went so swiftly that they made a whir of following wind that blew her hair across his eyes.

And the sudden contrast caused a shock that put a blank, perhaps, upon his mind, so that he lost the standard of remembered things. For it was no longer merely a particular adventure; it seemed a habit and a natural joy resumed. It was not new. He knew the momentum of an accustomed happiness, mislaid, it may be, but certainly familiar. They sped across the gravel paths that intersected the well-groomed lawn, they leaped the flowerbeds, so laboriously shaped in mockery, they clambered over the ornamental iron railings, scorning the easier five-barred gate into the park. The longer grass then shook the dew in soaking showers against his knees. He stooped, as though in some foolish effort to turn up something, then realised that his legs, of course, were bare. *Her* garment was already high and free, for she, too, was barelegged like himself. He saw her little ankles, wet and shining in the moonlight, and flinging himself down, he kissed them happily, plunging his face into the dripping, perfumed grass. Her ringing laughter mingled with his own, as she stooped beside him the same instant; her hair hung in a silver cloud; her eyes gleamed through its curtain into his; then, suddenly, she soaked her hands in the heavy dew and passed them over his face with a softness that was like the touch of some scented southern wind.

"Now you are anointed with the Night," she cried. "No one will know you. You are forgotten of the world. Kiss me!"

"We'll play for ever and ever," he cried, "the eternal game that was old when the world was yet young," and lifting her in his arms he kissed her eyes and lips. There was some natural bliss of song and dance and laughter in his heart, an elemental bliss that caught them together as wind and sunlight catch the branches of a tree. She leaped from the ground to meet his swinging arms. He ran with her, then tossed her off and caught her neatly as she fell. Evading a second capture, she danced ahead, holding out one shining arm that he might follow. Hand in hand they raced on together through the clean summer moonlight. Yet there remained a smooth softness as of fur against his neck and shoulders, and he saw then that she wore skins of tawny colour that clung to her body closely, that he wore them too, and that her skin, like his own, was of a sweet dusky brown.

Then, pulling her towards him, he stared into her face. She suffered the close gaze a second, but no longer, for with a burst of sparkling laughter again she leaped into his arms, and before he shook her free she had pulled and tweaked the two small horns that hid in the thick curly hair behind, and just above, the ears.

And that wilful tweaking turned him wild and reckless. That touch ran down him deep into the mothering earth. He leaped and ran and sang with a great laughing sound. The wine of eternal youth flushed all his veins with joy, and the old, old world was young again with every impulse of natural happiness intensified with the Earth's own foaming tide of life.

From head to foot he tingled with the delight of Spring, prodigal with creative power. Of course he could fly the bushes and fling wild across the open! Of course the wind and moonlight fitted close and soft about him like a skin! Of course he had youth and beauty for playmates, with dancing, laughter, singing, and a thousand kisses! For he and she were natural once again. They were free together of those long-forgotten days when "Pan leaped through the roses in the month of June...!"

With the girl swaying this way and that upon his shoulders, tweaking his horns with mischief and desire, hanging her flying hair before his eyes, then bending swiftly over again to lift it, he danced to join the rest of their companions in the little moonlit grove of pines beyond...

III

They rose somewhat pointed, perhaps, against the moonlight, those English pines—more with the shape of cypresses, some might have thought. A stream gushed down between their roots, there were mossy ferns, and rough grey boulders with lichen on them. But there was no dimness, for the silver of the moon sprinkled freely through the branches like the faint sunlight that it really was, and the air ran out to meet them with a heady fragrance that was wiser far than wine.

The girl, in an instant, was whirled from her perch on his shoulders and caught by a dozen arms that bore her into the heart of the jolly, careless throng. Whisht! Whew! Whir! She was gone, but another, fairer still, was in her place, with skins as soft and knees that clung as tightly. Her eyes were liquid amber, grapes hung between her little breasts, her arms entwined about him, smoother than marble, and as cool. She had a crystal laugh.

But he flung her off, so that she fell plump among a group of bigger figures lolling against a twisted root and roaring with a jollity that boomed like wind through the chorus of a song. They seized her, kissed her, then sent her flying. They were happier with their glad singing. They held stone goblets, red and foaming, in their broad-palmed hands.

"The mountains lie behind us!" cried a figure dancing past. "We are come at last into our valley of delight. Grapes, breasts, and rich red lips! Ho! Ho! It is time to press them that the juice of life may run!" He waved a cluster of ferns across the air and vanished amid a cloud of song and laughter.

"It is ours. Use it!" answered a deep, ringing voice. "The valleys are our own. No climbing now!" And a wind of echoing cries gave answer from all sides. "Life! Life! Life! Abundant, flowing over—use it, use it!"

A troop of nymphs rushed forth, escaped from clustering arms and lips they yet openly desired. He chased them in and out among the waving branches, while she who had brought him ever followed, and sped past him and away again. He caught three gleaming soft brown bodies, then fell beneath them, smothered, bubbling with joyous laughter—next freed himself and, while they sought to drag him captive again, escaped and raced with a leap upon a slimmer, sweeter outline that swung up—only just in time—upon a lower bough, whence she leaned down above him with hanging net of hair and merry eyes. A few feet beyond his reach, she laughed and teased him—the one who had brought him in, the one he ever sought, and who for ever sought him too...

It became a riotous glory of wild children who romped and played with an impassioned glee beneath the moon. For the world was young and they, her happy offspring, glowed with the life she poured so freely into them. All intermingled, the laughing voices rose into a foam of song that broke against the stars. The difficult mountains had been climbed and were forgotten. Good! Then, enjoy the luxuriant, fruitful valley and be glad! And glad they were, brimful with spontaneous energy, natural as birds and animals that obeyed the big, deep rhythm of a simpler age—natural as wind and innocent as sunshine.

Yet, for all the untamed riot, there was a lift of beauty pulsing underneath. Even when the wildest abandon approached the heat of orgy, when the recklessness appeared excess—there hid that marvellous touch of loveliness which makes the natural sacred. There was coherence, purpose, the fulfilling of an exquisite law: there was worship. The form it took, haply, was strange as well as riotous, yet in its strangeness dreamed innocence and purity, and in its very riot flamed that spirit which is divine.

For he found himself at length beside her once again; breathless and panting, her sweet brown limbs aglow from the excitement of escape denied; eyes shining like a blaze of stars, and pulses beating with tumultuous life—helpless and yielding against the strength that pinned her down between the roots. His eyes put mastery on her own. She looked up into his face, obedient, happy, soft with love, surrendered with the same delicious abandon that had swept her for a moment into other arms. "You caught me in the end," she sighed. "I only played awhile."

"I hold you for ever," he replied, half wondering at the rough power in his voice.

It was here the hush of worship stole upon her little face, into her obedient eyes, about her parted lips. She ceased her wilful struggling.

"Listen!" she whispered. "I hear a step upon the glades beyond. The iris and the lily open; the earth is ready, waiting; we must be ready too! *He* is coming!"

He released her and sprang up; the entire company rose too. All stood, all bowed the head. There was an instant's subtle panic, but it was the panic of reverent awe that preludes a descent of deity. For a wind passed through the branches with a sound that is the oldest in the world and so the youngest. Above it there rose the shrill, faint piping of a little reed. Only the first, true sounds were audible—wind and water—the tinkling of the dewdrops as they fell, the murmur of the trees against the air. This was the piping that they heard. And in the hush the stars bent down to hear, the riot paused, the orgy passed and died. The figures waited, kneeling then with one accord. They listened with—the Earth.

"He comes... He comes..." the valley breathed about them.

There was a footfall from far away, treading across a world un-ruined and unstained. It fell with the wind and water, sweetening the valley into life as it approached. Across the rivers and forests it came gently, tenderly, but swiftly and with a power that knew majesty.

"He comes... He comes...!" rose with the murmur of the wind and water from the host of lowered heads.

The footfall came nearer, treading a world grown soft with worship. It reached the grove. It entered. There was a sense of intolerable loveliness, of brimming life, of rapture. The thousand faces lifted like a cloud. They heard the piping close. And so He came.

But He came with blessing. With the stupendous Presence there was joy, the joy of abundant, natural life, pure as the sunlight and the wind. He passed among them. There was great movement—as of a forest shaking, as of deep water falling, as of a cornfield swaying to the wind, yet gentle as of a harebell shedding its burden of dew that it has held too long because of love. He passed among them, touching every head. The great hand swept with tenderness each face, lingered a moment on each beating heart. There was sweetness, peace, and loveliness; but above all, there was—life. He sanctioned every natural joy in them and blessed each passion with his power of creation... Yet each one saw him differently: some as a wife or maiden desired with fire, some as a youth or stalwart husband, others as a figure veiled with stars or cloaked in luminous mist, hardly attainable; others, again—the fewest these, not more than two or three—as that mysterious wonder which tempts the heart away from known familiar sweetness into a wilderness of undecipherable magic without flesh and blood...

To two, in particular, He came so near that they could feel his breath of hills and fields upon their eyes. He touched them with both mighty hands. He stroked the marble breasts, He felt the little hidden horns... and, as they bent lower so that their lips met together for an instant, He took her arms and twined them about the curved, brown neck that she might hold him closer still...

Again a footfall sounded far away upon an unruined world... and He was gone—back into the wind and water whence He came. The thousand faces lifted; all stood up; the hush of worship still among them. There was a quiet as of the dawn. The piping floated over woods and fields, fading into silence. All looked at one another... And then once more the laughter and the play broke loose.

IV

"We'll go," she cried, "and peep upon that other world where life hangs like a prison on their eyes!" And, in a moment, they were across the soaking grass, the lawn and flowerbeds, and close to the walls of the heavy mansion. He peered in through a window, lifting her up to peer in with him. He recognised the world to which outwardly he belonged; he understood; a little gasp escaped him; and a slight shiver ran down the girl's body into his own. She turned her eyes away. "See," she murmured in his ear, "it's ugly, it's not natural. They feel guilty and ashamed. There is no innocence!" She saw the men; it was the women that he saw chiefly.

Lolling ungracefully, with a kind of boldness that asserted independence, the women smoked their cigarettes with an air of invitation they sought to conceal and yet showed plainly. He saw his familiar world in nakedness. Their backs were bare, for all the elaborate clothes they wore; they hung their breasts uncleanly; in their eyes shone light that had never known the open sun. Hoping they were alluring and desirable, they feigned a guilty ignorance of that hope. They all pretended. Instead of wind and dew upon their hair, he saw flowers grown artificially to ape wild beauty, tresses without lustre borrowed from the slums of city factories. He watched them manœuvring with the men; heard dark sentences;

caught gestures half delivered whose meaning should just convey that glimpse of guilt they deemed to increase pleasure. The women were calculating, but nowhere glad; the men experienced, but nowhere joyous. Pretended innocence lay cloaked with a veil of something that whispered secretly, clandestine, ashamed, yet with a brazen air that laid mockery instead of sunshine in their smiles. Vice masqueraded in the ugly shape of pleasure; beauty was degraded into calculated tricks. They were not natural. They knew not joy.

"The forward ones, the civilised!" she laughed in his ear, tweaking his horns with energy. "*We* are the backward!"

"Unclean," he muttered, recalling a catchword of the world he gazed upon.

They were the civilised! They were refined and educated—advanced. Generations of careful breeding, mate cautiously selecting mate, laid the polish of caste upon their hands and faces where gleamed ridiculous, untaught jewels—rings, bracelets, necklaces hanging absurdly from every possible angle.

"But—they are dressed up—for fun," he exclaimed, more to himself than to the girl in skins who clung to his shoulders with her naked arms.

"*Un*dressed!" she answered, putting her brown hand in play across his eyes. "Only they have forgotten even that!" And another shiver passed through her into him. He turned and hid his face against the soft skins that touched his cheek. He kissed her body. Seizing his horns, she pressed him to her, laughing happily.

"Look!" she whispered, raising her head again; "they're coming out." And he saw that two of them, a man and a girl, with an interchange of secret glances, had stolen from the room and were already by the door of the conservatory that led into the garden. It was his wife to be—and his distinguished cousin.

"Oh, Pan!" she cried in mischief. The girl sprang from his arms and pointed. "We will follow them. We will put natural life into their little veins!"

"Or panic terror," he answered, catching the yellow panther skin and following her swiftly round the building. He kept in the shadow, though she ran full into the blaze of moonlight. "But they can't see us," she called, looking over her shoulder a moment. "They can only feel our presence, perhaps." And, as she danced across the lawn, it seemed a moonbeam slipped from a sapling birch tree that the wind curved earthwards, then tossed back against the sky.

Keeping just ahead, they led the pair, by methods known instinctively to elemental blood yet not translatable—led them towards the little grove of waiting pines. The night wind murmured in the branches; a bird woke into a sudden burst of song. These sounds were plainly audible. But four little pointed ears caught other, wilder notes behind the wind and music of the bird—the cries and ringing laughter, the leaping footsteps and the happy singing of their merry kin within the wood.

And the throng paused then amid the revels to watch the "civilised" draw near. They presently reached the trees, halted, looked about them, hesitated a moment—then, with a hurried movement as of shame and fear lest they be caught, entered the zone of shadow.

"Let's go in here," said the man, without music in his voice. "It's dry on the pine needles, and we can't be seen." He led the way; she picked up her skirts and followed over the strip of long wet grass. "Here's a log all ready for us," he added, sat down, and drew her into his arms with a sigh of satisfaction. "Sit on my knee; it's warmer for your pretty figure." He chuckled; evidently they were on familiar terms, for though she hesitated, pretending to be coy, there was no real resistance in her, and she allowed the ungraceful roughness. "But are we *quite* safe? Are you sure?" she asked between his kisses.

"What does it matter, even if we're not?" he replied, establishing her more securely on his knees. "But, as a matter of fact, we're safer here than in my own house." He kissed her hungrily. "By Jove, Hermione, but you're divine," he cried passionately, "divinely beautiful. I love you with every atom of my being—with my soul."

"Yes, dear, I know—I mean, I know you do, but—"

"But what?" he asked impatiently.

"Those detectives—"

He laughed. Yet it seemed to annoy him. "My wife *is* a beast, isn't she?—to have me watched like that," he said quickly.

"They're everywhere," she replied, a sudden hush in her tone. She looked at the encircling trees a moment, then added bitterly: "I hate her, simply *hate* her."

"I love you," he cried, crushing her to him, "that's all that matters now. Don't let's waste time talking about the rest." She contrived to shudder, and hid her face against his coat, while he showered kisses on her neck and hair.

And the solemn pine trees watched them, the silvery moonlight fell on their faces, the scent of new-mown hay went floating past.

"I love you with my very soul," he repeated with intense conviction. "I'd do anything, give up anything, bear anything—just to give you a moment's happiness. I swear it—before God!"

There was a faint sound among the trees behind them, and the girl sat up, alert. She would have scrambled to her feet, but that he held her tight.

"What the devil's the matter with you tonight?" he asked in a different tone, his vexation plainly audible. "You're as nervy as if *you* were being watched, instead of me."

She paused before she answered, her finger on her lip. Then she said slowly, hushing her voice a little:

"Watched! That's exactly what I did feel. I've felt it ever since we came into the wood."

"Nonsense, Hermione. It's too many cigarettes." He drew her back into his arms, forcing her head up so that he could kiss her better.

"I suppose it is nonsense," she said, smiling. "It's gone now, anyhow."

He began admiring her hair, her dress, her shoes, her pretty ankles, while she resisted in a way that proved her practice. "It's not *me* you love," she pouted, yet drinking in his praise. She listened to his repeated assurances that he loved her with his "soul" and was prepared for any sacrifice.

"I feel so safe with you," she murmured, knowing the moves in the game as well as he did. She looked up guiltily into his face, and he looked down with a passion that he thought perhaps was joy.

"You'll be married before the summer's out," he said, "and all the thrill and excitement will be over. Poor Hermione!" She lay back in his arms, drawing his face down with both hands, and kissing him on the lips. "You'll have more of him than you can do with—eh? As much as you care about, anyhow."

"I shall be much more free," she whispered. "Things will be easier. And I've got to marry some one—"

She broke off with another start. There was a sound again behind them. The man heard nothing. The blood in his temples pulsed too loudly, doubtless.

"Well, what is it this time?" he asked sharply.

She was peering into the wood, where the patches of dark shadow and moonlit spaces made odd, irregular patterns in the air. A low branch waved slightly in the wind.

"Did you hear that?" she asked nervously.

"Wind," he replied, annoyed that her change of mood disturbed his pleasure.

"But something moved—"

"Only a branch. We're quite alone, quite safe, I tell you," and there was a rasping sound in his voice as he said it. "Don't be so imaginative. I can take care of you."

She sprang up. The moonlight caught her figure, revealing its exquisite young curves beneath the smother of the costly clothing. Her hair had dropped a little in the struggle. The man eyed her eagerly, making a quick, impatient gesture towards her, then stopped abruptly. He saw the terror in her eyes.

"Oh, hark! What's that?" she whispered in a startled voice. She put her finger up. "Oh, let's go back. I don't like this wood. I'm frightened."

"Rubbish," he said, and tried to catch her by the waist.

"It's safer in the house—my room—or yours—"

She broke off again. "There it is—don't you hear? It's a footstep!" Her face was whiter than the moon.

"I tell you it's the wind in the branches," he repeated gruffly. "Oh, come on, *do*. We were just getting jolly together. There's nothing to be afraid of. Can't you believe me?" He tried to pull her down upon his knee again with force. His face wore an unpleasant expression that was half leer, half grin.

But the girl stood away from him. She continued to peer nervously about her. She listened.

"You give me the creeps," he exclaimed crossly, clawing at her waist again with passionate eagerness that now betrayed exasperation. His disappointment turned him coarse.

The girl made a quick movement of escape, turning so as to look in every direction. She gave a little scream.

"That *was* a step. Oh, oh, it's close beside us. I heard it. We're being watched!" she cried in terror. She darted towards him, then shrank back. He did not try to touch her this time.

"Moonshine!" he growled. "You've spoilt my—spoilt our chance with your silly nerves."

But she did not hear him apparently. She stood there shivering as with sudden cold.

"There! I saw it again. I'm sure of it. Something went past me through the air."

And the man, still thinking only of his own pleasure frustrated, got up heavily, something like anger in his eyes. "All right," he said testily; "if you're going to make a fuss, we'd better go. The house *is* safer, possibly, as you say. You know my room. Come along!" Even that risk he would not take. He loved her with his "soul."

They crept stealthily out of the wood, the girl slightly in front of him, casting frightened backward glances. Afraid, guilty, ashamed, with an air as though they had been detected, they stole back towards the garden and the house, and disappeared from view.

And a wind rose suddenly with a rushing sound, poured through the wood as though to cleanse it, swept out the artificial scent and trace of shame, and brought back again the song, the laughter, and the happy revels. It roared across the park, it shook the windows of the house, then sank away as quickly as it came. The trees stood motionless again, guarding their secret in the clean, sweet moonlight that held the world in dream until the dawn stole up and sunshine took the earth with joy.

MOORS OF WRAN

A. Lloyd Bayne

It is perhaps fitting that a collection of weird tales features an author of which there seems to be little available information. "Moors of Wran" proved A. Lloyd Bayne's sole contribution to *Weird Tales*, published in the September 1931 issue alongside works by regular pulpists such as Robert E. Howard, August Derleth and Clark Ashton Smith. Compared to the other poems in this collection, "Moors of Wran" strikes a distinctly apocalyptic tone. The ambiguity of Pan recedes, here, among imagery of a vengeful nature spirit leaving death in its wake.

I smell Blood and Death tonight
 On the Moors of Wran,
 On the Moors of Wran,
And o'er the plain stalks the dread of man,
 'Tis the fear of Pan
 And the laugh of Pan.
Terror shall strike while the night is young,
And the souls of the lost that in space are hung
Tonight toward Earth will be awfully flung,
 And the shrieks of the Damned will quiver.

Blood will bubble and flow tonight
 On the Moors of Wran,
 On the Moors of Wran,
And dreadful Things will be shown to man,
 'Tis the face of Pan
 And the hoofs of Pan.
Fear will burn in the hearts of all,
And Death descend like a ghostly pall:
The Dance of Life's on a spinning ball,
 And corpses float in the river.

HOW PAN CAME TO LITTLE INGLETON

Margery Lawrence

Margery Lawrence (1889–1969) was an English author born in Wolverhampton. Her fiction drifted between the genres of romance, fantasy, the detective story and the supernatural. As with Browning before her, an early collection of her poetry, *Songs of Childhood, and Other Verses*, was published by her father in 1913. Subsequent works included the *Club of the Round Table* series (1926–1932) and the *Miles Pennoyer* stories (1945), inspired by Algernon Blackwood's own supernatural investigator, John Silence. Notably, two of Lawrence's novels were adapted into films, with *Red Heels* (1924) becoming *Das Spielzeug von Paris* (1925) and *The Madonna of Seven Moons* (1931) reworked into a British drama directed by Arthur Crabtree.

"How Pan Came to Little Ingleton" is taken from the first of Lawrence's *Club of the Round Table* collections, *Nights of the Round Table* (1926). The story concerns the Reverend Thomas Minchin, who has brought his own puritanical values to the town of Little Ingleton. When the children of the village fail to turn up for Sunday School, Minchin sets out in search of his flock. Instead, he finds Pan in the labyrinthine wilds. Lawrence's tale touches on a unique association of Pan: his alignment with Christ. Developed during the Renaissance, through authors such as Edmund Spenser, the demon of antiquity came to be seen in parallel, not opposition. Though decrying the Christian faith, here Pan echoes the role of redeemer, saving the wayward priest's soul by playing the role of parson.

Dear old Father Pring had been a regular member of the Round Table ever since that happy January night when I joined it, but it had never dawned on me that he was anything of a story-teller—knowing the custom at Saunderson's, I yet imagined vaguely that the gentle old priest was, like the deep chairs, the cosy-shaded lamp, the hospitable red-tiled hearth, merely a pleasant part of the charming *mise en scene*, a "stage-prop" rather than one of the actors. I thought too soon, though. It was a perfect June night, Midsummer Night, and the windows thrown open upon a purple star-splashed sky, while from the far-below streets the hum of London rose like the faint boom and thunder of a distant sea. I was sitting with whimsical, charming Dan Vesey, in the wide window-embrasure looking out over the black peaked roofs, a jagged Cubist silhouette against the marvellous sky, when Father Pring joined us; staring out across the roofs to where in the distance, low down behind the line of black, a few streaks and slivers of livid green and gold showed the last ragged traces of the sinking sun, the old man sighed a little, then smiled as I raised questioning eyes to his.

"A wonderful night, Laurie, my child! An enchanted night... the night on which they say, the Old Powers have sway once more over mortals, and the Church must stand aside—strange, strange..."

But the hint was enough—greedy, I clutched his hand and called to the company.

"Knights of the Round Table—here is a story! No nonsense, Father... I'm sure there is—tell us the story!"

Blinking at the lamplight and the chorus of shouts and encouragement that greeted him, the old priest, smiling, half-hesitating, drew out an envelope, thick and bound with a rubber band.

"Yes... there is a story. I—it may seem a strange one for a priest to tell, but I can vouch for its truth indeed. It was written down shortly after it happened, by the dear friend to whom it happened, many years ago. He died, and in his will he left it to me, the one person to whom he had ever told the story, and till tonight its sacredness to me as well as its singular strangeness has kept it locked in my private safe. But with you, my friends—who do not see fit to laugh and jeer when you hear of things that seem beyond mortal knowledge eerie and inexplicable—there, I will read you this true story, only changing the name of my friend, lest he might have been known to any of you. I will call him Minchin—and the tale, 'Mr. Minchin's Midsummer,' or 'How Pan came to Little Ingleton.'"

Little Ingleton, drowsy in the summer sun, lay curled like a sleepy child in the hollowed arm-curves of the mothering green hills that cradled it. Warm and white and frankly sleepy on a Sunday afternoon lay Little Ingleton, and the Reverend Thomas Minchin was cross.

In the inexplicable absence of Potts the bellringer, Mr. Minchin was tolling the school-house bell for Sunday School. He tolled the bell industriously, but the wooden lych-gate gave no click to announce an entering scholar; the waiting cypresses stood tall and grim beside the old green-mossed headstones jostling each other up and down the little hill-perched graveyard, and the Reverend Thomas peered out now and again and gave the bell an extra angry tug in his annoyance—but sleep and the idleness of Midsummer Day held his parishioners, and not even Miss Rosamond Perkins, the lady teacher in the Sunday School, seemed to mean to turn up; so at last, with a primmed-up mouth and a scowl that rivalled those on the faces of the grimacing gargoyles that watched him go, the Reverend Thomas Minchin, newly installed incumbent of Little Ingleton, clapped on his black shovel-hat and stalked forth to find his strayed flock.

The Reverend Thomas did not yet know his way about the village very well—he was aware, as he plodded up the twisting little main street looking vaguely for the turning to Miss Perkins' lodgings, that he looked an incongruous figure in his dusty black garb against the prevailing glory of blue and gold and white, and the knowledge somehow gave an added edge to his already-ruffled temper.

He was a lean, stooping ascetic of a man with narrow lips and pale intolerant eyes, and his primly-buttoned black clerical coat over tight black trousers and clumping square-toed boots, his flat black felt hat jammed squarely down on his head, expressed his personality as surely as any courtesan's painted smile and shadowed eyes express hers. Though, to be sure, he would have been mightily enraged at the comparison—for was he not a man of God, a celibate, a teetotaller, a non-smoker, and in a word, all the other things that a clergyman (*vide* the Press) should be?

This being so, surely he should have earned the respect and obedience of his people, so that they flocked to listen to the Word—but the remembrance of the empty school-house that afternoon brought a fresh scowl of sour anger to the face of the Reverend Thomas, and as he turned into a winding lane that seemed to resemble Miss Perkins' description of her "road" he muttered a word that in a layman's mouth might have resembled profanity.

Had he not instituted fresh services, countless in number and strict in their ordinances? Suppressed dancing in the village hall or on the green? Closed down the "George and Crown" except for the sale of ginger ale and such innocuous drinks—banished from the chemist's shop *poudre de riz*, lip rouge, scents and other snares of the devil? Who but he had worked unceasingly for the regeneration of Little Ingleton—sunk as he had found it, in idle happiness, with but one or at most two services 'a Sunday, and used (low be it spoken!) to the lax ways of his predecessor, old Father Fagan, frail, gentle, kindly, who, it was whispered, at times so far forgot his duties as a clergyman as to watch and even take part in dancings and singings and junketings on the village green? Even Miss Rosamond Perkins, who wore pretty summer dresses of pink or blue and yellow patterned with gay little flowers, and had bright eyes and cherry lips—though to be sure, the Reverend Thomas had never noticed whether her lips were red or no—even Miss Perkins was reputed to have danced and laughed and played with these unregenerates before the advent of sterner ways.

Now he came to remember it, Miss Perkins had actually once or twice been guilty of murmuring on a fine Sunday in the hot classroom that it might be better to take the children out in the woods "to play with God"—to quote her own unusual phrase— "to play with God in His lovely world"—than drone sleepily over their Bibles; but this had greatly scandalised the new vicar, and he had spoken so severely to Miss Rosamond Perkins about it that she had wept, and looking up at his austerity with eyes like bluebells drowned in tears, subsided into silence. Subsequently, he remembered with satisfaction, she had discarded her frivolous-patterned cotton frocks, her hat with its wreath of floppy roses, and taken to brown holland and a severe straw hat with a band of ribbon only... This had pleased him, as showing a commendable wish to improve, but today he remembered the earlier rebellious murmur, and reviewing things grimly in his mind, decided that for some reason Miss Perkins had suddenly "broken out" and taken her little band of scholars to the woods or fields.

He quickened his step, sending up a little cloud of light floury dust, and his lips tightened as he peered through his short-sighted eyes at the names on the gates of the cottages. "Rose Nook" was the name of the cottage, he knew—but it was strange, it seemed much further down the lane than he had surmised from Miss Perkins' description.

"Just round the corner of Pan's Lane—you can't miss it!" Now he came to think of it, he supposed this *was* "Pan's Lane"? Curious name, that—must have some connection with the old Roman times, and their crude gods; curious how traces of that sort of thing linger. The Squire had told him that King's Panton, the little town in the valley's hollow, far below high-perched Little Ingleton, was so called for its old name: "Kynge Pan hys towne." Strange old heathen days—how thankful one should be for modern education, and enlightenment—now where *was* "Rose Nook"? It was tiring, plodding along in this heat, and the mental picture of Miss Rosamond Perkins, cool and happy in some sylvan dell, with the adoring children around her listening to some absurd fairy story—the sort of imaginative rubbish she was far too fond of telling—made his ill-temper, already sour, more acid still. He would find out from old Mrs. Calder, where Miss Perkins lodged, where they had gone, and follow after them—he would come upon them suddenly in their idleness, and see them cringe in shame and confusion before his righteous wrath, hurry tearfully back to the school-house to their books and catechism!... And as for Miss Perkins? She must be spoken to severely—more than severely...

He was walking so fast in his wrathful energy that in the cloud of dust he was raising he could not see anything distinctly, and stumbling over an obstacle in his path came down full length on his respectable nose, knocking himself completely breathless.

When, winded, angry and thoroughly undignified, he sat up at last, he found the obstacle over which he had stumbled was not one, but two—the long legs of a shabby young man in travel-stained grey flannel trousers, no shoes or socks, and a torn blue shirt, who sat surveying him gravely over a half-eaten hunk of bread.

"My goodness!" said the young man, "you did come a cropper!" He laughed and took another bite.

The Reverend Thomas was still too breathless to reply, but he blinked and stared, endeavouring to recover a touch of his lost dignity; but as he stared around him interest in his dignity was lost in his growing astonishment. Little as he knew of Little Ingleton, he was under the impression that he certainly knew by now all the lanes that ended in field-paths or *cul-de-sacs*—but it appeared he did not, for this lane was certainly new! Somehow it seemed to have fizzled out into a mere field-path winding away over the sloping hill-side. Glancing back, Mr. Minchin's puzzlement increased, and he concluded that, lost in his thoughts, he must have tramped further and faster than he meant, and left the village itself far behind him.

A copse of trees, through which the tiny path wound, stood at his back, and all around the stillness of a summer afternoon brooded over green hill and sleepy valley, sentinel woods and white-flecked shining sky... under the lee of a steep bank the strange young man sat, nodding cheerfully at him, and continued to munch his bread, throwing the crumbs to an impertinent red squirrel, that, to Mr. Minchin's great amazement, sat perched and chittering at his elbow.

Transferring his attention to the young man himself, Mr. Minchin frowned. He wore no hat, and his face was brown as a pine-cone, his hair bleached and wiry with the sun and wind; it stood up over each eye with a comic alert whisk that gave him a curiously impertinent appearance—his face was long and thin, with a narrow chin that ran to meet a hooked nose that stood out like a wedge between two light eyes—dancing, irreverent eyes, the colour of a hawk's. The Reverend Thomas winced and looked away from those eyes, and his resentment increased. What business had this ragged vagabond to survey him with such obvious amusement! He should have lowered his own eyes in shame at his garments—they were well-cut enough, but disgracefully torn and travel-stained, and that shirt! Well, not only were the sleeves rolled up to the shoulder, but the unbuttoned front lay open almost to the waist, showing skin burnt brown as the merry face, or very nearly—thus proving indubitably that this graceless fellow was in the habit of doing without even a shirt very often!...

"It's so much cooler in this hot weather!" said the stranger.

He took another bite, and Mr. Minchin jumped. So astonished was he that he remained sitting on the path, his hands spread each side to support him, staring at the young man who had so curiously guessed his question and answered it. Coincidence—but—odd, very!...

"Decent clothing is scarcely a question of convenience," he said stiffly.

The hooked nose came down over the lean chin and the young man grinned, surveying the dusty figure before him.

"Obviously, from your point of view, or you wouldn't wear those horrible black things! Why do you?"

Mr. Minchin gasped in amazement; not only at the revolutionary suggestion contained in the remark, but at the stranger's temerity at making it.

He answered severely, rising and dusting the insulted clerical garments as best he could—though he was conscious, under the scrutiny of the merry-eyed stranger, that he was not cutting his usual dignified figure.

"You do not seem aware, sir, that I am a man of God!"

The stranger twinkled again, quite unimpressed.

"I can see you are a clergyman all right—is that what you call a man of God?"

Mr. Minchin was outraged.

"Sir! Are you not a Christian, that you ask me such a question?"

The stranger threw a last handful of crumbs to the waiting squirrel, and clasping his hands round his dusty knees, surveyed Mr. Minchin again. Then laughed, softly, oddly.

"A Christian? I don't think I've ever been asked that before!"

"Then it's quite time you were," said Mr. Minchin virtuously.

"Time—ah, there's so much time, isn't there?" said the stranger, rather irrelevantly. "But to continue, O Man-of-God! What brings you wandering out here this Sunday afternoon—when presumably all Men-of-God should be herding their flocks willy-nilly into church?"

The faint flavour of insolence in the stranger's tone, strangely matching his impertinent upflaming hair, stung Mr. Minchin, and his response was severe.

"I agree with you. But unfortunately... my Sunday School class did not appear, and I came out to find them..."

The young man, hunching his shoulders back against the warm red earth of the bank, laughed suddenly, amusedly: a gleeful spurt of laughter like the uprush of a spring to the sunlight.

"So for once Pan won, eh? The old gods against the new—the lure of the sun and the hills and the blue, blue sky... ha, ha! Well, my worthy son of the Christian church, go on... so you came a-wandering to find your straying flock, eh?"

"Er—yes..." for the life of him the Reverend Thomas could not quite help an odd little feeling of trepidation under the fire of the yellow hawk's eyes that watched him, and he finished lamely, "And I—er—wandered considerably further than I meant..."

"You did indeed!..." said the young man grimly.

There was a moment's silence while he eyed the clergyman up and down, then down came the hooked nose again in a grin, and rolling over, he stretched for a shabby knapsack reposing against a giant root.

"Down Pan's Lane—into Panton Wood—over against Pan hys towne—and all on a Midsummer Day! Oh, wonderful—amazing—my poor dear earnest-minded friend!"

He extracted a fat round bottle and tin mug from the bag as he talked—sheer nonsense to the puzzled clergyman—and uncorking the bottle with a pop that certainly sounded more than luscious and tempting to the thirsty ears of the Vicar of Ingleton, poured out a foaming crimson draught and held it out invitingly.

"Have a drink, old boy? But I'm thirsty too—so drink fair!"

Despite his iron Prohibition principles it was with quite a considerable effort that Mr. Minchin waved the mug away.

"Thank you, no. I quite realise you mean it kindly—but my cloth forbids."

"Your cloth? Good Lord!" The stranger's laugh was faintly scornful—"I've had many a cheery drink with other fellows of your cloth, as you call it! Come, drink up!"

"I am—fortunately—not concerned with the irregularities unfortunately committed by others of my calling," said Mr. Minchin stiffly.

Unmoved, the stranger quaffed the rejected wine; over the top of the mug his piercingly bright eyes stared at the clergyman.

"Mistakes? Are you then so much better than your fellows?" He set down the mug with a flourish. "I seem to remember—somewhere—something about a Pharisee who thanked God he was not as other men..."

The Reverend Thomas flushed angrily, confounded and momentarily speechless. Before he could think out a sufficiently crushing answer the young man was off again.

"So you're the new vicar of Little Ingleton? I've heard of you! Round about King's Panton—we've been talking quite a lot about you lately..."

This was a sop, and though Mr. Minchin was feeling a little distrustful of this remarkable young man, he smiled; cautiously, warily, but he smiled. The allusion to King's Panton relieved his mind. This was probably—now he came to think of it—one of Mr. Imray's fellows from King's Panton Manor House down in the valley; the verger had told him he always had five or six studying for exams, reading for the Bar, being coached... doubtless this was one of his pupils. Eccentric, of course—but obviously a gentleman... and to a gentleman even going barefoot and wearing an open-necked shirt might be excused, though Mr. Minchin secretly hoped most devoutly that the stranger would not walk down the main street of Little Ingleton thus arrayed! King's Panton—that was fifteen miles away as the crow flies—it was certainly gratifying to hear that fifteen miles away they were talking of him and of his work in cleansing, in regenerating Little Ingleton...

"I don't know that I should quite call it that!" said the stranger coolly.

The Reverend Thomas jumped again, and the young man laughed.

"Oh, I'm a thought reader—one of my hobbies!" His eyes danced as he watched the other's chapfallen expression. "Great fun it is—I often guess what our fellows are thinking about, and it makes them no end annoyed. But what makes you think you have done so much for Little Ingleton?"

Mr. Minchin stiffened.

"I think, if you have heard as much about me as you say, that I need hardly answer that question?"

The young man looked at him reflectively.

"That, of course, is a matter of opinion!" he commented lazily. "You may think that driving your school-children into a stuffy room on a gorgeous day like this is doing good..."

Mr. Minchin exploded.

"Doing good? Doesn't the Prayer Book say—"

"I know all the Prayer Book says—read it all before you were born!" said the stranger brusquely.

In his annoyance Mr. Minchin failed to note this remarkable assertion from a young man of at most twenty-four.

"I know God demands a certain amount of attention..." His curious, half-wistful, half-insolent gaze strayed over the brooding hills, and he paused, then went on briskly—"but I fancy, you know, that God is a fair-minded Deity... and if folk come to worship Him on a Sunday morning, what harm is there if for the rest of the day they give worship to other gods—and maybe older gods than He?"

Mr. Minchin gasped in horror and amaze—the poor young man was mad, surely!—Mr. Imray should not have let him go out without a hat in the sun... As the alarming thought that he might be consorting with a raving lunatic crossed his mind, the young man jumped up, and bursting into a frank laugh, stood arms akimbo in the sun watching him. Through all the bewildered fright and anger that confused him Mr. Minchin was aware of a quick stab of sheer masculine jealousy of the slim wiry frame that confronted him, muscular and lithe and brown—why, he was only just thirty-four himself, and he should be like this long-limbed, sun-tanned vagabond, not a lean shrivelled bone of a man buttoned into a black coat and deliberately turning away his eyes when a pretty girl glanced at him! Through the heat and confusion of his thoughts the stranger's mocking voice came to him, taunting, accusing...

"... Done for them? That's what you're trying to do—*do* for them! Kill joy and youth and laughter in them to implant your wizened mean little creed instead! Because of your own dour miserable narrowness, you're trying to bully them into living life your way—you, with your bigotry and prudishness that sees sin and temptation in a flower in a hat, the gay colour of a pretty gown..."

"Black is the Lord's colour," croaked the Reverend Thomas, though he was growing more and more dreadfully frightened, confused, puzzled... why, oh why, had nice quiet Mr. Imray imported this crazy young man? His inquisitor's laugh was contemptuous.

"Are you sure you know Him? He never said anything like that to *me*! And as far as that goes, isn't it in your dour creed that He created all things, so, what of the scarlet poppy-flower, the blue-and-purple of the hills yonder, the gold of Rosamond Perkins' hair?"

"I have never noticed the colour of Miss Perkins' hair!" said Mr. Minchin stiffly—the laugh that answered him stung him like the flick of a whip.

"Poor fool! You've kept your nose so long between the leaves of your dusty Book of Duty that you almost forget you are a man at all... almost, almost you have remade yourself into a hard religious machine grinding out texts and platitudes and conventions! And yet still because I love my people—and perhaps a little because under those black absurdities of yours I discern the germ of a real man still, one worth saving—"

"A crazy revivalist... must be!" muttered Mr. Minchin to himself, catching at the explanatory straw. Above his shrinking head the voice went on, light, laughing, yet faintly menacing in its very laughter.

"... Didn't you stop little Molly Isitt from wearing a pink sash? Tell the Squire that to start a cinema in the village meant encouraging immorality—since it would be held in the dark? Get Miss Bank's maid, Ellen, sacked because you caught her kissing a gypsy in the lane? Abolish the kindly old custom of giving bread to beggars each Friday night because it encouraged pauperism? Abolish beer-drinking and the use of perfumes? Forbid dancing and singing, and refuse permission for the yearly pageant to be held in the Vicarage grounds?..."

"All vanity—and turning their thoughts from the Lord," snuffled the Reverend Thomas feebly, for he was very frightened—above him the voice seemed to be shaping itself into a song of triumph and of scorn together, and he was shaking, cold, despite the glowing heat...

"From the Lord! Oh Allah! Oh Set and Horus and Osiris! Oh Kali, Shiva, and all forgotten gods!" Oh, the ringing scorn of that laughter—shrivelled tiny the wretched listener felt as the voice boomed on. "Oh Zeus, Apollo and goat-footed Pan! In the great world is there not room—is there not room for more than one God?"

*

It was evening when Mr. Minchin awoke, and the slanting rays of the sun were touching his bare head over the bank. Staggering to his feet, stiffly enough, for it seemed he had slept a long time, he dusted and shook himself and turned to the copse behind him. The path opened out into the end of "Pan's Lane" up which he had trudged so wearily in the afternoon, and as the clang of the bell for Evensong rang out he hastened his steps. He had slept too long indeed—it was still a little way to the church, and he always liked to be there a good while before service, fussing about the choirboys, heckling the patient little humpbacked organist, arranging and rearranging his books and papers. As he came down the darkening graveyard he could see the people already filing into evening service, the single bell swinging in the square tower, and he frowned.

He would have to hurry to get into his surplice and head the procession—he almost ran down the incline to the crooked little vestry-door that hid slyly behind a buttress, and rushing to the cupboard, reached for his surplice... and gasped! It was no longer there! Neither his own, nor the clean white surplices of the choir-boys, ironed and carefully hung up every Sunday by Mrs. Kitson... as he stared, unable to believe his eyes, the organ burst forth into full volume and he realised the dreadful truth. The service had begun without him!

Staring vaguely round the vestry, Mr. Minchin pinched himself, at first doubtfully, then viciously—the shock of the pain made him realise quite definitely that he was not dreaming, and a wave of anger took possession of him. How dare they—meek little Mr. Lycett, his curate, Kitson the verger, Clubb the organist, all the rest? How dared they venture to open the service without him? Was it possible that he had invited a brother priest to conduct Evensong for him, and forgotten? No—it was impossible. Frazer of King's Panton was not free, and he knew no other... The organ boomed and surged around him, the choirboys sang lustily and the crowding people sang too... Though the church was full, it seemed that a long line of dark figures, black silhouettes against the violet evening sky, still streamed towards the door, and as they came, they sang...

Staggering to the little window, Mr. Minchin watched them come—never in all his life, certainly never since his ministry in Little Ingleton, had so great and eager a congregation besieged his church, and beneath all his bewildered anger he felt a sharp pang of compunction, of shame. Surely, surely, had he known his work as he should have known it, this throng should have trooped before to listen to his teaching?... Suddenly his anger left him—gave place to bewilderment and a nameless deep-seated fear—and slipping noiselessly into the dimlit church, he crouched down in a distant pew, his heart for the first time in his narrow life humbled, abashed before a thing he could not understand.

The tall windows were slips of gleaming purple where the night sky showed through, and the one rose window in the nave, of gorgeous old painted glass, shone like a glorious jewelled buckler—the high-hung gas-lamps down the centre aisle shone out, round globes of yellow, like pale marsh-flares in the velvet gloom, but it seemed either a few of these had failed or else this summer dusk was heavier than usual, for the church was dimly lit on the whole.

From his far corner Mr. Minchin could see the old pulpit with its supporting stone angels shrouded in their drooping wings; a corner of the lighted choirstalls, the carved oak lectern that bore the great leather-bound Bible with its gold-tasselled marker. As he looked at this his eyes bulged and he drew an astonished breath... it passed in a flash, but for a moment Mr. Minchin had imagined he saw an audacious red squirrel, own twin to the furry creature that had eaten crumbs so tamely from the brown hand of the strange young man, dash down the stem of the lectern and vanish beside the pulpit! It was a mere impression, of course—must be—but Mr. Minchin was not quite so sure of himself as he had been a few hours ago, and the supreme assurance with which he would have said "Imagination!" had its tail between its legs and was already sneaking ignominiously away... A little way beyond him stood a slim girlish figure, a child clinging to either hand: Rosamond Perkins, adorable in her pink-flowered gown, crowned with the rose-wreathed hat, her pretty mouth open as she sang, heartily, happily, her eyes fixed on the stall where sat the strange priest, grave and sedate, in the place usually sacred to the Vicar of Little Ingleton. From his position Mr. Minchin could not see anything but a white-sleeve laid along the carved chair-arm, the back of a head... yet he had the impression that the head was young, and suddenly, completely, a miserable jealousy seized him, and he knew that he would have given anything in his lonely world to have had Rosamond Perkins look up at him like that... Fool that he had been—oh, fool and blind! The choir sang on; the people sang, and strange voices from every side took up the chant; voices strange and, to Mr. Minchin's dazed ears, barely human at times... gruff and squeaky, shrill, batlike, or deep and ringing, as one, in an insane dream, might think a goat's or ram's might be... Old Miss Banks stood hand in hand with pretty Ellen, her dismissed maidservant, dressed gaily as for a wedding in white muslin and ribbons, and beside Ellen stood her gypsy swain: and grim old Miss Banks' face was gay with smiles, and she wore a flower-spray pinned to her cloak! Molly Isitt's pink sash gleamed beside a pillar, and a pink frilly hat accompanied it—all the village was there, and behind them and beside them in the shadows there seemed a thousand creatures more, strange and elusive, indistinct to see, yet present, a great concourse of tossing heads and rustling hairy bodies bringing with them the scent of leaves and trampled grasses and flowers!... And behind these, more elusive still, others that Mr. Minchin did not dare to look at; slim, elflike shadows, bright-eyed and wild, yet singing shrilly, lustily with all their hearts...

The singing stopped, and shivering, not daring to glance up, Mr. Minchin knew that the Strange Preacher was in the pulpit—yet without glancing up he knew who stood there well enough—for it was the Young Man of the road, the mad student! In the lightning brilliance of those hawk's eyes that played upon him now, Mr. Minchin knew the truth, and shivering, cowered in sheer terror in his shadowy corner—above him, his twin peaks of bleached shining hair like two flames under the flaring gaslight, the Preacher gave out his text... "I will lift up mine eyes unto the hills!"

With all his theology-trained heart the Reverend Thomas longed to shriek "blasphemy, blasphemy," for was it not blasphemy to have to listen, in God's Own House, to This that preached... why did not the outraged heavens open, the earth split and swallow up church and congregation, the very stones, consecrated by austere bishop and celibate priest, crumble upon them for this impiety? But in the hush that settled over the dusk-veiled church there seemed no note but attention, no hint of action from an outraged God... At last, raising his head from his hands where he had thrust his fingers into his ears, fascinated, Mr. Minchin listened too, as the Preacher spoke on.

He spoke of the grave eternal hills and of their story. Of the hills in whose cradling generous arms nestle grim Druid Grove and pagan altar—fairy ring and Christian church alike. Of the rains and dews that settle in their folds and run together into streams and pools, deep lakes and mighty rivers; of the little bright unconsidered flowers that grow on the hills, and the myriad unknown creatures that live out their coloured lives of but a day, the gossamer moths and lazy painted butterflies, the grey-velvet ground spider and his black neighbour the busy ant... Of the forgotten forts that, built by a long-dead people, still face the sea, the green turf weaving a winding sheet over the sturdy bones of the old builders; of the cromlechs and dolmens—the strange stone rings, so old that even their purpose is forgotten now—of the battered altars to ancient creeds, so old that their very names are dead; the green groves in hidden woodland places, groves planted in honour of goddesses that rule no longer...

He told of trees; of the bent and crooked pine trees that face the sea-gales, the sturdy sentinels that stand guard over England and her shores; of the green willow that trails her long hair in the brooks, the sad yew with its clustering red berries; the brittle lanky elm and its twin sister the larch, slim and elegant in delicate flutter-ing green, like a Watteau lady, all powdered and panniered, ever whispering to her other still lovelier sister, the silver birch, superior as any Bond Street miss, and twice as fair. Of the grave oak, whose roots are planted in a Britain older even than we dream—of secret ash, and subtle thorn, that Trinity of pagan magic... of the little furry creatures that scamper and fight and hide beneath the great tree-boles, the quiet-eyed deer peeping wary from the thickets, all the thousand-and-one shy people of the woods that live and love, happy in their untaught way... And then he spoke of Man and his wonder and his strength, and Woman, in her beauty—and of how Man and Woman were made for love and joy, and for the dear companioning of each other through laughing youth to hale old age. He spoke of the loveliness of love, of frank kisses betwixt honest man and maid, of the close pressure of hand in hand and heart to heart; the murmured holiness of loving speech, of marriage, and mating, and the proud bearing of sturdy children... and as he listened the Reverend Thomas thought of the red lips and uplifted eyes of Rosamond Perkins, and smiled and trembled, and did not turn away...

And above him, under the flaring gaslight, his twisting spirals of hair like pale horns, his yellow hawk's eyes roving the crowded audience, the Preacher preached on... and now he spoke of Others—of careless and happy things that roam the green woods in vivid lovely life, if not life as mere humans know it... of Those that knew and loved their Mother Earth ere ever Man had set foot upon it! Those Older Things that, retreating before Man and his noisy dusty cities, yet laugh and, shaking their windblown hair, withdraw deeper and deeper yet to their old fastnesses in mountain and cave and forest... Unbaptised, perchance—knowing no creed nor caste—merry pagan Things that own no church, yet should there not be room for all beneath the mantle of Him whose name is Love?... Room for even these, for elf and satyr and white-browed nymph, merry brown gnome and wandering fairy, fauns with their goat-feet, and green-eyed nixy with her dripping hair? All the Old Ancient Things that Man denies, since dust of cities blinds his once-keen sight... Yet strangely, amazingly, the listener understood, and nodded happily, though his face was wet with tears, as the great Voice boomed on, that Voice that held in it the pattering of rain on summer leaves, the sweep and majesty of thunder on the cowering hills, the shrilling clearness of the stars that sing eternally in the Outer Spaces!... And as he listened, it seemed to the Reverend Mr. Minchin that his soul shrank within him in shame at his past littleness; shrank to the smallness of a shrivelled pea, and yet swelled to a greatness and happiness utterly beyond his knowledge, a happiness too immense to even grasp as yet. Yet remembering his past harshness, his bigotry, the narrow foolish laws with which he had sought to bind and straiten the great and laughing World—his mean, harsh judgment, and lack of charity—in the shelter of the kindly pew he wept and trembled, afraid, as the Voice boomed and shouted above him, and he knew Who, for the saving of his little soul, had supplanted him to teach the people truth!

"... Lift up your eyes to the hills, whence cometh your help indeed! The hills whence came your fathers; The woods, the seas wherein dwell strange and lovely things undreamt of in your little lives—the aged, the eternal Mother Earth! Mother Earth from whose heart we are come, and to whose arms we return at the last. Man and Beast and stranger Folk alike! Sing praises, my people—to the dear and goodly Earth and All Those that dwell therein, each in their kind and every kind, and to all gods old and new that love the world... for beneath the mantle of the Great God, is there not room to shelter smaller gods?..."

Abruptly the wonderful voice ceased—confusedly, dazed by the tumult of emotions that possessed him, yet dimly afterwards the Reverend Thomas seemed to remember a great and wonderful acclamation in which he joined, calling feebly, his face wet with joyful tears... the singing of a great Magnificat in which he vaguely remembered such happy lines as he had never dreamt the dourly thunderous Psalms possessed...

"God is gone up with a merry sound... with the sound of the trumpet!..."

He remembered stumbling out into the churchyard, ghostly, beautiful with its black tall cypresses in the moonlight, its crowded gravestones leaning against each other in the shadows as if to listen to the happy chanting, the chorus of praise that followed him out into the open.

As if in a dream from his place on the sloping bank above the path he watched the congregation file out, two and two, like the figures in a Noah's Ark, a strung-out line of black shadows against the gorgeous sunset, rose, green and gold, singing jubilantly as they went—and smiled, without surprise, but with happy knowledge, as he saw, mingling with the village folk, Those of a different world, beast and satyr and elvish unnamed creature, all come to shout their gladness in one great festival of praise! He saw old Kitson, arm-in-arm with his wife... and a faun, goat-footed, leaf-crowned, pranced beside them and tweaked old Kitson's hair... and the old man laughed and hugged his old wife the closer! He saw sour Gertrude Pring, who ran the post-office, companioned by two merry small Things, brown-eyed and saucy, and Miss Banks, unscandalised, walk beside a sly-eyed young Bacchante, whose white breasts gleamed shamelessly beautiful in the dusk...

Wee Molly Isitt held a fawn in leash, that trotted sedately at her side, and two slim green nixies bestrode Dame Calder's pig—sweet-breathing cows came by beside the tossing antlered deer, the snarling village dogs, now harmless and friendly, playing between their pacing feet. Singing and waving branches of trees and garlands in the air, they wound away over the ridge that hid the village from the little church, and the sound of their singing was an echo in the listening air... yet Mr. Minchin waited, afraid, for the Preacher had not yet come forth.

The last chanting figure vanished, silhouetted against the blazing golden sky, and from the dark church door two figures came, shadowy among the shadows of the darkened churchyard, moving each by each—and as they went they gazed into each other's faces, rapt, enthralled—and suddenly, horribly, a pang of dread caught at the Reverend Thomas's once cold heart! For it was the Preacher—the Strange Young Man, his gay hawk-eyes bent upon his companion, his arm about her waist... and that companion, slim and young in pink flowered gingham, swinging her rose-crowned hat by its dangling ribbons, Rosamond Perkins!

Held by a spell he could not break, the wretched listener watched them approach, whispering, murmuring to each other, with little tender foolish sounds and laughter and beneath him on the path, pause and turn, rapt in each other's eyes. He saw, sharp in the moonlight that now strove valiantly against the fading gold, the face, upraised, ecstatic, of Rosamond Perkins, her red lips pouted, her blue eyes starry with love! He saw, bending to that kiss, the profile of the Stranger, hooked nose meeting lean chin, those dancing light eyes triumphant beneath those hornlike tufts of curling hair, his arms, now no longer surpliced, lean and muscular in the tattered shirt of the afternoon, clasped about the slender body of the girl that the miserable Thomas Minchin now realised he loved with all the yearning passion of a man at last awake to love!

How it happened exactly, the clergyman never knew, but at that moment the spell seemed to snap and he stumbled wildly forward, shrieking, desperate... for a moment the entire universe seemed to swing round him in a whirling dance, clouds and moon and sinking sun, crowding trees and reeling churchtowers, to the tune of a wild shouting and glorious laughter... and shaking, dazed, Mr. Minchin found himself standing on the path, a shaft of moonlight on his face, and Rosamond Perkins, quivering, smiling in his arms, her lips upturned to his! Dimly through a haze of rioting emotions he heard her voice—loving, eager, human.

"Yes, yes! I love you—I've loved you all along! Darling—I felt you loved me—and after your sermon tonight I knew, I knew!..."

"*My* sermon?" The Reverend gentleman was still dazed, but she patted his cheek with her hand and laughed triumphantly.

"Your sermon—your wonderful sermon! If you could have heard yourself—the glorious theme—the fire and eloquence!... If I had not loved you from the beginning, I should have loved you after tonight! You seemed all of a sudden to have dropped all your funny little stilted ways, your stiffness—the grim hardness and intolerance, that—(forgive me!)—seems to have so long enclosed your great and generous heart like the hard shell of a nut that is all sweet and wholesome and tender within... but tonight all this fell away, and you spoke like one who, long-prisoned in a dark tower, looks out into the open and sees the wide and lovely sky..."

Still dazed, but with his hand fast-locked in hers, Mr. Minchin turned towards the listening hills, the dark woods that seemed to watch him, the dusk-filled valley from which he still vaguely thought came an echo of joyous singing... They had gone again back to Their secret places, these dear strange People who had turned aside to teach him wisdom, and his heart swelled within him in love and sorrow that he could not thank Them, bless Them, tell Them his humility, his deep-hearted gratitude!

Mystified, the girl watched him, as, moving away a step, on an irresistible impulse he flung out both arms to the deep and smiling sky, and his voice, limpid, tremulous, rose to a joyful note that was almost a song.

"Oh great god Pan, I know Thee!—I thank Thee—I bless Thee... Thee and all Thy People great and small—for indeed, indeed beneath the mantle of the God whose name is Love, is there not room for all in His world to shelter?"

*

So Pan and his merry crew came to Little Ingleton, and so departed—and so the Reverend Thomas Minchin learnt humility. But deeply as he is now loved and revered by his flock—and indeed you would not know him for the same man—it is generally admitted that he has never again attained to quite the pitch of eloquence of that memorable Midsummer Day.

Through cautious questioning of his betrothed, the young clergyman established, much to his own private relief, that not one of the congregation that night, not even Miss Perkins at the moment when Pan, playing his last elvish trick, literally thrust them into each other's arms, had the remotest idea that any but their own accustomed priest had led the service... the truth lay hid in Mr. Minchin's breast, and there it was buried, gratefully and thankfully. Not one had dreamt of the Things of so strange life and shape and form that had elbowed them during that amazing Evensong—and in his undreamt-of happiness with his pretty wife the Reverend Thomas looks back upon that enchanted Midsummer Night with a deep and humble thankfulness,... For since that marvellous hour of sight—when for a little while the veil before his eyes was torn away and he saw horned beast of the field, wilful elf and goblin, faun and nymph, mingling with village maid and man, jostle together singing prayer and praise in the Church of Christ, he has walked humbly, tremblingly before men, and in his gentleness and understanding, his loving-kindness and readiness to forgive sin, his old cruel bigotry is long forgotten.

Only on one day in the year does he mystify the village a little, and that is on Midsummer Day—now a great holiday in Little Ingleton, when parson and flock betake themselves to the fields and woods, dancing and singing and feasting as in the old days, for joy of the dear green world, the warm sun and the merry pagan winds of heaven... And there is no stinting of the feast these days— good ale and foaming golden beer shoulder prim lemonade and gingerpop, and there is no lack of junket, and syllabub, of Granny Calder's recipe, to eat with the cakes and pies, the plum-starred buns... and the village foots it to the tune of ragged Peter's fiddle and old Dad Verity's drum till the moon rises glimmering over the tree-tops, and busy little Mrs. Minchin begins to gather up the food for distribution on the morrow to her beloved poor. But then her husband comes, and despite her eager puzzled questions, so frequent at first (though now she laughs and shrugs and lets it go, since he merely smiles and shakes his head!) silently, reverently the Reverend Thomas chooses a portion of cake, of fruit and wine, the best that remains, and disappears silently into the wood with his offering. There on a log or clear space of mossy turf, he lays his tribute, and after standing a moment with bowed head, goes softly away through the green shadows back to his flock, leaving behind him his yearly offering, libation to the old God who taught him wisdom, the God who was old when Christ was a stammering babe... the Great God Pan, who, in a whimsy moment, came and played parson to save a parson's soul.

THE DEVIL'S MARTYR

Signe Toksvig

Signe Toksvig (1891–1983) was a biographer, novelist, translator and writer born in Nykøbing Sjælland, Denmark. In 1905, Toksvig moved to New York with her family, where she graduated from Cornell University and went on to become assistant editor of *The New Republic*. Over the course of her career, Toksvig wrote two biographies: *The Life of Hans Christian Andersen* (1933) and *Emanuel Swedenborg: Scientist and Mystic* (1948). Her fictional works include the novels *The Last Devil* (1927), *Eve's Doctor* (1937) and *Life Boat* (1941). Toksvig was further published in the *New York Times*, *The Popular Magazine* and *Tomorrow*. She was the great aunt of author, comedian and broadcaster, Sandi Toksvig.

"The Devil's Martyr" was originally published in the June 1928 issue of *Weird Tales*, with the cover devoted to it. The story follows Erik of Visby, a young man living alongside staunchly devout monks with a fascination for flagellation. Following the arrival of a family friend, Michael of Lynas, Erik is taken to his rightful home as Count of Visby. Here, he learns that the Christian tradition is not the only way and is welcomed into the cult of Pan. Opposing modern religion with ancient beliefs, "The Devil's Martyr" aligns Pan with his satanic sibling, Baphomet. Suitably Gothic, the story explores themes of worship, ritual and martyrdom.

In the garden of the episcopal palace only the dragon-flies were stirring. They gleamed and darted over a little fountain pool, iridescent, energetic, careless of the summer heat that weighted the still leaves and the drooping flowers. They skimmed close to the thin silver line spouting from the statue, a small dilapidated faun; they circled in patterns of light around his weather-beaten head, making a vivid but hardly appropriate halo for it.

A boy lay close by the fountain, watching them. He was fifteen, tall for his age, and too slim for the black clothes he was wearing. Except for their colour they were those of any noble youth of his time: a doublet, close-fitting hose, a short surcoat, a fall of white lace around the throat. His brown wavy hair had a glint of gold in it, and framed a handsome face with definite features, black brows, dark blue eyes and curving red lips, contrasting oddly with his air of shy sensitiveness, his white thin cheeks, his pallid hands.

At the moment he was smiling as he watched the dance of the dragon-flies. He loved this spot; it was the only brightness in the great stiff garden where even in summer the cathedral aisles of elm and beech were dim and gloomy. His uncle the Bishop, whose ward he had been since his parents died, disliked the frivolity of flowers and advised the solemn avenues for ambulatory meditation. Young Erik of Visby had been sent out for that very purpose; a book of prayers lay forgotten on the moss beside him, but now if he noticed it at all it was only to see that the coruscating wings were more like jewels than the precious stones with which the missal was encrusted.

But a prayer-book will not be forgotten with impunity. Erik had no sooner discovered the living halo around the head of the queer little statue than a tall, thin cleric in a dark cowl appeared at the end of the avenue and looked about. He soon saw the boy and came noiselessly toward him.

"Do you call this devotion?"

At the sound of the metallic voice the boy jumped up and swung around, his hand flying nervously through his hair.

"Father Sebastian—I—" He choked with apprehension.

The monk lifted a long, slender hand and his large, light grey eyes widened.

"What were you sent out for?"

The boy hung his head, saw the missal and hastily picked it up.

"Not to lie here, gaping at a heathen stone! What made you do it?"

The boy rubbed the book with his sleeve but was silent.

"You don't know? Didn't something seem to pluck at you; didn't something draw you away from the avenue where prayers are easy to this place where you forget them?" Father Sebastian's face blazed into sudden anger and he shouted: "That was the Devil!"

Erik cast a terrified glance at the little grey faun, and his bewilderment was so evident that the tense, meagre face of the monk relaxed. He laid a pitying hand on the boy's shoulder.

"You didn't mean to let him. You forgot. But *he* is always watching; he took the shape of one of those gaudy flies to lure you away. My fault, too; I should not have left you so long."

Erik, looking down, could not see the watchful tenderness trembling in the thin lips; he only shivered to hear the words, "Come, we must do penance in the chapel, for the Lord is angry with us," and the monk walked toward the trees, bidding the wilting boy precede him, as if unwilling to leave him out of his sight again.

Erik went in a daze. When he passed from the hot, golden sunshine into the chill dark green of the avenue, he felt buried; it was like an endless tomb. It ran straight for nearly half a mile, walled in by ancient elms that branched sideways until they arched impenetrably into each other, high overhead. There was dead silence here, and awe. Had he been alone he would have run breathlessly to the far end where the sun shone. The anger of the Lord was ready to overwhelm him anywhere, but most terribly here and in the chapel. He shed a few unmanly tears. He would never have done that in his father's castle, five long years ago. But he was tired now, and weak with fasting and vigils, and his back still hurt from the last time he had done penance with the whip. It was no consolation that Father Sebastian, too, flagellated himself.

They were half-way up the avenue. Drops of light dappled it here and there. He could see two human specks moving about at the end of it. One had a reddish look, an unfamiliar colour. The other was wide and black; that was likely to be Father Laurence, the bishop's thrifty almoner, who had no taste for the whip.

It *was* Father Laurence. But to whom was he bowing?

Erik was dazzled. Dominant against the green leaves stood a big, broad-shouldered, dark-bearded knight, clad entirely in shimmering vermilion. Soft white plumes drooped from his hat, and a heavy gold chain about his neck glinted fierily. As Erik approached, staring childishly, the stranger watched him smiling; then as the two came into the sun he turned to Father Laurence:

"Is this the Count of Visby?"

Father Sebastian pressed forward and said sharply, "This is a boy entrusted to our care."

"True," the stranger deferred with a slight bow, "but is he not also Count of Visby?"

The almoner waved Father Sebastian aside. "You are quite right, my Lord, of course! What our brother means is simply, as you know, that Count Erik is the ward of his uncle the Bishop until he comes of age."

But the ascetic would not be denied. "This boy was vowed to us by his dying mother, and he should not be reminded of the empty title which he is about to forsake."

"As well as the domain of Visby which so conveniently adjoins the estate of the Order," the knight said, flicking his boot with his riding-crop.

Father Sebastian was about to answer hotly, but folded his arms, bent his head, and said with dignity, "Come with me, Erik, to the chapel."

"Not so fast, not so fast," the knight laughed, stretching out a long arm and gathering the boy to his side; "the reverend Father Laurence here will tell you that I have just come from the Bishop, who has given me permission to take away Count Erik for a month to my castle of Lynas."

The almoner nodded deferentially and drew his colleague aside, hissing at him, "Let him go! It is the Bishop's orders." Father Laurence was plump, but he had a firm jaw and small, practical eyes. Every gooseberry in the kitchen garden was known to him.

Erik stood quiescent within the arm of the red knight, not daring to take his eyes off Father Sebastian's white, pained face, and more than a little afraid of this man who had said he was going to take him away. But when the monks turned their dark backs to them and walked down the corridor of trees, he felt a strong hand press his shoulder.

"They're gone now, Erik. Would you like to come with me? I am Michael of Lynas. I knew your father."

A vague memory stirred in the boy and he looked up, shyly. The bronzed, bearded face was smiling, and the narrow dark eyes were full of kindliness. In a rush of confidence he begged, "Let us go now, before flagellation in the chapel!"

"By a thousand devils we will go!" swore the knight, shaking his gauntlet at the retreating monks. "My horse will carry us both."

They hurried away, the boy half hidden in the swirl of the vermilion mantle, and the clerics, turning back, saw them disappear around a corner.

Father Sebastian doubled his stride and began to mutter rapid prayers.

"What demon are you exorcising now?" sneered Father Laurence. "Surely the fasting and whipping you do is affecting your mind!"

"I see the Prince of the Air, robed in the red of eternal fire, carrying off a soul that was entrusted to me," cried the monk, beginning to run, "and he shall not!"

The other pursued him, clutching his cowl.

"You'll stay here or the Bishop will deal with you! I told you the Earl of Lynas is not known to you because he has been away in the East for ten years or more."

"Is that why you would trust him with a boy whom I have been preparing for the novitiate?"

Father Sebastian was icily scornful, Father Laurence endlessly sweet:

"Because you've prepared him so well he's certain to choose us when the time comes, and besides—but you wouldn't understand—for one month of his young kinsman's company the Earl is willing to drop the lawsuit about the western meadows."

"Sell all thou hast—" murmured the other, then asked bitterly, "Was Lynas right? Does the domain of Visby go to the order if Erik enters it?"

"Or if he dies. It does," said Father Laurence casually and bent down to uproot a presumptuous dandelion. "And what other heir is there, or who will administer it better?"

Father Sebastian stared into the sky, his face contracting. "I shall spend the month in prayer for him."

"If you want work," his colleague smiled, "I hear that witchcraft has broken out in the town again—healing with magic herbs and so on. They say that Dame Agnes and her pretty little daughter Karin—"

But Father Sebastian was walking rapidly away in the direction of the chapel. The almoner smoothed out the hole where the dandelion had been.

Twilight arose from under the trees and veiled the garden. The dragon-flies of the fountain folded their wings, and a serf came out to turn off the tinkling water. The world was still as the hovering moths.

There was quiet, too, between the blossoming hedges where Erik was riding. In the courtyard four men-at-arms had been waiting for them, and Earl Michael had caught him up in front of himself on a black stallion. Through the town it had pirouetted a little, but now it was trotting ahead peacefully enough. The rhythm almost put the boy to sleep, tired and weak with hunger as he was, and he soon found himself gently drawn back against the broad chest of the Earl. There he rested. A soothing warmth came from the firm strong body, and he marvelled dreamily at the even, magnificent thud of the heart. Now he remembered this man. Long ago, in the castle of Visby—he must have been very young—he had been brought into the great hall by his father, who had laughed and flung him into the arms of his friend, where he had lain still and heard the same reverberant heart-beat. He wondered would he ever see Visby again. He had given up asking Father Sebastian to let him.

The Earl reined in the horse violently. Erik nearly slid down but he was held in a steady grip. In the diaphanous northern evening, he could see that a body was lying across the road, the slight body of a girl, her kirtle torn and her long light hair tossed about her.

One of the men dismounted and brought her to his master. Thick amber hair fell away from a face as white as the hawthorn flowers. The Earl looked at her. "She's not badly hurt," he said. "Take her to the last house of the town."

Erik's heart sank. Often indeed had he been told that women were the favourite aids of Lucifer, but now he was only hoping that this poor hurt pretty thing would be helped by the powerful arm sustaining himself.

"Wait!" the Earl commanded, and Erik, following his gaze, saw a bundle of plants by the roadside. They were brought to the master, who examined them carefully. The boy waited breathlessly. Never had he seen anything so pitiful as the round white shoulder cut by a red gash.

At last the Earl said something in a foreign tongue; one of the men lifted the inert body in front of him; and the little cavalcade continued in the darkening shadows.

After a while the Earl remarked, as if he had been put in mind of it by the feel of Erik's ribs under the thin clothes, "Your Father Sebastian, what does he do besides starving you? I mean, what is he famous for; does he illuminate beautiful books of hours?"

"Oh, no," Erik answered with some pride, "before he came here he was a great exorcist of devils—four thousand and five hundred and forty-seven he drove out of one person's body once, he told me. And he has got sixty-nine witches burned—but only when they wouldn't renounce the Evil One; he says he doesn't hold with burning them if they confess and repent."

"Was that in the Bishop's town?" The Earl's voice was steely.

"I don't know, I think not; there's been none there for some years. No, now he practises austerities. He can fast longer and sleepless and pull the girdle of spikes tighter than anybody I know, and he hardly feels flagellation," Erik trailed off disconsolately.

"A proud martyr."

"He often tells me about the martyrs and how he envies them that they were let suffer for the love of the Lord—I can't understand—" he broke off, terrified at himself.

"The word 'love' seems strange to you?" the man asked tentatively, at the same time drawing the mantle closer. But Erik only shook his head, not wishing to risk injudicious confessions.

They rode more slowly now. The hoofs were sinking in a sandy road, and Erik could smell the salt tang of the sea and the spicy little shrubs and flowers that crouched near it. The strong air made him drowsy; he wanted to rest and ride forever. But the road turned, and soon there was the sound of sliding summer waves on a long beach. He started up.

"The sea?"

"The sound you'll hear day and night at Lynas. The place where I'll teach you to swim. Look!"

There was a wide bay in front of them, and into the bay a high tongue of land, and on that, dark and formidable against a pale green sky, rose a tall, square, turreted castle. One of the men sounded a horn, and lights gleamed in the deep slits of masonry, and the smoky red of torches flared below. With a grating whine the drawbridge was lowered, and hoofs clattered hollowly over it. Inside the gloomy courtyard forbidding grooms were waiting, men as tanned with another sun as their master himself.

Earl Michael dismounted. Losing his support, overwhelmed by weariness and the sharp air, Erik saw everything whirl about him. He was caught then, in the same strong arms, and carried into the castle like a child.

Darkness slid over his mind in long purling waves like the sea. When he began to rise out of it he heard low voices speaking a foreign language. He was conscious of hands running smoothly along his limbs, rubbing his feet, restoring heat to his body. If it were a dream, he would not wake up. He clenched his eyelids, he would force himself back to sleep, but soon he feared the cold grey matins bell would ring!

They were lifting him now; what a pity! they would see how hideous his back was with the scars from the whip. And then he heard a full round oath in a ringing voice that he knew—Earl Michael's. He was not dreaming! They were caressing his back with velvety oils; something silky descended over him; something pungent was held to his nose. He opened his eyes.

He was in a small but high-vaulted room suffused with marigold light and hung with verdant tapestries. Two women were leaning over him, but he saw only the anxious face of Earl Michael. He smiled to banish the concern, and the man touched his cheek gently.

"I was afraid they had left only your bones!"

He was given something strong and delicious to drink, and the light feeling in his head vanished. He looked around, first at the loose crimson silk mantle in which he was wrapped. The Earl was stately in a green, wide-sleeved, fur-brimmed tunic. The two women stood attentively in a corner. Their skin was brown; their eyes were black and humid. They were so dark to Erik's wondering glance that he involuntarily thought of a white fairness he had seen, and hair the colour of yellow amber.

He tried to sit up. "What happened to her?"

The Earl was puzzled. "To whom?—Oh, the girl we found! I forgot. I must—" He rose. "You'll hear later. To sleep now."

He was gone. The boy sank back to rest.

In another room of the castle, simpler and barer, the young girl of the road sat in half-darkness by an open fire. Shadows flickered on the walls and she did not notice that a door opened. Like a sudden apparition a figure stood before her, a tall man hid in a curious cloak of vivid green, terminating in a hood that was crowned by two small, hornlike plumes and a great emerald shining between them. His face was muffled, showing only the steady, burning eyes. He did not speak nor make any gesture, but the girl had no sooner looked up than her pale passivity changed into joyful awe. She threw herself at his feet.

"Lord!" she sobbed. "You have come back at last!"

"Have you kept the laws?" he asked in a thick, unnatural voice.

"Always," she replied; "my mother taught me what you taught her and the others of our faith. We have helped the good and hurt the cruel. Today I was going home with a bundle of healing herbs when the boys stoned me and called me witch."

"You know that they will always call you 'witch' and the god 'devil'?"

"I ask only to suffer for the god!" There was rapture in her face.

"You must stay at Lynas for a month and serve the young Count Erik, who will be one of us."

She nodded and sank down to adore him again. When she rose he was gone. She showed no surprise.

Erik woke with a start, his heart palpitating; had he overslept for matins? But slowly he worked forward to reality; thrilled with delight he looked out, not on imprisoning trees, but on an opal sea, calm and brightening into blue. A shining speck moved out beyond the far foamy line of the third reef. It came nearer; it was the Earl. Down on the strip of hard, white, sandy beach, sheltered by dunes that held the sun, Erik went to meet him. Laughing at the boy's fears, the man assured him that soon he, too, would be swimming, if not beyond the third, at least beyond the second reef; while Erik shivered, undressed against his will, pitifully thin and pale beside the other's brown muscularity. But after he had thrust himself into the clear, bracing saltiness, had come out alive, and lay baking in a fragrant nook of the dunes, he began to feel a new strength pulsating in his blood, and saw his skin turn pink in the sun.

There were meals with wines and savoury meats, and in the evening they went to a curtained hall lit by many candles held in sparkling flowers of glass. Silk hangings glistened along the walls, and rugs of strange patterns silenced the floor. Otherwise there was nothing except a divan wide and long, and soft as morning sleep. Here they lay, and musicians came with flutes and citherns while the two Eastern women danced for them. Erik felt he should hide his face, yet he did not, following with big eyes the whirling veils, the glittering bangles, the pliant movements. The Earl watched only him. They salaamed away, and in came the girl of the road with a guitar which she strummed while she sang plaintive songs of the people in a sweet, slender voice. Erik went to sleep.

The days went by, long days full of satisfied curiosities, the vigour of sea and sun, food and wine, dance and music and sleep. Erik seemed to grow visibly taller, heavier, stronger, and the monkish pallor soon gave way to a hard, clear tan. In the evening now, one or other of the Eastern women remained frankly coiled up by the side of her master. Karin, the girl of the road, stayed, too. Erik was teaching her to read, proud of at least one of his former accomplishments.

One night, the next before last of the end of the month, the Earl saw their lips meet over the big, black-letter book, and he stroked his pointed beard with satisfaction. When they were alone he said, "Now will you forsake the world, the flesh and—the devil?"

The boy ran his fingers gayly over the guitar. "I have a few surprises for Father Sebastian." At the thought of his former preceptor he pulled his black brows together. "You worship another god?" he dared.

Earl Michael was startled out of his bronze calm.

"What do you know of that?" he asked sharply.

"Nothing—except that Karin has told me that there is another— who loves love."

The Earl gazed at him, the long dark eyes narrowing intensely. Then he drew him down by his side, and while the yellow wax candles guttered in the glass candelabrum, and the night flitted in from the sea, he whispered to the boy.

There was indeed another god. He had many names, but the most unjust of them was the "devil." He was far older than that, and far different, but he had been branded with that name for so long that now even most of his worshippers knew him by no other. Among them there were both simple and gentle, and when they met together the priest of the god had to disguise himself even as a horned devil. He, Earl Michael himself, was now the priest here. Erik's father had been, and his mother must have suspected it. Later, when he was older, he too should be initiated into their community, and he should know the secret of the name of the god.

Suddenly Erik clung to him, half in feverish entreaty to know the god at once, half in panic fear, for a wind sprang up from the bay, puffing out the last of the candles, and they lay in a darkness that seemed to rustle and moan. But he was calmed by the strong steady presence so near him, and passionately he begged again to be let adore the god of the man whom he adored.

The Earl took his hand, and they went through the dark to a little door behind the hangings. Through it they stepped into absolute blackness. They stumbled along damp, dreadful passages where soft things flew past their heads and wet things hopped across their feet. At last a thin wand of light split the moist darkness, as an invisible door opened.

They were in a gleaming white colonnaded room that held, like the inner calyx of a flower, a golden cell in its centre.

Earl Michael clapped his hands, and the light vanished. Only one ray came like a shining path to them from this inner cell, and from there came also, faintly at first but approaching louder, a sobbing, thrilling music of flutes, strange, thin, reed-like flutes, evanescently and plaintively divine. The cell opened, and black polished stone glistened around them from circular walls. A black altar stood before a drawn curtain.

The boy knelt with bent head. The clear, frail music danced about him. Of a sudden it stopped. He looked up.

Doubly bright against the darkness of a deep niche stood a Greek marble statue—a naked god, a tall, young, beautiful, smiling god, with his head turned and his chin tilted a little, if he were following the last echoes of the air he had been playing on the reed flute in his right hand. Two small, stubborn horns were half concealed by his curls, and his ears were mischievously pointed.

But awe veiled the neophyte's eyes, vivifying the antique god, making him seem to breathe, to be on the point of raising the reed flute to his lips again.

Sonorously the priest vowed a new worshipper to Pan.

"He swears to be thy servant forever, never to reveal thy pact with him, never to renounce thee."

"I swear." Erik bowed his head. Again the aerial music floated about him, gayer, more lilting, more argent than before. The Earl touched his shoulder, and he rose. The curtain was drawn, the vision gone.

"How can I wait to begin the service of the god?"

"You have begun; in less than a year, when you come of age, you shall know everything."

"How can I go back to them, the torturers!"

"It will not be for long, and every night when you fall asleep you will be brought to me. Look at me! You will come to me!"

The dark eyes grew darker, more burning, boring into him; he felt drowsy. Every night he must come back to Lynas.

A horn shrilled insistently. It pierced at last even into the semi-hypnotic sleep of the young Count of Visby, and he sat up. He was in his own room, and a moment later the Earl came in.

"The Bishop's men are here, a day too early. Father Sebastian has had evil dreams and must have you back at once."

The boy whipped up, slim, tanned, lithe, confident.

"Shall I go? And you will stay here, at Lynas?"

The dark face brightened. "Go! I will travel no farther than just beyond the third reef!"

Erik rode under the Bishop's gate an image of radiant youth. The wind whirled out his short crimson cloak and the sun glittered in gold embroideries. Spurs jingled on the heels of his long, soft doeskin boots as he ran up the carved staircase of the palace, and louder even when he crossed the white oak floor of the Bishop's private room. He had seen his uncle rather seldom; this time he meant to make an impression on him.

The Bishop, a hawklike man, small and withered, sat in a high throne-chair, Father Sebastian on one side and the almoner on the other. They were ominously still, but the Bishop winced.

"You make a military noise, Brother Erik."

Erik scowled. He already felt himself Lord of Visby.

"My uncle," he began, and at the hardy sound of his voice the monks looked quickly at each other, "I will tell you that if ever I thought I must carry out my mother's wish, I think so no longer. When I come of age I go to Visby Castle. I do not remain here."

Then he strode out, leaving anger and bewilderment behind, yet he was a little anxious at the thought of Father Sebastian's face. The large, light grey eyes had scrutinised him in a new way, not with zeal, not with wounded affection, but with an icy, dangerous sort of interest.

Erik was no sooner back in his white-washed cell than there was a swift step in the corridor and a key turned in the lock. The jailers! He beat and kicked on the door, shouting imperiously that he, the

Count of Visby, demanded to be let free. When he had exhausted himself, a chilly voice came from the other side. Father Sebastian bade him go to bed and substitute penitential prayers for supper; then he went away hurriedly lest he should betray the tears he was shedding, bitter tears over the long years of soul-saving whose work had been undone in a month.

To bed! Erik looked at the narrow window high up and tested his climbing skill. Yes, he could perch up there. It was on the third floor; a combination of ledges on the outside wall could support daring feet to the ground. But as he looked down he grew dizzy, nauseated. Impossible!

He threw himself on the pallet. If he could only go to sleep! There had been a promise. The long black lashes would not stay down. He turned and fretted. The bell tolled twelve before the warm weariness of approaching sleep flowed through his body.

Then he thought he was awakened by flutes, and that the little fountain-statue from the garden was alive and sitting near him, but golden, not grey, and with clear laughing features, short stubby horns half hidden in curls, ears mischievously pointed. It beckoned to him, and he followed it without the slightest fear, through the narrow window and down the perilous ledges. Without exactly knowing how, he found himself at Lynas. As if in a lovely haze he saw Earl Michael, and there were dancing and music, food and wine, while Karin hovered over her guitar. Yet all was misty and brief and faded away in a troubled sleep.

He was still asleep when Father Sebastian came into the cell. The monk went whiter at the sight of him, and stepped back into the corridor.

"Is he there?" whispered Father Laurence.

"He is, but he was just as surely gone when I came in the night.

He must be watched today. It is best to let him run free and see what the evil spirit will prompt him to do."

The almoner began to smile, then suddenly he looked shrewd.

"Do you suspect him of dealings with—?"

"With Satan! How else would his whole character have changed in a month? Is it natural? And who took him out of the cell to which I alone had the key?"

"Watch him," said Father Laurence eagerly, suppressing the theory that Erik with the sure step of a sleep-walker could easily have got down from the window. "The Bishop will bear no witchcraft, even in his kinsman. And the law will be with him."

"Tomorrow," sighed Father Sebastian, "I will examine and have put to the question this Dame Agnes and her daughter of whom you spoke. Rumour has it that she was at Lynas too, and you say that they are both suspected—?"

"They are!" the other encouraged him. "But remember it is more important to root out the black art in high places!"

Erik awoke, his clothes soaked with dew, his body stiff, but with the glowing sense that the promise had been kept, and he would be prisoner only in the day. Karin had been there. He closed his eyes again and thought with leaping pulses of what she had told him of the joyous sabbaths. But could he not see her now? She, too, had left the castle.

Later in the day a servant came in with bread and water, and Erik, looking abstractedly at him, flamed with interest when the fellow made a little sign, a little secret sign which he had often seen Karin make. It flashed into his mind that the god had many worshippers, gentle and simple, and he waved the sign back. Instantly the man was changed from surly clay to humble alertness. Yes, he knew where Dame Agnes lived; he knew Karin. He would bring her that very day to a place near the garden, known, he felt sure, to him only. He scurried away.

The door was left open. Erik went out, cautious, watchful, but no one appeared to hinder him. A warm, bright day brooded quietly over the garden. He sauntered down to the fountain. Crimson-edged flowers grew by it, and he laid a few on the head of the chipped, unrecognisable statue. Then he flung himself on the soft moss, lulled by the crystal tinkle of water.

Someone was calling, "Master, master," in a low voice. It was the servant beckoning to him from the shrubbery. He ran after the man, who glided ahead of him along hidden paths that twisted in the thick underbrush surrounding the garden.

A monk, livid and haggard, attended by two big lay brothers, came out from the dark avenue, taking the same paths.

In a high outcropping of limestone, there were several hollows hidden by grass and creepers. Erik entered one to which the servant pointed, but the sun through the foliage made a flickering tracery on the floor of the little cave, and he saw nothing for a few seconds. Then he felt two smooth arms about his neck and heard Karin whispering his name. He held her hard against his body; he kissed her throat, her mouth; he felt himself infinitely removed from boyhood.

Into their bliss a sharp dry voice cut suddenly: "Bind the young witch. Seize Count Erik."

Lamed with surprise, he felt the girl torn from him. He tore out his little dagger, but it was sent spinning by one of the lay brothers and his arms were held behind him. Peering into his face were the terrible grey eyes of Father Sebastian, and the thin mouth was uttering strange words:

"Sathanas, I adjure thee to speak! Your name, tell me your name, and who sent thee into the body of this innocent lad?"

Erik gritted his teeth at him for an answer. The two were brought out. The lay brother with Karin went first, having bound her hand and foot and flung her over his shoulder as if she were dead. Her long, fair hair hung down, shining in the sun against the black cowl. Her eyes were closed, and no sound came from her. Soon she was out of sight.

Erik was locked into his cell, and his day went in wild apprehension for Karin and in vain attempts to dare an escape from the window. But dizziness overcame him whenever he climbed to the sill, and night found him sitting motionless. He did not even look up when the key grated in the lock and Father Sebastian entered.

The monk put a hand under his chin, forcing him to return his gaze.

"I have not lost hope for you. I will save you, the demon shall be cast out; only confess your sin and then renounce Satan!"

Father Sebastian's emaciated body trembled with suspense, and all the emotion that had not been flagellated out of him welled into his eagerly supplicating eyes.

But Erik was silent, cold. Boy no longer, he knew it would be worse than useless to ask about Karin. He sighed with relief when the monk abruptly quit him and he was left alone to try to sleep, to try to reach Lynas again as he had the night before.

It happened again, the little guiding faun, the bright hall of Lynas, Earl Michael's thrilling voice adjuring him to be steadfast, the sweet embrace of the girl, but all as if in a mist, more dimly seen than the first time. Under his joy there was a heaviness in his mind, a foreboding not clear to him.

*

He was dragged out of his sleep by Father Sebastian, who violently shook him.

"Unhappy, miserable boy! I came here in the night and found you gone. What choice had I but to tell the Bishop that you were off, unrepentant, with the Evil One? His Lordship's verdict is that even he can not save you from the death of a sorcerer. But confess, confess—renounce the Devil, and I will beseech the Bishop, your good uncle, to forgive you!"

He shook him again, in a passion to save him, but Erik remained silent. Father Sebastian knelt down to pray, and just then the door opened and Father Laurence came quietly in.

"Has he confessed?"

"He has not, but—"

"Then leave us. It is the Bishop's orders. He desires your presence. I have come from the witches."

The other left sorrowfully, reluctantly.

"Kind Father Laurence," Erik asked, "tell me about the—witches."

The almoner smiled calmly.

"They have confessed."

"Karin?" the boy shouted.

"No, not Karin, yet. But the mother has confessed that she knows you have sold yourself to the Devil. And now they are bringing the girl into the torture-chamber where she, too, will confess."

"Never!"

"Never?" Father Laurence brought his smooth face quite close to the boy's and almost purred, "Never? But you don't know what happens. First they will strip her quite naked. Then she can not conceal any devilish charm to keep her from speaking. One can never be sure about that. Such things can be kept even in the hair. So they will cut her hair off, and shave her. Everywhere, do you understand? The hangman and his helpers will touch her fair white skin everywhere."

Erik leaped up. "Where is my dagger? I'll kill you with my hands! Where is Earl Michael?"

The almoner chuckled, "His master the Devil drowned him the day you left when he was swimming out beyond the third reef in his foolhardy pride. But the girl is still alive and you can save her, if you will!"

"I will do anything!"

"Confess then," he suddenly thundered, "that you have made a pact with the Devil!"

Erik sank back on the pallet, exhausted, his head whirling with the half-understood words about Earl Michael, but his voice was firm: "I can not."

Father Laurence was suave again. "And then when the hangman has shaved her body, he will take a long sharp needle and puncture her with it. For where the Devil has put his mark on a witch she has no feeling, at any rate Father Sebastian says so, and if she doesn't scream when the needle is pushed far into her flesh they know they have found the mark. Even so she may not confess. But there are ways—I think perhaps they will lock her legs between two iron plates and screw them together. They can break the bones and start the marrow from them—" He paused expectantly.

"I will confess. Only save her!" Erik moaned.

The monk called, and a clerk entered carrying a parchment.

"Write down," the almoner commanded, "that Erik, Count of Visby, confesses of his own free will that he has entered into a compact with the Devil—"

Erik nodded. "Save her," he whispered.

"Wait—the said Count Erik now renounces the Devil and all

his works and is ready to expiate his sin in whatever way we decide to recommend to the secular arm."

With shaking fingers Erik signed this, and Father Laurence started to leave when he was met by Father Sebastian, white and strained.

"Has he confessed?"

"He has."

"Praise God!" the other declared ecstatically. "I have obtained grace for him from the Bishop, should he confess."

Erik burst out, "Father Laurence just promised me that Karin would not be tortured."

Father Sebastian looked blank. "The young witch? But she has been tortured already. As she would not confess she is to die by fire. Think about your own immortal soul, my poor boy!"

Crying out, "He tricked me, and I recant my confession; I lied, I said what I did only to save her! I lied, I lied!" Erik fell unconscious to the floor, looking suddenly as pallid and thin as he had looked a month ago.

Father Sebastian bent over him tenderly, tears flowing.

"This is very terrible—"

"It is—I can not understand," said the almoner, "why the Bishop should have changed. When I left him he understood he could not pardon even his own nephew if he confessed so abominable a crime. Especially as the accomplice must die—"

"She dies because she would *not* confess. Then there can be no mercy. That is the law. Who knows it better than I? Alas, if Erik persists in recanting his confession, he too must die for his soul's sake. But I may yet save him!" He buried his face in his hands.

The placid, practical face of the almoner twisted suddenly into fury. He thrust out an unyielding jaw and hurried off to hammer the Bishop again.

*

When Erik recovered consciousness he found he was clothed in his former black garb. The two monks were both beside him, but as he looked from one to the other they seemed changed. They were mild and grave. He determined to test them.

"I do not confess," he said defiantly.

Father Sebastian bent his head.

"I accept that," he said.

"What will you do with me?"

The almoner said hastily, "You will soon be of age now, and the Bishop, although he is not well and can not say good-bye to you, desires us to take you to Visby Castle."

Erik rose unsteadily. He could hardly walk, but they were ready to lead him. Father Sebastian supported him down the stairs. In the courtyard a carriage was waiting. They drove away in stony silence through the long tomb of sad dark trees, and he glanced at the little fountain where the sun was bright on the water and the statue sat grey and pensive. His thoughts hovered like the dragon-flies above the tragic contents of his mind without touching it, without remembering anything except when they rolled cumbrously into the great park of Visby full of gracious open spaces and gay with flowers. It suddenly came to him that here he had been happy. He pointed out childishly that there he had learned to shoot arrows at a target, and there he had learned to ride. But his companions were grimly still.

As if wandering in a dream he walked between them into the castle, and then Father Laurence opened a door. Erik stepped back. The cry of a terrified animal broke from him.

The room was hung from ceiling to ground, from door to window, in long, dead, merciless folds of black, and it was empty—empty except for a low block in the centre, and by this there stood immobile a masked man in black with a cold bright sword in his hand. His eyes rolled white through the mask and he took hold of the boy.

Father Laurence read in a voice of iron from a large parchment.

"Erik, Count of Visby, as you are a nobleman and a kinsman of his, the Bishop has recommended you to the favour of death by the sword, although the death for an unrepentant sorcerer is by fire. Executioner, do your duty."

Then he strode out, his sandals clattering on the stone.

Erik tore himself loose. The ultimate fear crazed him. He shrieked: "Father Sebastian, I confess, I renounce! Let me live!"

The monk took him in his arms. "You shall live, by all the Martyrs!" he exclaimed, but even as he held the boy he felt him cease shaking. He saw him raise his head, saw the colour come back into the pale handsome face, saw that Erik was listening intently to something. He too listened, but heard nothing, except a starling that fluted sweetly on a branch beside the open window. Erik stood straight now, with a radiant, exalted air.

"Forgive me," he said, as if to an invisible presence; and then to Father Sebastian, "I do not renounce the Devil. I *am* his. If I were not I would be. I love him. Make me his martyr."

With sure step he walked over, knelt and laid his head on the block. He smoothed the brown wavy hair with a glint of gold in it down over the dark-blue eyes.

Father Sebastian hid his face.

*

Afterward he wrote his side of this true story in the Latin chronicles of the Bishopric, and his last words were:

"And so, without a groan of pain or a word of piety, his head fell to the ground—God grant that his soul did not fall into eternal fire."

BEWITCHED

Willard N. Marsh

Willard Marsh (1922–1970), published here as Willard N. Marsh, was an American author and professor born in Oakland, California. Known by the nickname "Butch", Marsh funded his place in college using his musical talents, performing as Will Marsh and the Four Collegians. He was a prolific genre writer, publishing works in *The Magazine of Fantasy and Science Fiction*, *Worlds of Tomorrow*, *The North American Review* and dozens more periodicals. He was also brother-in-law to John Williams, author of *Butcher's Crossing* (1960) and *Stoner* (1965), until his divorce. Marsh's fiction includes the short stories "Astronomy Lesson" (1954), "Machina Ex Machina" (1956) and "Forwarding Service" (1963), as well as the collection *Beachhead in Bohemia* (1969).

"Bewitched" was first published in the March 1945 issue of *Weird Tales*. Familiar themes return in this poem: that of the untamed wild, rustic music, a long-departed Pan and the ancient world resurfacing for those who would hear it. Here, the speaker finds themselves trapped among the harmonies of the horned god. When read alongside "The Haunted Forest" by Edith Hurley and "Forest God" by Dorothy Quick, we can see how the Pan poems of *Weird Tales* often struck a note of longing and loss.

This timeless garden, like a thing diseased
Has flung a green veil round its leprous face
And deathless evil blooms are tightly squeezed
Within the unkempt vine's obscene embrace.

In other days this setting must have heard
The cloven hoofs of Pan, and as he spun
The witching harmonies that lured the bird
From flight, its growing for a time was done.

And now the whisper of a magic pipe
Has filtered through to me from yesterday:
An ancient, half-forgotten dream is ripe—
And caught, I grope and cannot find the way.

THE GOLDEN BOUGH

David H. Keller

David H. Keller (1880–1966) was an American author and psychiatrist born in Philadelphia, Pennsylvania. Having graduated from the University of Pennsylvania Medical School, Keller then served as a neuropsychiatrist in both World Wars I and II. Publishing dozens of short stories in contemporary pulp magazines, as well as writing numerous essays, Keller's work is often marked by its conservatism and pessimism. Notable publications include the novels *The Human Termites* (1929), *The Metal Doom* (1932) and *The Devil and the Doctor* (1940), as well as various short works such as "The Revolt of the Pedestrians" (1928) and "The Thing in the Cellar" (1932).

"The Golden Bough" was first published in the November 1942 issue of *Weird Tales* and shares its name with an influential treatise on mythology and ancient religion by James George Frazer. The story follows the newlywed couple, Paul Gallien and Constance Martin. Constance, following a vivid dream, pleads with Paul that they find the house that she imagined. However, when they eventually do so, she starts to hear the music of Pan. With familiar themes of temptation, trickery, rustic music and the moon, "The Golden Bough" is a haunting Gothic tale which presents the unique ambivalence of Pan.

"**L**ast night," she said, "I had a dream. In that dream I saw a house in a dark forest. Now that we are married let us travel till we find that house, for it is there that I want to live."

Paul Gallien smiled as he looked at his bride of a few hours. This was her first request, and long ago he had promised her that her first request after their marriage should be granted, no matter what it was. This idea of hunting a dream house seemed a peculiar one but he decided it would be fun—and besides he had promised.

Gallien was of royal blood, but it was in an age when royalty was no longer fashionable; so he contented himself with the other things he had inherited and forgot about the title. He had been bequeathed money, pride which held his head high, courage and a kindly manner. He had married Constance Martin knowing little, and caring less, about her ancestry. All that concerned him was the plain fact that they were in love.

So Gallien and his bride started eastward through Europe, with no definite destination, simply sliding over the hills and down through the valleys in search of their dream house. For Constance often said to her husband:

"I shall not have any trouble in knowing the house when I see it. When we find it we shall rest there a long time till the remainder of my dream comes true. It is a house in a dark forest and it is as real as the pot of gold at the end of the rainbow. I know you are laughing at me, but it is not a wild goose chase. We are seeking an actuality."

*

As they slowly drove through the country or sat over their meals at little taverns or enjoyed the sunsets at the close of the day, they talked of the dream house and Gallien asked a thousand questions. Was it a house or a castle? How large was it? Was it habitable or just a mass of ruins? Were they really to live there? Was there a library? Fireplaces? Thus, through long conversations they discussed the most important details of their search.

Gallien did not care, so long as he could spend twenty-four joyous hours with Constance; he did not care if the journey never ended, if only she remained contented and happy. On and on, day after day, they went and finally came to a dark forest. There the giant pines rose a hundred feet upward before branching. There was a hush in the air and a peculiar absence of little living things, which made all still and unusually quiet. The ground was covered with a heavy matting of pine needles. In some of the little open spaces thick moss shone softly green against the copper background of the dry spills. Circles of moist ground were ringed round about by toadstools which glowed waxy-white in the dim, uncertain light; on high bare rock shelves fool's gold glittered in the occasional sunbeams.

From the lofty branches of the pines, cones had fallen on the road; these crackled loudly under the tyres, but this and the throb of the engine were the only sounds that broke the eerie stillness. The road crossed over other roads, yet here and there, bunches of wild grass grew in the wagon ruts, showing how old the road was and how seldom used. Gallien throttled the engine down till the car made only a few miles an hour; they drifted rather than rolled; seeming to sail into a dreamland of ethereal beauty. At times an unexpected ray of sunshine illuminated a part of the forest, like light breaking through the multi-tinted windows of a Gothic cathedral, and for a moment the heart paused in its beating with the beauty of it all.

They came at last to a fork in the road. The main road went on down into the valley; the other climbed in tortuous curves, up the mountain. When the woman saw that up-winding road merging into the pines she whispered, as though anxious that no one, save her husband, should hear:

"Let us go that way. What a beautiful road! Where will it take us? What shall we find at its end?"

"I know," replied her husband, as he turned off the main road. "We shall go on and up and on and up, and at the end we shall come to the home of a woodcutter or a charcoal burner and, after much trouble, we will turn around and come down again."

"Let's do that!" she urged enthusiastically.

Gallien was not correct, however, in his prophecy, for at the end of the road was neither hut nor peasant burning charcoal. Rather, there was a house in the woods. Constance Martin Gallien looked at it once and looked at it twice; then covering her face with her hands started to cry. Her husband, who now was accustomed to her moods, gently drew her to him saying nothing until her sobbing ceased. At last she lifted her head from his shoulder and turned a smiling face to him, saying:

"How stupid! But it was joy, Paul, that made me cry and nothing else. Now we have come to the end of our search, for this is the house of my dreams—and in it I want to live a long time—till I know what life is and the real definition of love."

Gallien looked at her, surprised and slightly disappointed.

"I did not know your plan included really living here. I am sure it would be a splendid place to stay for a little while if we had servants and could entertain and had all the little accessories to make life comfortable and pleasant, but none of these things can be had here. Still, if you want to, we will stay here, if possible, for a few days. Perhaps after a day and a night of it you will be glad to go on with me to some city where there is light and laughter, music and dancing."

Constance jumped out of the car.

"At least we can see what it is like! I called it a house, but it is really an old castle. I am sure it must be very old. Do you remember anything about castles, Paul? Could you tell how old this place is just by looking at it?"

He looked at the rough stone-walled building; the weathered parapets, then shook his head.

"How can I tell? But there is a part of your answer. See that tree? The one growing near the wall? That was not there when the castle was built. It would have afforded too easy an access to the windows. No doubt when the place was built all the trees within a hundred yards were cut down so if an enemy attacked the castle they would have no shelter. This one tree, surely, and perhaps all the others, must have grown since that time. Some of them are five feet in diameter. This road must have been built by the Romans. Maybe part of this castle was built by them. Shall we go inside? No one lives here save bats and toads. However, we can look around and go on until we reach a town."

But again he was in error for, circling the wall, they came to an old woman, seated on a three-legged stool, herding a few goats and geese. Gallien spoke to her first in French and then in German, but she only smiled at him toothlessly. Constance tried Italian, and at once there followed a conversation that glittered in explicatives as a summer storm is forked with lightning. At the end of ten minutes the bride turned to her puzzled husband.

"You did not know I could do that?" she asked. "I was raised in a convent in Rome. This old dame says she is the caretaker of the castle. Years ago the owner went to war and simply told her to look after the place; that if anyone came who wanted to live here, to rent it for a certain sum in gold. She says there is everything in the place for comfort and she will serve us. Her people live in the valley and will bring us food. She prefers to live here with her pets."

The aged woman took the bride's hand and whispered. Tears brimmed Constance's eyes as she translated:

"She says the man who went to war years ago was her lover. They were happy here for a month and a day. Since he has gone she just stayed here, with her memories for companions."

The dame showed them through the castle. They were surprised to find it so comfortable in its homely simplicity. Throughout there were signs of great age; but all had been well and lovingly cared for. A slight chill was over all, but it was not dampness; the walls were dry. The woman asked if they wished her to build fires. Constance looked pleadingly at Paul. Half reluctantly he handed the woman five pieces of gold, the price of a month's service. Thus it was that they came to live in the dream house, now materialised as a castle in the Dark Forest.

Many were the rooms in the castle which the lovers thrilled over, but two delighted them especially, each in a different way. One was a library, with solid walls and a long, horizontal slit of a window through which the sun came from morning to night, and time could be told by the position of the beam of light. The first streaming light of morning fell on Eve, graven in pink marble, conscious of the knowledge gained by the fall in the Garden. Just before night came the last light which fell on a bronze man, tortured by the surety that he must die before he achieved to the wisdom greater age might have taught him. Between the marble Eve and the bronze man were books of every size, cover and age. Paul Gallien knew that he would be very happy in this room.

The other room was a bedroom. The floor was of wide, oaken boards covered here and there with bear skins. A bridal chest was the only furniture, save a large four-poster bed standing central in the room, and was, according to the ancient guide, the best bed in the castle. Her eyes glistened as she looked at it—glistened through tears. Many narrow windows completed one side of the room; casement windows, which could be opened, giving the night full freedom to enter. Decorations there were none; no pictures nor draperies; simply the chest and the bed.

Constance, beholding the bedroom, quivered with delight.

"This will be our room," she said and requested that the bed be aired forthwith and made with fresh clean sheetings. Thus, one was happy because of the library and the other because of the bedroom and each pleasured in the joy of the other.

For a week they did nothing but explore the castle and the dark woods surrounding it. During that week the automobile stood where they had left it.

The road ran past the castle and on through the woods to a sudden ending at a sharp precipice, making an edge to the mountain. A mile below they could see a little mountain stream decorating the mottled green of the valley like a silver ribbon, lying haphazard. Standing on the very rim of the world one day the lovers felt that here was truly the end of a long trail. Constance turned to her husband saying:

"Will you do one more favour for me?"

"If it will make you happy," he replied with a kiss.

She looked at him anxiously, twisting in her indecision.

"All my life, dear, I have wanted to be happy in just this way. I do not understand my emotions—but I do know that I am happy and that I am fearful lest something spoil it all. I want to stay here. At night I wake up crying, and I know the tears come because I cannot bear to think of leaving. Ever since I dreamed of this place I have wanted it, and in it I have found, not quiet peace, but a tumultuous rapture—expectation of what I know not nor why.

"This I do know; that if I have to leave here I shall die with longing to return. I can't bear to look at the car; it is a symbol of roving; it means that some day you will ask me to sit on the seat beside you and ride to the cities you delight in. When I see it standing there a dark despair fills my heart."

"Suppose I take it down to the village and store it?"

"No! Because then you can claim it again. I want— Oh! I know it is silly, but I want—I must have you do it! Start it and let it go down over the side—here. When I know that it is down there, crushed and broken, a mile below me, I shall sleep in peace—the fears of the great cities will no longer torture me with the menace of their nearness!"

Gallien drew a deep breath. "'Tis a good car," he said simply.

For answer she clung to him, trembling in the fierceness of her desire. And, because he loved her, he asked her to wait for him. Without looking at her again he went and drove the car within ten feet of the lip of the ledge. Stepping out, he threw on the gas and let it go free. Up it plunged into the air and down it fell—like a fallen star, striking so far below that no noise came to tell them of its destruction.

The man looked at the woman, and on his face was a twisted, bitter smile, but the woman, with eyes shut, breathed deeply, peacefully. Nor did she rouse from her seeming sleep for a long time and then only to kiss him passionately, lapsing again into her dreams. Thus it was dark before they returned to the castle.

The old woman was anxious about them, for seeing the car gone when she returned from her herding, she thought they had left for further adventuring; a new life, perhaps, in the great, to her unknown, cities, where her lover had gone whistling in the days before the war.

Thus the springtime came and went, and summer brooded warmly over the dark forest, in all its sweet majestic beauty. Time passed happily, though slowly, through long months. More and more time Gallien spent in the library, while Constance, in a long, happy daze, spent hours on the bed dreaming of the future and of dreams already come true. The dame had shown her dresses of ladies long dead, and more and more frequently the bride wore these gay things of past ages, and more and more she wore her hair braided down her back in two long ropes, falling below her knees; and more and more she passed the minutes looking through the windows into the dark forest.

One day she noticed that the room was but twenty feet from the ground and that the ivy covering the wall formed a perfect ladder for adventurous feet. That night she could not sleep. The old woman in her walled-off bedroom slept, dreaming of her long dead lover and the beautiful wild thing in the forest that had come to her through him. Gallien, tired from a day of study, slept dreamlessly. Under the flagstones in the kitchen the cricket slept, but Constance Martin Gallien, wide-eyed and pulsing-hearted, lay with her face in the moonbeams. Sleep she could not. In the dark forest there was neither song of bird, hoot of moon owl nor howl of far-away wolf. There all slept.

*

Then came the near music of a pipe, the thin-trilling, few-noted music of a pipe, and Constance, without knowing that she knew it, realised that the tune was the oldest in the world contained in one octave, but encompassing every dread and exultation known to mankind throughout the ages. Even in bed her fair body wove from side to side as she lay listening to the music of the pipe. Not being able to bide longer she ran to the casement where she saw a man making the music, and around him in silent circles, were geese and goats. The man sat on a rock and made mad music in the moonlight.

The woman put on a pair of slippers, crept into a black silken robe, and inching to the window climbed down the ivy. Her feet hardly touched the ground as she sped to the rock, broke through the circle of goats and geese and came near to the man who was making the olden music. As he came to the end of his song, and the music died in the murmuring notes, mixed with the mellow moonbeams, he looked at her with a glad smile.

"You like my music?"

"It's wonderful! Who are you and where did you learn to play?"

"I have always lived around here; this is my home. I never learned to play. I always knew how. Only one piece, but it can be played in an infinity of ways. Would you like to hear more? Come here, beside me, while I pipe for you."

Then he played in a livelier manner, and the goats and the geese stepped a gay measure to the music. Round and round the rock they went till at last Constance joined them. Between a goat and a goose she danced till there was an ending to the music. She rejoined the man on the rock, flushed and breathless, happier than she had been in all her life.

"Oh! I am so happy!" she whispered, entranced.

Throwing back his head he laughed, revealing glistening white teeth in the moonlight.

He tossed his arms upward. In one hand was the pipe, in the other there was nothing, and with that hand he clutched at moonbeams. Again he laughed gaily.

"'Tis wonderful to be happy. Men and women used to be happy. I seem to remember this place being filled of a night with bravely dressed men and dainty women in love, and sometimes the men piped for the ladies to dance, sometimes the men loved for the entrancing of their women, and which pleased the women the more, the music or the loving, how can I, being a man, tell? Those days are gone save in my memory, and I am not sure even that serves me honestly. At least, I now have no audience save such as you see."

Suddenly she turned to him and asked:

"Who *are* you?"

"What does that matter so long as my music thrills you?"

"It does make me glad. Weeks ago I dreamed of this place and asked my husband to find it with me. He did. I asked him to destroy the car so we would not be able to leave. He did. I want a son—a gay, gladsome son—who will be able to catch the moonbeams and play the pipes. Can he give me that son?"

"Perhaps, but what odds? If you want a son, I will tell you how. Have you seen the pool of dark water over the hill on the other side of the castle? No doubt the old lady told you not to drink there—that it was poison. Near the water is a giant oak. Now you must do thus and so—"

Slowly, for an hour he held her hand, telling her just how she should do and why and if she did this and the other as he directed, the desire of her heart would be granted. He promised that on every moonlit night he would sit on the rock, playing the pipe for her pleasurance and thus, when her child was born, it would be a child of great joy and wondrous beauty; a player of ancient tunes upon the pipes; a gatherer of moonbeams and star dust.

She walked slowly back to the castle, climbed the ivy, put off her shoes and her black silken robes, she stole again to her husband's side, while he, never having wakened, snored peacefully, for that he had never knowingly wronged anyone. Constance, awake beside him, heard him snore and still in her soul rang the unearthly sweet music of the stranger's pipe, she could not help contrasting the two. Placing one ear against the pillow she covered the other with a mass of hair and a pink palm. Thus she slept, lulled to calm by the memory of that soul-engulfing liquid music of the moonlight. The next morning she woke and could not tell whether it had been a dream or a reality. Her husband was still asleep but she woke him with a torrent of kisses and then was unable to tell him of the night or her desires.

The same day the old woman left the castle and wandered through the dark forest till she met the man who had played the pipes. She kissed him tenderly and ran her fingers through his tight-curled hair and over his pointed ears. At last she took courage and asked him to play no more at the castle till the woman and the man departed.

"But you were asleep last night," he answered her.

"Yes, but I saw the tracks around the rock and the woman's footprints, mingled with those of the animals and the birds; so leave her alone, for the sake of your mother."

For reply he only laughed and ran away in big skipping leaps.

The mother was worried. She had never been able to tell whether she had created a simpleton or a God.

Constance began to prepare according to directions of the man who piped in the moonlight. There had to be a ladder, a sickle and a white sheet. Some of those things could only be got by the wiles of a cunning woman. Finally all was ready. With burning heart she undressed and pretended to sleep on her pillow. But while sleep came swiftly to her husband she remained wide-eyed and anxious till she was sure of his slumber. She donned her robe and slippers. Tying the sickle in the sheet and the bundle to her back, she went out the window to the ivy and down to where the ladder rested against the wall. Lifting the ladder to her shoulder she tiptoed westward from the castle to the place of the pool of dark water.

It was moonlight and the shadows and the moonbeams made curious fairyland of the dark forest. Though her heart was beating fast—fast—there was a song on her lips, a very old song, such as could have been sung within one octave or upon a very simple pipe. She came at last to the old oak tree which grew by the dark pool and drank of its water.

Placing the ladder against the scabby bole she looked upward. On the first branch, just a little above the ladder, grew a spray of mistletoe, its green leaves, white berries and grey stems all shimmering in the eerie moonlight. Taking the sheet she spread it evenly over the ground under the parasite plant; on the sheet she placed the sickle. Now she loosened the two long braids and let those dark, wondrous tresses come in freedom, one in front and one behind her body, which she freed from her silken robe and white gown. Taking the sickle in hand, she, trembling, started up the ladder.

Near the top she paused. The mistletoe was within her reach. She still hesitated, and while she did so—was it the wind?—a long strand of hair reached over and entwined around the grey branched parasite. The woman looked at the union of plant and hair, then slowly reached and freed herself. With the curved knife she began cutting the plant from the oak, being careful to take a large piece of the bark with the roots of the plant in it. With the last slash the mistletoe fell earthward, but on the shadowed sheet, which was as it should be, for all in vain had it touched the heart. Then this last of the Druid worshippers descended the ladder carefully and placed wet moss over the cut bark, tying it tenderly in the white linen sheet. The ladder she slid into the dark pool and did up her hair and put on her clothes. With ineffable joy in her heart, she tripped back to the castle. Somewhere in the dark, moon-spangled forest a laughing man piped a very old tune, and she, hearing him sang the song to his music.

Back in the bedroom she found it still light from the moon. On the headpost of the bed, on the side on which she slept, she fastened the freshly cut bark placing the wet moss over and around it, and wrapped it all with the white sheet which she tied in hard knots. Thus was the mistletoe grafted onto the oaken bed, just a foot above her pillow. She kissed the white fruit, and loosening her hair fell asleep.

Thus Paul Gallien first beheld her in the morning; on her face the smile of infinite peace. Her slippers, kicked wantonly from her feet, he found were wet, and her silken robe stained with dew.

"She is a queer little wild thing, and so far I cannot tell what she is doing. Perhaps the old woman can help me," he spoke to himself as a feeling of frustration and futility settled over him as a raincloud envelopes a mountain peak.

The next time one of the girls came up from the village with fruit, Gallien took her and the old woman into the kitchen where by the girl's little knowledge of French made the woman understand what he needed to know. Sighing, she bade the girl leave them.

She then led Gallien to the library where she found him a very old book with pictures in it, and, crossing herself, left him. Gallien began the study of that book, even as young men have studied it in all centuries past.

The young bride woke, saw the mistletoe, smiled and went to sleep again. When next she woke, she dressed. After dinner she took the silver pitcher and in it carried water from the dark pool, as was her wont each day, for the moss must be moist for the grafted parasite to grow. And it grew. Finally it spread all over the head of the bed, fastening here and there to the ancient oak, and seeming to sap the life from it.

At last Paul Gallien solved the secret of the book and understood the conduct of his wife. Now while in the library he slept so when night came he was able to stay awake. The full moon passed, the dark of the moon had come and gone; now the crescent moon was growing larger, thriving on her diet of stars.

The first night of the watch Constance slept as though drugged. So satisfied was her husband with her sound sleep that he arose, lit a candle, and sat on the bridal chest, watching her. It was dark in the room and he decided that when she stirred he would blow out the candle, even though by so doing he would be alone with the shadowless things.

Her girlhood beauty was now ripening into the full bloom of womanhood; her white face shone like a pearl amid the blackness of her loosened hair which covered the pillow. Above her shadowed masses of the grey mistletoe, green leaves and white berries. Even as he looked a branch drooped slowly, until it rested on her breast. The ringlets of her hair seemed to curl upward from the pillow to interlace, caressingly, with the green leaves. All her fair body was at last covered with black hair and green plant. She smiled as though her dream were giving her great joy. Now and then her lips moved—as if caressing a lover.

The next nights were the same. Then came a fuller moonlight and the woman was restless. She tossed by her husband with little murmuring cries.

"I cannot sleep," she sobbed. "Life is too full. There is so much love and happiness in the world, why should a woman spend her life sleeping?" She flung herself passionately into her husband's arms, smothering him with kisses, wrapping her hair all about him.

"Life is too short!" she cried again and again.

He tried to satisfy her and calm her, but at last pretended to sleep. She lay quietly by him, but he knew by her short, sharp breathing that she was wide awake and restless. Then, through the sweet, resinous air of the moonlit forest came the sound of music. Constance sat upright. She listened to her husband, then satisfied that he was asleep, she ran to the window. There on the rock sat the laughing man, surrounded by the goats and the geese and the tune he played was a very old one, all within one octave. Drawing on her leather slippers, she climbed down the ivy, hurrying on eager feet to join the dance.

Paul Gallien stood in the shadow and watched her dance, all lovely and exotic in the moonlight with the goats and the geese who paced sedately with her. After the dance she sat on the rock with the man who clutched moonbeams.

"Is all well with you?" he asked her.

"All is well. The plant is growing on the oak bed. Every night the spirit enters my body. I never knew how exquisite real happiness could be. The thought of your love and your music fills my every thought."

"Life is naught without love," replied the man, laughing, as he reached into the air for the moonbeams. "Keep the plant well watered, my dear. Whenever you are not sure of yourself, follow me."

As Gallien watched from his window he thought of the old book with its pictures and knew that he had but little time to spare. Below, in the little room next to the kitchen, the old dame heard the music, crossed herself, kissed the silver cross which hung from her neck, prayed and remembered other such nights, long years gone by. She determined to ask the strangers to leave before it was too late.

The next day the young woman made her usual visit to the dark pool, carrying her little silver pitcher, while her husband went to the little village at the bottom of the valley for letters and food. There he talked with some of the young men and they went far away with a mule team, and in a week came back with a number of long iron pieces of pipe.

Came a day when Constance went to the dark pool, carrying her little silver pitcher and instead of the dark pool of water there was but a mud spot; nothing save the slime of the ages, and on the slime rested the ladder. Angry, she walked around the edge of the muddy hole and at last found where the water had all drained through long iron pipes. She looked at the giant oak and saw all the mistletoe on it was turning golden, a sign of dryness; death, decay. Crying, she ran back to the castle with her empty pitcher. Up to her bedroom!

Her husband was there arranging some of his ties. She ignored him as she ran to her side of the bed. There was no mistake. The love plant was indeed golden, on the bed as on the tree. It must have water every day from the dark pool; and now it was dead from the lack of it. She touched it, pityingly, and the leaves dropped off. All the dried berries rolled in a pitter-pattering across the floor; all the dark green had turned to golden brown. She faced her husband.

"Why did you do it?"

"Do what?"

"Drain my pond?"

"I was afraid of malaria. It was the only place like it on the mountain and I did not want you to be sick."

"Fool! Fool! FOOL!" she shrieked. "If you had only asked me. Now all life is dead for me!"

"I still live," he said kindly.

At that she burst into tears and ran to him and caught him in her arms.

"I didn't mean it," she sobbed. "I didn't mean it. I was just worried and sorry because my beautiful plant died. I do have you but it may be that you die as the plant and the moon and the song of the laughing man. Everything dies, and perhaps your candle will go out in the dark some time. Take me away from here. I am afraid! I fear the dark, and the moon will soon pale, shrink and die also."

He soothed her as best he could, caressingly, telling her they would leave in a few days; just as soon as he could get another car.

They spent that day as lovers and for long moments Constance seemed to forget her fears in the embraces of the man. At other times she looked furtively into the dark forest. They told the dame they were leaving and she sighed, saying she wished they had never come. None too happy, the bride and her husband returned to their bedroom, discussing plans for their future.

"And I think," said Paul Gallien suddenly, "that before we go we had better throw out that dead mistletoe and clean the room. Suppose we do it now? I will borrow a shears from the old woman."

He returned shortly with a great pair of shears, such scissors as the oldest Fate used to clip the thread of life. While Constance sat on the bridal chest and cried a little, he cut all the ropes and rotten sheet, then threw the dead plant and other things with it out the window. As he wiped off the oaken bedstead he remarked:

"This wood is all dry and powdery. I believe I could break it in two in my hands. The mistletoe must have taken most of the life out of it."

"It has taken most of the life out of me," the woman added under her breath.

"No. We are just beginning to live. There are so many happy days to come."

Thus and so he tried to cheer her. The work done, he placed the shears on the bed and then coaxed her to come to supper. She said she was tired and asked that they go to bed early that evening.

Returning to the room she noticed the shears on the bed, exactly in the middle of the coverlet.

"How odd you are," she said to her husband. "You left those shears on the bed, exactly in the middle. If it stays there, it will be between us all night."

"That would be a good idea," he answered gently, "you are tired and this has been a hard day for you. Thus in olden times the knights did with their swords when they wished to assure their damsels of an undisturbed night. So, you stay on your side of the shears and I will stay on mine. Thus we shall both waken refreshed on the morrow."

Half an hour passed.

"I am frightened, Paul," she whimpered. "Is that thunder I hear? Hold my hand—tight!"

He did so and went to sleep.

Then came the full moon lighting the room with its yellow beams, and the woman heard the sounds of the pipe in the dark forest. At once she knew she must go out and dance or die from desire. As she tried to rise her hair held her back. She started to pull the long braids but they still held her. At last she took courage and slid her hand down the braid till she found it wrapped round the neck of the man who had held her hand. Her hair, those long, black, snake-like tresses, was wrapped around his neck; covered his face.

She screamed; for she knew that Paul Gallien was dead; and she knew the manner of his death.

Yet the pipe called her to the dark forest.

She took the shears and cut her hair, close to her head she cut it. Strand by strand, she cut it till she was free, and as the hair loosened it clung closer to the man's face and throat as though not quite satisfied that the deed was done.

Constance took off her silken robe and spread it over the thing that lay on the bed. Under the silk all was still, save for the final convulsive twistings of the ropes of hair, tightening uselessly round the throat of the dead. Then the woman ran to the window and climbed feverishly down the ivy. This time she did not wait to put on her slippers.

Once she reached the ground she ran to the rock. The laughing man was gone; the goats and the geese were gone; but through the woods, down the road, she heard the tones of the music, a very old tune, all within an octave, and she hastened after the song, crying:

"Oh, Pan! Wait for me! Please wait for me so I can love you and be happy."

But the laughing man walked on. The running, panting woman could come no closer to him till at last she saw him standing on the edge of the cliff. There he stood and played, waiting for her. She reached out to catch him and kiss him, but failing to touch the fantasy of his body, she plunged over the cliff, her white body curving like a falling star, till she silently became one with the crushed automobile.

The laughing man, lurking in the shadows, ran out into the moonlight and threw his open hands into the air as though to pluck the moonbeams with his questing fingers. Then he began to play his pipes anew. From the dark woods came the goats and the geese and gathered silently round him, and the song he played was all in one octave and very old. He laughed, and laughed.

"These mortals are never content. They always try to gather moonbeams—and even I cannot do that."

FOREST GOD

&

THE CRACKS OF TIME

Dorothy Quick

Dorothy Quick (1896–1962) was an American author, poet and playwright born in Brooklyn, New York. A prolific writer, Quick published a range of short stories and poetry in various pulp magazines including *Weird Tales*, *Strange Stories* and *Fantastic Adventures*. She also published the novel *Strange Awakening* (1938) and the one-act play *One Night in Holyrood* (1949). In 1907, while aboard the S. S. Minnetonka, Quick met Mark Twain, who had just received an honorary degree from Oxford University. The two developed a fast friendship that would last until Twain's death three years later, and he offered encouragement to Quick's writing ambitions. Quick reflected on this bond in *Enchantment: A Little Girl's Friendship with Mark Twain* (1961).

To close this collection, we turn to two of Quick's contributions to *Weird Tales*. The first, "Forest God", was reprinted in the November 1949 issue after its first appearance in August Derleth's poetry collection *Dark of the Moon* in 1947. Here, Quick seems to encapsulate the dichotomy of Pan, and why so many tales speak of encounters with the horned god. Connecting each of the previous texts, she highlights the joy that meeting Pan might bring, even if it signals one's end. "The Cracks of Time", meanwhile, is a short story first published in September 1948. Returning to the theme of Pan as a conduit for suppressed sexuality, the tale follows Sheila, who notices a cracked mosaic of Pan in her home. As the mosaic slowly starts to repair itself, as the image of Pan becomes more alert, so too does Sheila's infatuation continue to grow until she eventually succumbs to her passions.

FOREST GOD

Keep out of the forest
    Harken to advice,
For those whom Pan caresses
    Never see him twice.

Those who know Pan's touches
    And those who feel Pan's kiss
Know that there is nothing
    Ever to equal this.

Those who hear Pan's music
    And look into Pan's eyes,
Will always hear his laughter,
    Will always be too wise.

Still it's worth the risking
    Loneliness and pain,
To have the hope to cherish
    Pan might come again.

I t was when the cocktail party I was giving for Myra was at its height that I first saw the face.

I had been listening to the one hundred and fourth "But my dear, your engagement was such a surprise—You know you have all my best wishes—Now I want to congratulate the lucky man," and wondering how Myra ever found the right words to reply. Marvelling, too, at the ease with which she did so, and passed the people on to Henley, who managed them equally well. They were a good pair, my younger sister Myra and Henley Bradford. They'd have a happy marriage.

It was to hide the rush of tears to my eyes that I looked down, and saw the face. The sun room's floor was done with tiles Jason and I had brought from Spain while on our honeymoon—when we had been happy. They were a sea green-blue, some with geometric designs, some perfectly plain, their only ornamentation the patina of the glazing and the dark lines, or cracks, which time had given them. In this particular tile that caught my eyes the cracks had patterned a face. It was only a vague outline, the profile of a man with full, thick lips—sensuous lips, slanted eyes, and a forehead from which the hair rose up into a point that looked like a horn. There was nothing more that was definite. The rest was blurred and vague, like some modern, impressionistic picture, of the shadowy school which suggests its subject, rather than portrays it.

I was about to call out and tell the crowd what I'd discovered. I thought I'd make a game of it, because, in a way, it was like "statues," or finding shapes in clouds. The words "See what I've found!" were actually on my lips when the eye of the face looked a warning from under its slanting lid, and then the lid came down, covering the eye.

It was a trick of lighting, of course. The fact was in profile and the eye was open. The shadow of someone's foot in passing must have made the effect of the lid closing. The eye looking at me in warning was imagination plus several cocktails. But what I had been going to say was still-born. I didn't mention the profile but kept looking at it as the afternoon progressed, and it seemed to me that the face became clearer and more sharply etched. I began thinking it resembled the ancient sculptures of Pan.

By the time the guests had drunk themselves into a state of hilarity I had forgotten the face. I didn't notice it again until Jason came over to me and, in a rare mood of affection, put his arm around my shoulder. "Sheila," he whispered in a voice liquor had thickened, "you're the best-looking girl here. Why don't we kiss and make up?"

I knew he wouldn't have said that, sober. I also knew that our quarrelling had gone beyond the point where we could follow his suggestion. Jason's charms were legion but so was his drinking and the other women that went with it. I had out-forgiven myself—there just wasn't any more of that virtue left in me. Still, perhaps I should try once more. Maybe it wouldn't be right to reject this offer.

It was then I looked down and the face was moving from side to side, obviously saying "no" to my charitable inclinations. "No, no, no!" I caught myself up sharp. This was ridiculous; I was letting my imagination run away with me. The afternoon shadows were tricky things and I certainly couldn't let shifting light betray by better impulses.

So, when Jason repeated his question, kissing the place behind my ear that he called his, I said "Yes, Jason."

It seemed to me then that the one eye of the face completely closed and that I saw a tear trickle down the high-boned cheek. It was ridiculous but that's the impression I received.

"Hi, folks," Jason was calling, as he swirled me around in a wild dance. "Let's have another round. I'm celebrating the fact I've got the loveliest wife in the world, the kindest, the sweetest—"

I didn't hear the rest of the adjectives. My handkerchief had dropped during the turns we'd made. As Jason talked I bent down for it. The tiny square of white had fallen over the face. When I picked it up, it was wet. Liquor? Something spilled from a cocktail? That's what I thought, but when I lifted it to my nose there was no alcoholic odour. I touched it to my lips, the tip end of my tongue, and there was the bitter salt taste of tears.

And I had seen a tear roll down the face! Incredible, but in my mouth was the tang of a man's tears. I looked down. The face *was* much clearer; the back of the head was completely filled in, with the hair clustered on it dark and curly. The eye was open now and it had acquired depth and perspective. It looked down at me with admiration and a kind of pathetic appeal. The full lips trembled. It was as though they were calling out for me to lean over and touch them.

So strong was the illusion that in another moment I might have done so, but Jason came back just then with two cocktails. "Here you are, darling." He handed one to me.

I took it, and he encircled me with his arm. "Sweet, let's drink to us!" He was very tight, but his charm was in the ascendancy. I drank with him and forgot about the face.

The reconciliation proved very absorbing. Not since our honeymoon and the first year of our married life had Jason been so completely devoted. It was as though the five miserable years through which we had quarrelled had not existed. We were suddenly back, continuing the first twelve months of our felicity. I had fully intended to examine the tile with the face most carefully, the next day, when there would be no feet to cast shadows, no liquor to give ideas. But as it happened it was over a week before I went in the sun porch.

To begin with, there was the new devoted Jason, a round of parties for Myra, and several days of rainy weather, which always put the desirability of the sun porch at low ebb.

The cocktail party had been on a Saturday. It was exactly ten days later—Tuesday, to be definite—that the sun shone so brightly I said I'd have my lunch in the sun room. I had completely forgotten the face by then.

But once seated on the red bamboo chair with my lunch tray on a matching table before me, the face obtruded itself into my vision. It was slightly to my right and not as much *en profile* as I'd thought. It was more three-quarter; there was a glimpse of the other cheek, more than a suggestion of the other eye. The original one looked at me reproachfully.

I caught my breath. The effect was really amazing. Since I'd seen it the face had gained dimensions too. There was depth and thickness to it now, and it was larger—the hair had spread over to the next tile. I leaned over and examined the lines—the cracks of time. They were deep, almost fissure-like, quite outstanding against the blue-green glaze. It was almost as though some artist had made a sketch freehand of Pan, before the tiles went to the kiln, and it had lain under the glaze for years until time and wear had brought it back to the surface. I had no hesitancy about knowing it was meant to be Pan; the little forehead horns were very clear now, and the full, sensuous lips could have belonged to none other. Pan in the deep wood, admiring a dryad, with all the connotations of a satyr.

I wasn't particularly interested in my lunch but I went on eating it automatically, watching the face as I did so, surprised to see the reproach melt away to admiration, then longing, and finally desire undisguised.

At that point I caught myself up sharply. "Sheila, you're being ridiculous," I said aloud.

Johnson, the maid, appeared in the doorway. "Did you call?" she asked.

"No." I was amused. She'd heard me talking to myself. "But now you're here, you can take the tray. I'll just keep my tea."

When she came over I pointed down to the tile. "Look, Johnson. Don't you think it's funny the way those lines on that tile make a face?"

She peered down and then drew back. "It is, indeed, Madame, a strange face—not quite human, although it's not very clear, is it?"

The outlines weren't vague to me now but they had been when I had first seen them. Suddenly there was a voice in my ear. "You have tasted the salt of my tears; that is why you see more clearly."

The tea cup I had been holding crashed to the floor, the china ringing hard against the tiles as it shattered into bits. I found control of myself quickly. "Oh, Johnson, I am sorry. It just slipped out of my hands."

"And your good china, too," she sighed. "I'll clean up, Madame, and give that tile a bit of an extra rub, too. Maybe we'll be able to wipe that ugly face out."

But I knew she'd never be able to erase it from my mind.

Or the floor, either!

In fact, her efforts only made it more distinct to me, although she seemed to think she had obliterated some of it.

When she had finished and gone, I sat there trying to figure it out. There *was* an outline of a face on the tile. Johnson saw it, so it wasn't entirely imagination. She wasn't educated enough to know about Pan; if she had been, she too would have seen the resemblance. So I wasn't completely off track. There was a face. It was inhuman, but there actuality stopped. The rest had to be imagination. The cracks of time could make a face but they couldn't make it weep or speak. That had been my own mind, and yet what it had said made sense in a way: "you have tasted the salt of my tears; that is why you see more clearly."

There was a fairy tale I remembered from my youth and Andrew Lang's coloured fairy books. It was called "Elves' Ointment" as I recollect, and it was the story of a midwife brought to attend the birth of an elf. Given ointment to put on the new baby's eyes she had inadvertently gotten some on her own, and had seen everything differently thereafter—that is, until the elves caught on and took her new sight away from her, with quite tragic results, as I remembered.

But the analogy held. I looked at the face again. The full lips were parted. I could almost feel the hot quickened breath on my nearby ankle.

This was getting beyond sense. I was making myself see things that couldn't be, hear a voice, feel emotions that should be kept under cover. It was incredible, yet it was so real! It was uncanny. It made me a little afraid.

I decided I would go up to the attic and see if there were any leftover tiles and if there were, I'd have this one, with its cracks of time, removed as quickly as possible.

"Of course," I told myself sternly, "it's only because you've been emotionally stirred up these past days. What with Myra's engagement and Jason, no wonder you're full of imaginings."

Then I heard the voice again, an ageless voice, thin and reedy, yet with a curious appeal. "Don't fight me. Just listen to my music."

The music was soft at first, fleeting into my brain with gently vibrating notes. From its first sound I didn't think any more. I couldn't. I could only listen to something indefinably lovely—music that soothed and made me know that nothing apart from it really mattered. It held the essence of life.

Suddenly it changed and became little tongues of flame licking around me, touching me here and there like caressing winds. Then there were waves of sound that vibrated through my entire being. And it seemed as though all the magic there had ever been was in them, weaving itself around me until I was a part of it, and I knew that nothing so lovely had ever happened to me before. I was suddenly a part of nature. Soon all its secrets would be known to me, and—

Jason's voice: "Hi, Shelley, where are you?" came from the living room, driving the music away. I didn't answer. I didn't want Jason to find me. I wanted the music back again. I wanted to lose myself in it.

"Shelley." Jason was calling. "Shelley." His pet name for me, part nickname for Sheila and partly made up from my admiration for the poet.

I looked down at the face. There was a finger touching the lips, as though to enjoin silence. Another crack of time, but it looked like a finger and its meaning was plain: the music was to be our secret, there was no mistaking that. And I wasn't imagining it. There *was* a finger on the thick lips.

For a minute I thought of them touching mine, and I knew that was what I wanted most in the world—that, and the music.

"Soon. It will be soon." The thin, reedy voice was like the notes of a pipe, coming from far-off enchanted places. A pipe, Pan's pipe.

Then Jason was in the room, exclaiming: "What the—! Why didn't you answer me? Didn't you hear me call?"

"No. I—I guess I was half asleep."

He leaned over and kissed me. There was warmth in his kiss but it left me cold. The wonderful music had deadened my senses to everything but its own magnificence, and Pan's, the god who had called it to being.

I looked down at the tile. The finger was no longer against the full lips. Instead, they were forming a word, "Wait." It was as plain to see as though I had studied lip-reading.

Jason's eyes followed mine. "Hello! Look at that cracked tile. We'll have to change that. You know, those cracks make a face, a horrible, repulsive face that gives me the shivers. I'll go to the attic tomorrow and fish out another tile and get rid of that face on the bar room floor."

Against my will I laughed. Against the hurt look in Pan's eyes. But suddenly the expression changed to one of cunning, combined with determination.

Words came to my lips. Without any volition of my own I found myself saying, "There's a piece of broken china still there. I broke a cup."

Jason bent down, picked up the piece of the tea cup the maid had overlooked, which I hadn't even known was there. He swore softly and shook a few drops of blood from his finger. Aghast, I watched the full lips catch them, suck them in.

"Jason," I cried. "You're hurt!"

He laughed. "Don't look so horrified; it's only a small cut." Again he shook off a few drops of blood, which the mouth on the floor caught.

I shivered. There was something so horrible about the mouth and the blood that I forgot the music.

"Come on." Jason caught me up. "I'll let you put a band-aid on it and then we're stepping out. The Crawleys are waiting for us at Agello's."

Agello's was our local "21." Going there was always an event. I was quite excited. There in the bright lights, with the gay music, I could forget the face and the silly things it provoked me into imagining.

I thought that, and I was happy, looking forward to fun at Agello's with Jason and the Crawleys, a couple we both liked tremendously. I was quite elated. Jason had his arm around me and it felt fine— warm and vibrant.

But as we left the porch I saw the face again. The lips had colour, and they formed a word, "Soon." And as we left, an echo of the thin, fluting pipes sounded in my ear.

At Agello's I managed to forget. I had to forget, otherwise I would begin to think I was going mad. The face on the floor was genuine enough; Jason and the maid had both seen it. They had sensed evil. The maid had said it was inhuman, Jason that it was repulsive. So the face was all actuality. The rest had to be an over-worked imagination, and I didn't like the implications of that. I made up my mind there on the crowded floor dancing with Jason that I'd help him find another tile and get rid of the one with the cracks of time as quickly as possible. After that, I proceeded to enjoy the evening.

It was late when we left Agello's. Once we were home, Jason didn't give me time to think. It was like our honeymoon all over again, and I was glad of that.

The next day was Sunday. Sunday was the day we usually had breakfast on the sun porch in our pyjamas. In the light of day I wasn't worried about the face, but it was comfortable in our room. "Let's be sissies," I said, "and have breakfast in bed."

"Lazy." Jason laughed. "But it's too nice a day to be on the north side of the house. No, Shelley, we're going to bask in the sunlight. And just to pamper you, I'm going to carry you thither." He leaned over the bed and gathered me into his arms.

"This is fun," I grinned, "but in the interests of modesty you'd better let me have a negligee."

He held me down so I could retrieve my blue crepe housecoat from the foot of the bed. I clutched it to me, and we were ready.

On our way, Jason paused a minute before the mirror set into my closet door. "See what a pretty picture you make," he whispered in my ear. "You're like a slim dryad of the woods, and I—" he squared his massive shoulders and I felt the muscles of his chest hard against me—"am Pan."

There wasn't any music—no thin fluting or wondrous tones; only a resentment and a feeling of instinctive recoil—as though anyone could be Pan but the face. I made myself look in the mirror. Just as we were we might have posed for a calendar picture of a dryad being abducted by a satyr—not Pan. Jason's face was lascivious enough but there was no suggestion of the god in him. He was of the earth.

I, in my white satin nightie had a classic look, for the satin moulded my form and was a startling contrast to my red-gold hair.

Jason, in blue foulard pyjamas, looked like an advertisement straight out of "Esquire." Direct physiological appeal. But I knew instinctively that within him there were no nuances, none of the subtle approach that is so dear to a woman's heart. His was not the knowledge that Pan possessed.

It was at that moment I heard the music—the faint, thin piping that shivered against my nerves and made them vibrate to its tune, music that grew louder even as I listened.

Jason started towards the door.

The music was calling to me. Calling to me to come, to give myself up to it completely.

Suddenly I was afraid. Jason was very dear, human and near. I clung to him. "Don't go downstairs," I begged. "Let's stay here." I tried to put allure into my voice. Anything to keep him here where it was safe, where I could shut the door and drown out the music that attracted me, as something evil that is yet beautiful can always do.

Jason's mind was one track. "Breakfast first, darling." He walked on, and the music swelled in tone. It was making me forget everything but my desire for it—and Pan, for the two were inescapably one.

Still I tried to hold to reality. "Do you hear music?" I asked Jason, as he descended the stairway.

"Music? Lord, no! But I do hear a vibration like the jangling note of a wire that's off-key. After breakfast we'll look for it."

"There may not be time." The words said themselves.

"We've got all day, darling." He was at the bottom of the steps, advancing to the living room. The music was becoming more and more pronounced. Like Wagner's fire music, little tongues of flame licking about me, growing larger and stronger.

I knew they were waiting to envelope me. I made a last effort. "Jason, we mustn't go to the sun room. There's something there— something—" "Evil" was what I'd meant to say but the word was still-born on my lips. The music had taken possession of me. I was encased in it as surely as Brunehilde ever was on her fire-ringed mountain. Little flames of music were licking about me.

Then we were in the sun room and Jason put me down.

My wrapping the negligee around me was mechanical, and wasted, for Pan's eyes looked through the material, yes, through the skin, into my very soul. He was complete now, a full-grown figure, and even as I watched he rose from the blue-green tiles, wholly dimensional. His boring eyes held mine and the music was like a flowing river of fire, touching me, everywhere.

"So, you have answered my pipings?" It was as though he were singing.

"Yes," I replied, "And now that I am here?"

"Shelley, what are you talking about?" Jason's voice was impatient.

The music diminished. "Didn't you hear?" I began.

"Wait." Pan's voice was thunder-clear.

Suddenly arrested, I stood still. But my gaze betrayed me.

"What is it?" Jason asked. Then, when I made no reply he became insistent. "*What is it? What do you hear?*"

That caught me up short with surprise. It didn't seem possible that he didn't hear that glorious, engrossing, enveloping music. I found words. "But you *must* hear the music. It's so wonderful. And you must see—"

I looked at Pan. He was regarding me strangely and shaking his head.

I stopped short. Jason followed my gaze. "It's that darn tile. You've been acting peculiarly ever since you saw those cracks. I'm going to dig it out."

"No," I cried. "No, Jason, let it alone. There's danger!" I don't know how I knew there was danger for Jason, perhaps it was the expression in Pan's eyes. But how, or why I knew Jason went in peril? And at that moment the urgency was upon me to save him.

"Don't be foolish, Shelley. How could there be danger in a tile—a cracked tile, at that?"

"But he's larger than you." I was struggling against Pan and the music now, trying to save Jason from something intangible, some danger I sensed but couldn't rightly name. I was afraid, and yet, what did Jason—anything—matter, against the vibrant music that was swelling around me?

"Sheila!" Jason exclaimed. "I think you must have a hangover—seeing things. A hangover, or be mad. That tile has bewitched you. I'm getting rid of it now—this second."

He went to an old sea chest where he kept tools and things. He opened it and took out a hunting knife.

I could see Pan's triumphant smile.

"No, Jason, no!" I shrieked, and then the music was so loud, so beautiful that I couldn't think of anything else. I was completely lost to the music, hypnotised as any snake by a master piper, enveloped by melody which was part of Pan.

As in a dream I saw Jason advance toward the tile, knife in hand. I saw Pan moving towards him.

For more Tales of the Weird titles
visit the British Library Shop (shop.bl.uk)

We welcome any suggestions, corrections or feedback you may have, and will
aim to respond to all items addressed to the following:

The Editor (Tales of the Weird), British Library Publishing,
The British Library, 96 Euston Road, London NW1 2DB

We also welcome enquiries through our Twitter account, @BL_Publishing.

The music accelerated. For one desperate moment I came to my senses. "Jason, come away!" I screamed, and rushed to him.

Pan was before me. With one hand he thrust me back; with the other he turned Jason's arm with the knife inward, so that the knife was toward Jason's body. I saw the blue tile gleaming, crackless and pure, just like the others. Pan had left it. He had materialised. Just as I realised this, Pan pushed Jason. My husband fell, and as he did so, impaled himself on his own knife as surely as any ancient Roman running himself through with his sword.

There was a funny gurgling noise. Then Jason rolled over on his back. I knew the danger had struck. Jason was dead.

But Pan was alive!

Alive and wholly man, and the music too was a living, throbbing thing, marvellous beyond human knowing, enveloping me until I was part of it.

The wonder of the music was completely mine now. It swept me forward, into Pan's arms.

I don't mind being in prison, or the fact that I am on trial for my life, charged with the murder of my husband. I don't even care that they are saying I am mad, perhaps because I know that if I told them the truth they would be certain of it.

I don't mind being confined in this horrible cell, or any of the rest of it. I don't mind, because the cracks of time opened for me, and now the wonderful music is always in my ears, and the remembrance of Pan's kisses on my lips.

And the certainty that at the end I shall feel them again!